the protocols of *Ambiguity*

the protocols of *Ambiguity*

B. B. Jacobson

ARCHWAY PUBLISHING

Archway Publishing books may be ordered through booksellers or by contacting:

Archway Publishing
1663 Liberty Drive
Bloomington, IN 47403
www.archwaypublishing.com
1-(888)-242-5904

ISBN: 978-1-4808-0903-1 (sc)
ISBN: 978-1-4808-0904-8 (e)

Library of Congress Control Number: 2014911881

Printed in the United States of America.

Archway Publishing rev. date: 07/17/14

For my wife and three sons.
I love each of you with all my heart.

Chapter 1

"He's just a boy," the old woman shouted to her excited peer.

It was true. The boy was merely six years old. And shy too. Severely shy. But still he stood there, undaunted, before the electrified apostolic crowd of three hundred worshipers. He slowly raised his hands to the heavens, and through stammering lips, he began to utter words.

Awareness … weeping … it was filling him … overflowing …

The volume of tears that streamed down his cheeks was in direct proportion to an expanding awareness of the words now flowing from his mouth. New words, different words, words he did not understand yet, words not foreign, words not without meaning. Tears poured from his eyes as though his tear ducts were fastened open. He was very aware—aware of the pressure on his toes from shoes a half size too small, aware of the bubble of snot beneath his nose, and aware of how happy he was. He didn't want this moment to end.

The Pentecostal preacher bellowed from the pulpit, "Theeus is thayt spowk'n of baa the prowphet Jowel sayith Gawd, 'I whill powur out maa speeritupon awl falesh in the layst days'!"

The boy didn't understand what the preacher was saying. But it didn't matter. Nothing mattered.

The preacher lifted the boy and held him to the microphone so the people could see and hear a child speaking in tongues.

The man's fiery expression unfolded from utter amazement—"Don't let nobody tell yall Acts 2:38 ain't the way any more"—to fierce and emphatic—"*Read it!* It's still the birth of the church!" The preacher broke into a smile and pointed to the crowd. "What shall I do to get right with Gawd? Acts 2:38 is the altar, laver, and the Holy Place. It's still the doorwhay to the kingdom! Thayt doorwhay ain't ever changed! Ain't no eemperor, no theologeen, no council of politishuns and popes ever hayd the autharty to chaynge eet. *No mayn*! *Ever*!"

The congregation roared with praises, shouting, and clapping. And in spite of the predicament, the boy didn't want to stop. He was comfortable. He allowed the new language to flow through him as the only language he ever wanted to speak. The preacher made marvelous, prophetic-style proclamations that nudged the congregation into a revelatory frenzy.

Music began with low, soulful tones from a Hammond B-3 organ, slowly at first, progressive and rhythmic. Bass notes pumped alongside the syncopating high-hat of a particularly skilled drummer. Deep percussions pulsed under shaking tambourines accompanied by brass, piano, and powerful vocal harmonies. Barefaced women in modest dress danced until their bouffant constructions crumbled to glorified lengths. The atmosphere was at once festive and repentant as contrite sinners flooded the altars.

Memories flashed in the boy's mind. He remembered three weeks before when he and his family lived in another town far away. He remembered his parents' announcement that the family must relocate. How sad he had been to part ways with the little church they attended, especially the Sunday school teacher. The man was a magnificent entertainer with a strong Brooklyn accent and a wry grin. He often called the boy "the little preachuh." An impossible shock of wiry hair jiggled loosely above the teacher's right eye as he screwed a light bulb into his mouth. From the corner of his mouth he would declare, "Look here, little preachuh. See what happens when I reach my hands high into the throne room of God and falip the switchaaa!" The light bulb would light up. The boy knew it was a battery-operated trick bulb; he could see the magician's tongue pressing the button. The smiling boy never spoke to the man.

The boy remembered every detail of the former neighborhood. He remembered the bully he'd punched in the nose at the incitement of his three older brothers, who giggled with delight as the bully lay screaming and bloody on the ground. That was the night his grandmother, visiting from South Louisiana, told him of the gift.

There was an air of affluence about his grandmother; a deep sensitivity not acquired in conventional circles; a sweetness that adequately masked her inability to read and write. Maybe she discerned his guilt, or fear, or something as she sat him on the chair and began to speak in her soft, French accent. "Shaa, yoo awlmoost six year ol now. Yoo need to know dat dare is a gif dat da Lowad Jesus wish to give yoo. Yoo need to know dat yoo gon need dis gif mar dan yool need anytin else for de res of yoo life. More dan dem puppy, more dan dat swim poowl, and more dan dem lil trahcycle. Dat gif gon open yoo eyes and guide yoo tru awl da dawrkness."

The grandmother didn't know the boy had taught himself to balance on a bicycle with no pedals. The boy didn't bother to correct her. There was something in the aged woman's words, something that quickened his heart. He studied the stately shape of her mouth, her mannerisms, and the way she davened slowly back and forth as she spoke in measured rhythms. The meter of her sentences moved from elliptic phrases to a seamless flow slowly painting a vivid image in the boy's mind.

"Shaa, dares many, many lights in da world dat yoo gon see. But awl dem lights oonly mix togethah to make biggah and biggah dawrkness. At dat midnight hour, awl dem lights in da worl gon come togethah, and dis whole world won't know da difference between light and dawrkness. Never let yooself believe dem lights. Dem devil lights want to hide dat one true light. Always remembah … *dar is oonly one true light. One oonly*!"

The boy pondered her words. He'd previously experimented with a flashlight in the darkness of his closet, waving his hand through the invisible beam.

"When yoo have true light, yoo nevah let yoosef stoop to earthy powah," she continued. "Holy powah is biggah dan yoo fist, biggah dan any sword, and biggah dan awl dem bombs. If dem people claim da neem of Jesus but still dey use da powah of da sword, and fear to force others to believe, den you know das not da true light. Shaa, God is love, but love was anvisible and noo man could see, until dat lil baby born in Betlehem."

The boy continued the heavenly communiqué as the congregation pressed in on all sides. A random hand wiped his nose with a handkerchief as images from the past flickered again. He remembered his brothers' excitement for the new city and how the church was a lot bigger than they had all expected. And though the boy found little comfort in crowded places, he didn't mind this new church. Often, during the Sunday-night service as the preacher vehemently expounded another message from God, the boy would lie under the church pew and pray. He would study the splintered underside of the wooden bench and marvel at the colorful blobs of chewing gum stuck finger length from the edge. He found he could stare right through the air, through the wooden bench to another place, the throne room, spoken of by the man with the light in his mouth. The boy would close his eyes and talk to Jesus with limited words.

From these moments a yearning was conceived. *I must be baptized in the name of Jesus.* It was a concept the boy found comprehensible and urgent as expounded by the preacher, who said, "You gotta be towtally sayturated, through and through, in the idantitey of Gawd. You must be covered in His name. Repent! Be baptaazed in the name of Jesus for the remeeshun of seeuns! And receive the Holy Ghost! Thayts the whole gospel! Death, burial, and resurrection!"

The boy's mother inquired of the preacher regarding the boy's baptism.

"Sister, we don't beptaaz babies," the preacher retorted. "But that boy certainly ain't a baby. As long as that boy has repented of his seeuns and has a good understandin of what it means, then praise Gawd, I'd be heppy to beptaaz him."

On the night of the baptism, they dressed the boy in a white robe and led him to the huge tank of water built into the platform of the sanctuary. He stepped into the water, and the people gathered around and began to pray.

The preacher held the boy by the hand and addressed the crowd. "Ya see, brethers and sisters, conversion is the most crucial moment in a human beeuns laaf. If thars ever a time the name of Jesus must be verbulley spowkn aloud, with claritee, it's at this moment. Here is the power of the pretrinitarian church. That name of autharty must be invoked. So without further adieu, upawn the confeshin of yer faith and the autharty of the Word of Gawd, I now beptaaz you in *the name of Jesus Christ*, for the remeeusshen of yer seeuns, and you shayall receive the geeuft of the Holy Ghost!"

The preacher pushed the boy's body into the tank, immersing him completely. The boy emerged waving his hands through the air, lunging for the gift. He felt something happen, for certain, and he reached for the gift as high as he could, crying out to God with everything he had. "Jesus, Jesus, Jesus, Jesus, Jesus."

He could hear the people around him praying toward a fever pitch, encouraging loudly, "Come on, boy! Let go! Receive it! Praise His name! Halleluiah!"

Nothing.

He was sure the gift was near, and he reached higher, crying out, "I praise You, Jesus! Halleluiah! Halleluiah!"

Nothing.

He lowered his head and hands, his cheeks turned red, and he exited the tank without eye contact as the people patted him on the back.

It was dark. He lay in his bed in a restless heep with visions of myriad staring faces. A lost, lonely, desolate mass hovered in the aether, expecting the boy to impart some essential word.

Morning broke, and he awoke to a different feeling, a particular newness. He could hear the birds singing just beyond the window as the dogs barked in the distance. The sun shone through the Venetian blinds to create an inclining ladder shadow over the floor. Above the shadow, the invisible ladder was betrayed by tiny particles of dust floating and disappearing again. The boy thought of the previous night. He had no doubt something had happened. And what was once a soft yearning now expanded to a fully bloomed, internal, desperate plea.

The following week, the church began a seven-day revival. A visiting evangelist was scheduled to preach every night for the next seven. Each night the evangelist delivered his message and gave the altar call, inviting souls to repent. Each night the boy was the first one to the altar, kneeling and hoping, straining and reaching for the gift, but each night it eluded him. Night after night he lay in his bed, deeply saddened, dreaming again of the throngs of faces, hopeless and dying. He tossed restlessly, caught in a quandary of increased longing and the impending sense that his window of opportunity would come to a close.

On the seventh night of the revival, the evangelist delivered the final altar call, and the boy ran down the aisle, crumbled across the altar in a supple mass, and gave up.

Then it happened!

Wind … peace … fire … joy …

The boy had become a conductor, the path of least resistance. He stood to his feet and raised his hands in total accession. He could feel the Holy Ghost filling his soul like a well of warm water from within. Immeasurable volumes of clarity flooded his deepest recesses. The steady rise delivered divine pressure to every emotional portal, expanding beyond containment, and spilling over in a teary deluge. The mouth became the last bastion as pressure increased on his lips, tongue, and vocal chords from the inside. He relinquished his tongue in deliberate, resolute surrender.

He must have been speaking in tongues for an hour. When he opened his eyes, the sanctuary was empty of all but a handful of saints with big, adoring smiles. The head usher and his wife gave the boy a gentle embrace. "You got the Holy Ghost," they said with faces beaming as if they were his blood relations. His brothers surrounded him too, saying, "Give me five," as they patted the boy on the back. One of his brothers offered an unopened Mr. Pibb from the coke machine. The mother laughed as the preacher prophesied, "Sister, mark maa words: that boy can see!"

It is dark and dusty, and I can barely hear beneath the roar of the giant air-conditioning unit. I rest my head on the wall next to the return-air vent and peer through the slats, but I can only see the carpeted floor of the balcony. My fingers aimlessly run the length of the electrical conduit, and I notice a child-size, wooden chair in the corner, and the moment I reach for it, the air-conditioning unit cycles off. The silence gives way to a plethora of voices rising through the louvers and reverberating high throughout the small hidden space. There is soft, low weeping and speaking in tongues. The people below are praying. I detect a familiar voice. I am trembling. I wipe the tears from my unshaven face with a dirty, determined hand. It is five minutes till six, Sunday evening.

Chapter 2

Gussie Mae was an elderly widow who belonged to the same church the boy attended. Her knee-length hair was pristine white, tastefully braided, and tucked into an elegant bun at the base of her skull. "I have power with God," she would say with a smile as she brushed out the silvery strands. As a young woman, she had been one of a number of traveling female ministers within the Oneness Pentecostal movement. The boy's mother often referred to Gussie Mae as the babysitter, but the boy thought of the aged woman as his friend.

Every day after school, the boy would walk to Gussie Mae's house and stay until six o'clock, when his mother would pick him up. Gussie Mae had a granddaughter, Donna, a twenty-something art student with a multiplicity of piercings along the helix of her ear. Donna dependably stopped by to borrow things, never failing to dismiss herself with a comment on Gussie Mae's religion. "They are actually sad, narrow-minded people," she would say with an inward cock of her chin. "Did you ever notice Granny never wears makeup or earrings? Ugh! What's with that? And no television? Hah!" The girl poked at her grandmother's modest lifestyle as she filled a grocery bag with items from Gussie Mae's cupboard.

Every day, Gussie Mae would greet the boy with two homemade peanut butter cookies, a glass of milk, and a big, adoring smile. Gussie Mae was always smiling. And the boy did notice the absence of jewelry and makeup, but he thought of Gussie Mae as pretty, though he would never say it. In difficult times, she would chuckle and say, "Dear, dear, and mighty God." The only times she didn't smile were the indiscriminate moments when she felt inclined to pray. Whether cooking, washing dishes, or tatting, it didn't matter. She'd hobble her walker across the living room, and all of the sudden a somber countenance would wash over her lighted face. Right in the middle of the room, gripping her walker with one hand, she'd wave her other hand freely through the air, instinctively speaking in tongues. "God, oh God, keep your hand on him, God. Protect him, Jesus! Anoint his life! Ooh, oh God!"

One day the boy was playing in his usual hiding place behind the chair in Gussie Mae's living room. He leaned back with his head in the corner and his feet propped straight up the back of the chair and pretended his hand was an airplane slowly arching across the sky. Gussie Mae hummed quivered notes from her rocking chair the opposite corner, "There shall be light—in the evening time—the path to glory—you will surely find …" All of a sudden, Gussie Mae began to weep.

The boy slid his feet across the back of the chair and quietly rolled to his knees so he could hear better. As he concentrated on the unknown words flowing from Gussie Mae, a reminder stirred within. He too could speak in tongues. With his eyes wide open, the boy whispered, "Jesus, I love you, Jesus," and suddenly the well of words flowed from his deepest parts. A warm, salty tear forged a path to the corner of his mouth. He spoke this language with greater ease than the language he used to speak to people. The boy had no idea what he was saying, but he knew these words. He knew, from the depths of his soul, God loved it when he spoke this language.

The boy wiped his tears and peered from behind the chair to discover the room empty. He guessed Gussie Mae had gone outside to check the mail. Perfectly content, he crawled from his hiding place to the click of the closing door and the familiar sound of Gussie Mae's wrinkly chuckle. He tiptoed into the kitchen and peeked around the corner, and there stood his old friend sifting through the mail. "Look," she said, waving a large gold-glitter envelope near his face. "I won one hundred thousand dollars!" She chuckled again and tossed the unopened envelope in the trash bin. The boy just stood there staring.

The boy loved the house his family currently lived in. It was a few blocks from the former house they'd occupied for three whole months, but this dwelling had only two bedrooms, so the rent was cheaper.

The dad was coming home for the weekend. The mother called all four boys to the living room to brief them on what to say and what not to say. The dad was Catholic. The boy was christened Catholic too when he was three. "But our new church was established *before* the Catholic Church," the mother explained, "so you had to be rebaptized calling on the name of Jesus, according to Acts chapter 19, just like the pastor said."

The mother wasn't asking the four sons to lie to the dad; she merely wanted to control the information the dad received and didn't receive. "Blessed is a peacemaker," she would say with a sage expression. The boy didn't understand, but it mattered little because *his dad was coming home*! He decided right away he was going to take his dad fishing—his brothers too. They all would have one fine weekend.

The dad arrived at eight Friday night on a Greyhound bus. The boy and his brothers piled into the back seat of the Chevy Biscayne. As they motored toward the bus station, they spotted the dad standing on the corner with a small duffle bag slung over his shoulder and a rectangular box under his arm. He tossed the bag into the trunk, climbed into the front seat with a nod, and the mother put the car in drive.

Few words were spoken on the ride home, but there was definitely excitement in the air. They pulled into the driveway, and the dad quietly commented on how pretty the trees were. The brothers tried to convince the dad to play hide-and-seek, but the mother reminded them of all the work planned for the following day. She ordered the four boys to bed.

The boy's heart was broken. All three brothers climbed into their bunk beds, and the boy reluctantly followed. In a short time, the brothers were snoring, but the boy lay on his bed with his eyes wide open, trying to focus in the dark. *Maybe if I sneak into the living room, I might catch a glimpse of Dad. Maybe Dad will go to the kitchen for a drink or snack or something, or maybe I could go to the bathroom and find Dad brushing his teeth.*

The boy quietly rolled out of bed, tiptoed out of the room, and approached the dim opening at the end of the hall. He slowly peeked into the living room. There sat his dad, staring directly at the boy and grinning ear to ear as if the boy was right on schedule for a covert meeting.

The dad gave the boy a great big hug. "Shhh, I know your birthday was two weeks ago." He held out a rectangular box. "Open it." It was a brand-new skateboard. "Happy birthday." The dad kissed the boy right on top of the head. The boy stood on his tiptoes with his mouth wide open and his eyebrows lifted as high as they would go.

Suddenly, the mother appeared, let out an irritable sigh, and stomped back into the bedroom, slamming the door behind her. The dad winked at the boy. "See ya in the morning." And he patted him to bed. As the boy and dad parted ways, the boy could hear the mother speaking to the dad with raised tones. The dad responded heatedly, and some object banged against the wall.

It's all my fault, the boy thought, resisting the urge to knock on the parents' door and apologize. He wanted to make them aware of the happiness in the moment, but he didn't know how. He climbed into his bunk and instinctively whispered, "Jesus," as he sank into his pillow. The unaffected peace permeated the dark of the tiny bedroom. He could hear his eldest brother snoring from above.

Another brother tossed in his bunk, causing a creaking. The boy closed his eyes and fell asleep.

In the morning he awoke to the sounds of cereal pouring into glass bowls and clanging silverware and two of his brothers arguing over the cereal box. With sleepy eyes and hair sticking straight up on one side of his head, he pulled on his tattered, undersized jeans and joined his brothers for breakfast.

The age gaps between the three elder siblings were only eighteen months. But the age gap between the boy and the brother closest to him in age was five years. This disparity left little in common between the older three and their younger brother.

"Where's Daddy?" he asked as he helped himself to a bowl and spoon from the cupboard.

"He borrowed the neighbor's lawnmower to mow our grass," one brother snorted.

"Can we help?" The boy emptied the powdery crumbs from the bottom of the cereal box into his bowl and added enough milk to make a cereal paste.

"No," both brothers replied simultaneously. "You have to stay inside with Mommy. Only the men of the house get to go outside and help Dad." The brothers discharged themselves in an oafish manner, neglecting their mess, and clambered out the door, sneering.

The boy finished his breakfast and hurried to find his mother.

"She must be sleeping," he said aloud, deciding he shouldn't knock again. As he turned to walk to his bedroom, the door flew open. "*What! What! What! What!* … Oh baby, I'm sorry. I didn't know it was you." The mother covered herself with her robe. "What is it, honey?"

"I want to go outside," said the boy. "I want to help Daddy and my brothers."

The mother winced. "Oh baby, you don't want to do that. You would rather stay inside with Mommy. Besides, they're too rough, and anyway, you'd be a big help inside if you'd dust the furniture."

The boy nodded and ambled straight to the cabinet beneath the kitchen sink where he found the Pledge and an old dust rag. He weaved his way through the unpacked boxes of household items that filled the living room. He thoroughly dusted one table and the next, but couldn't resist peering out the window.

The grass was three feet tall, so it took much effort for the dad to mow a small section. The eldest brother raked grass into random ample piles while the other two cleared the way of sticks and pinecones. The boy smiled from behind the curtain as one of the brothers zinged a pinecone at another brother's head, barely missing his right ear. In retaliation, the other brother bounded a pinecone off the backside of the culprit. War!

But the mother yelled his name, so he quickly closed the curtains and continued dusting.

"Who ate all the cereal?"

The boy, thinking he was in trouble, hesitantly confessed to finishing it.

The mother wrinkled her nose. "It's okay. I'll have an egg."

The boy returned to the window again to find the eldest brother filling black plastic bags with the piles of grass. The boy was startled as the dad burst through the back door into the kitchen. "I have a great idea!"

The mother glared at the man from her plate of fried egg as he stood there soaked in sweat and covered with grass. She put her hand over her nose as the dad announced his fancy. "Why don't you bake a chocolate cake, and let's have a birthday party for the boy, with candles and everything!"

The mother's grimace exposed a mouthful of egg. "That is the stupidest thing I have ever heard. We already gave him a party and a cake. You missed it!"

The dad frowned. "You won't have to do a thing. I'll bake the cake, and I'll clean up afterward. I want to see his face when he blows out the candles."

"Never mind, I'll do it! I'll bake the stupid cake!"

The dad smiled and backed gingerly out the door to finish the yard.

The boy continued dusting as cabinet doors slammed and pots and pans banged together. "Stupid, stupid, this is so stupid," the mother hissed. "I can't believe I am doing this!"

The boy hurried to the kitchen to offer help. He wondered if his parents knew that he didn't like cake. The mother slammed the oven door, set the timer, and huffed to her bedroom with another slam. The boy went to his room and climbed into his bunk.

He wanted to do something for the mother and dad, anything to calm their spirits. He wanted to bake a cake for his mother or clean the kitchen. He wanted to do yard work for his dad. Instead, he lay in his bed motionless with the feeling of a rod iron poking his chest. He closed his eyes and tried to fall asleep, but the smell of burning cake kept him sharp. At once, the door to his mother's room burst open, followed by the sound of heavy feet stomping through the hall. "Stupid timer, stupid timer, stupid timer!" The oven door opened. "Stupid, stupid, stupid, I knew this was a stupid idea!"

The boy pulled the covers over his head as the dad happened through the back door.

The mother unloaded, "Yours, yours, yours, the cake is burned!"

The dad grabbed a potholder, took the cake out of the oven, and set it on the stovetop."It's okay, it's okay," the dad said, with a sheepish grin. "It ain't bad."

He sliced a dried corner of the cake. "See, it's only a touch well-done around the edges. We'll put some icing on it. The kids will love it." He found some canned chocolate icing in the cabinet, spread it on the cake, and placed the cake at the center of the table.

"Where are the candles?" he asked.

The mother stared at the dad with her lips tight between her teeth. The dad began to boorishly open and close drawers. The spoons and forks jangled, another drawer slammed shut, then a striking match, and the smell of smoke wafted into the boy's bedroom. The dad opened the back door and called sternly to the brothers.

"Gather around the table. We have a surprise for your baby brother." He passed napkins around and called to the boy. The boy didn't answer. The dad called again and moved the direction of the bedroom. Seconds before the dad entered, and the boy quickly turned and pretended to sleep.

"Hey, little buddy, wake up. We have a surprise for you."

The boy opened his eyes and smiled. The dad held him by the hand to help him out of bed. "Upsy-daisy." They walked hand in hand to the dining room, and as soon as they entered, the dad yelled awkwardly and alone, "Surprise!"

The boy grinned ear to ear as if he were genuinely surprised. The mother and the brothers sat there blinking as the tone-deaf man sang "Happy Birthday" solo.

"Now blow out the candles."

Right away the boy noticed only five candles, but he dutifully drew a deep breath and blew the candles. The dad guffawed loudly and beamed as he sliced the cake and distributed the pieces to each member of the family.

Instantly one of the brothers said, "This cake smells funny."

Another brother replied with a mouth full of cake, "I think it's burnt."

The third brother chimed in. "Yeah, and how come there are only five candles?"

The dad stared at the floor for a moment, his lips turning white. "You will eat the cake, and you will like it!"

The boy quickly forked a piece of cake into his mouth and swallowed without chewing. "Mmmm!"

The mother sat on her chair, acrimonious and silent, glaring on the pitiful scene. The dad tried to nod her subtly into eating her share of burnt cake as the boy shifted nervously, taking tiny nibbles.

In a start, the dad's fist slammed violently on the table, knocking the boy's piece of cake to the floor. The boy bowed his head to small, fidgeting hands as the dad barreled out the back door.

Silence.

The mother whisked lightning fast to the living-room window, craning her neck, investigating. "See, I told you. Now you know what I go through every time. This is what *I* go through!"

The boy moved from the table and slipped unnoticed to his bedroom. It was five o'clock in the evening, and he was emotionally exhausted. He changed into his pajamas, crawled into bed, and drifted into a deep sleep.

He could see himself, a boy, standing at the edge of the veranda, gazing on the vast array of coexisting, coequal paths, and he winced under the complicit din. There were myriad beautiful mazes—each with a chorus bidding seductively from dark, colorful, and boundless corners. But a still, small voice atop a solitary, narrow path called his name. The boy had never seen Him but knew Him now. His face was true and kind, but His eyes were difficult—bright light with grief and knowledge. The friend led the boy to a stoop above the tree to rest beyond the shadow of endless branches. He showed the boy the wind as it stirred a colony of ants below. A velvet-black passerine lighted blue fell from the sky. The friend touched the boy's nose and whispered, "You're best."

The boy woke with a gasp. The house was dark and quiet, and the inhabitants slept soundly. The glowing clock on the wall broke the silence with urgent ticks as the minutes edged to midnight.

He crawled out of bed, tiptoed past his brothers, and felt his way along the short hall until he touched the doorway of the parents' room. He could hear his dad snoring beyond the partial opening. The boy leaned on the frame, slid silently into a crumpled ball, and began to weep.

He tried his best to stay quiet so as not to startle his parents, but it came out in sobs. He held his mouth with both hands and bent slowly to the floor until he felt something touch his shoulder.

"What's the matter, baby?" the mother whispered groggily.

The boy continued the suppressed sobs. The mother held his face in her hands, searching. "It's okay. Tell Mommy what's the matter." She spoke firmly now, and agitation crept into her cold fingers, which tightened slightly on his jaw.

The boy closed his eyes. "I want to go home."

"What do you mean? You are home."

The boy continued to cry.

"Do you mean where we used to live?" She was curious now.

"No, not there. I don't know. I just … want … to go home." The boy broke down completely.

The mother hugged him. "Shhh, it's okay. We don't want to wake your dad." She patted him to his room.

The boy pulled himself together as he eased into bed.

The next morning, he awoke to screams coming from the bathroom.

"I am telling Mom!" the eldest yelled from the shower.

"Mom's not here. Hurry up!"

The boy could hear impish giggles echoing from the kitchen. Two of the brothers entertained themselves by opening the hot water valve in the kitchen sink, which cut the hot-water supply to the bathroom, giving the brother in the shower an instant deluge of ice-cold water.

"If you don't quit it, you'll be sorry!"

"Shut up, we are not doing anything!" they replied, cracking up as they turned the faucet on and off again.

The mother was taking the dad to the bus station. Before she left, she gave the three older brothers strict orders: "All four of you better be ready for Sunday school when I return!" The three older brothers motivated each other to take quick showers using the cold-water trick. The boy opted not to take a shower. Besides, by the time it was his turn, there would be no hot water anyway. The boy brushed his teeth, combed his hair, and put on his Sunday clothes. All four boys were ready for church when the mother honked the horn from the driveway.

As they gathered at the door, the mother burst through carrying a jumbo, bright-purple, helium-filled balloon with enormous white letters.

"Who is that for?"

"It's not yours," the mother replied. "Get in the car. We're late!"

The boy could read. He caught a glimpse of the balloon on the way out. It was his name in big bold letters.

The Sunday school teacher was a big woman with a soft, sweet voice and long, wavy hair to the back of her knees. She taught of heaven and the essence of a name.

"A name is very, very important. There is a little signature at the bottom of every painting which tells us exactly who created the piece. The name identifies the artist. Our creator has a name. There is only one name which summons light and truth, and we must apply that special name, and everything His name represents, to our individual lives."

She spoke of the human need to give of oneself to God. "The world will never know true peace but through the name of Jesus. He is the true Prince of peace."

The teacher's words touched the boy. He could feel the words gently pressing like a Christmas cookie mold or a hand kneading Play-Doh.

After church, the three older siblings were invited to the youth picnic to take advantage of the windy day with kites and games. The mother and the boy would spend the afternoon alone. On their way to the car, they passed by the pastor of the church as he unlocked his Cadillac. He wore a fine tailored, pinstripe, silk suit with gold cuff links and a beautiful gold tie. The man greeted them with perfect white teeth and an oversized, diplomatic smile.

"Hey, there he is." The pastor shook the mother's hand and winked at the boy. "I've got my eye on that one. There is just something about him. Gonna be in church tonight?" The boy stared at the ground, and the pastor gazed expressionless into the distance as he eased into his Cadillac. "Good, we'll see you tonight."

The boy felt as big as a giant.

On the ride home, he stretched across the back of the family jalopy and thought of how much he loved Sunday school—as long as they didn't call his name. He found great discomfort being the object of attention.

As they entered the house, the mother informed the boy she would be taking her afternoon nap. The boy headed straight for his room, where he saw his prize floating: a giant purple balloon with huge, white letters spelling his name. The balloon had a long, white rubber band tied to the bottom for a handle. The boy quickly changed into his play clothes, grabbed his balloon, and headed outdoors.

When he crossed the threshold, a gust of wind nearly ripped the balloon from his hand. He held fast and carefully latched the door behind him. The balloon waved wildly in his rigid grasp as he stepped into the windy world beyond.

The yard looked and smelled different with the grass freshly mowed. Right away he noticed an enormous ant bed overrun by the mower barely a day ago. Thousands of tiny red insects scurried to and fro with exquisite cooperation, rebuilding their broken home. He walked toward the weeping willow at the center of the yard as a black and blue sparrow struggled against the wind. It came to an erratic landing on the clover patch at his feet.

The boy at once turned his face to the sky with a glowing awareness of a certain presence next to him, around him. As the whirling wind disheveled his hair, he stepped carefully backward, well away from the ant bed, lay on his back, and gazed skyward.

He marveled at the racing clouds and the sensation that he too was moving. He remembered his Sunday school teacher's words: "*Give … give to God.*" He wanted to give something to his Friend, anything, everything, but he had nothing to give. A gust of wind forced his balloon to collide with the earth, causing it to spin confusedly. Around, around, and around, the boy's name flashed again and again, *Ches, Ches, Ches*, *Ches*, with blurry elegance. The boy gripped his balloon and lifted it to the sky.

One finger at a time he loosened his grip on the rubber band—pinky finger … ring finger … middle finger—until his index finger and his thumb formed an O holding the balloon to the earth. Ches smiled, opened the O, and watched the balloon as it grew smaller and smaller until it disappeared into the clouds.

I run my hands through my matted hair, filthy with sand and seaweed. I stink of soured garments and seawater and sweat. Is this, hiding in a utility room, the behavior of one who knows the truth? What if someone opens the door? No. Irrational maybe, but my mind has never been so sound. I must do this. I move the little chair from the corner and position it next to the vent so I can hear the meeting in the next room. The music has begun with applause and shouts. The vent is at least thirty feet above the main floor behind the balcony's rail out of view of the congregation. The air handler cycles on again, but the sounds of worship from the sanctuary below can be heard in spite the noise. It is six o'clock.

Chapter 3

Multitudes of lonely, hopeful souls were there. Seeking. Five thousand gathered in the valley as rain gave way to dry, cool air. They'd heard of the boy. They heard he held the answer, the solitary solution to a plurality of confusion and pain. They waited.

The boy climbed a giant rock, held forth his hands, and began to speak.

"Get in the boat. The master is casting his net. There is life in the boat. There is fun, happiness, and safeness in the boat." The boy held high a little toy surfboard with a familiar Disney character in a surfing stance. "This is the boat of Jesus. There are lots of good things, and you have to come aboard." The crowd began to nod and sway like trees waving in a long-awaited breeze. A real tear formed in the boy's eye. "There is direction in the boat. There is no fighting in the boat. And best of all—"

Honk, honk, honk, honk!

The car horn startled the boy. He leaped from his perch atop the washing machine, dropped his plastic toy, and crouched to peer through the louvers of the utility-room door.

The mother yelled from the car to nobody in particular. "Where is he? We're late!"

The boy's view was limited through the louvers, but he could hear everything. The car door slammed a few feet from his head, and he peeked at a slant as the mother stomped past and disappeared. Ches stealthily exited the utility room and tiptoed through the bushes along the side of the house into the backyard. He found a bare spot in the grass where previous tenants had kept a swing set. He kneeled there, pretending to play with two acorns, just as the mother burst through the back door.

"Where is your stupid dad?! We've got to go! We're late. Go get in the car!"

Apparently, both the mother and the dad had forgotten the appointment for student enrollment at the new church school. The dad was nowhere to be found. As the car sped toward the church, Ches lay down in the back seat and gazed at the passing treetops.

"Straight A's? Really? My baby?" The amazed mother gave the boy a genuine hug.

The preacher showed the mother transcripts from the two different elementary schools of the boy's first-grade year. The preacher was twice amazed. He balked at the number of times the family had relocated within seven months, but he also could hardly believe the mother had no idea her youngest son was exceptional. The preacher chuckled. "He's gifted! Look at him!" Statue-still, Ches stared straight at the ground.

The preacher went on to explain how he'd requested the boy's transcripts, and the very next day he'd received the phone call from Palm Grove Elementary, the school Ches had attended the second half of the school year. The voice on the line was Ches's first-grade teacher, Miss Riggs. Ches remembered her for the colorful stories of Native Americans who, until the Europeans arrived, coexisted with the land and fellow tribes in perfect peace and harmony.

Miss Riggs was moved to tears as she spoke. "It's a curious thing," she said. "The boy doesn't speak, yet he completes every assignment without error. But when the boy is called upon to participate with the group, he simply will not respond. Of course we are all keenly interested, but when we administered the test for gifted students, he left the pages blank."

Miss Riggs disclosed that she considered Ches's behavior a sign of extraordinary potential, while other members of the faculty viewed his behavior as a cause for concern. "I think the boy has a special gift," she concluded.

The pastor offered the mother a tuition-free scholarship for Ches. The mother snatched the offer. "Hallelujah, praise the Lord, my boy is gonna make me rich!"

Ches was horrified by what had transpired. He knew he wasn't gifted. But the first semester at Sky View Elementary he had become familiar with the curriculum. The identical material was only just being covered when he enrolled at Palm Grove Elementary the second semester. He would study the familiar material every day, hoping to avoid the attention that comes to students who show signs of struggle. Nevertheless, by the end of the school year, his impeccable academic ability had drawn the attention of the students and faculty alike.

Except for the whirring of the washing machine, the utility room had become a peaceful escape from the encroaching instability and confusion. A raw rage had crept into the day-to-day bearing of the family. While the boy found violence contemptible, certain genetic compulsions pawed impishly at the boy's protective covering, persistently poking for opportunities to push any molecule of darkness to the surface. The family thrived in that world with a shameless disregard for boundaries. For a defenseless seven-year-old trapped in such a world, the only viable option was withdrawal.

Ches expended much energy deflecting impressionable moments. He strained to shake the sounds and contended to keep the vivid images from taking permanent residence in his mind. He worked to devalue the memory of the family motoring into a gas station where the dad and the eldest brother struggled in the restroom at the mother's behest. Ches sat in the back seat of the jalopy as blood-curdling screams echoed throughout the parking lot. He discerned the thud of a seventeen-year-old human body as it slammed again and again shattering the mirror on the wall.

The sound made Ches feel as though he were stripped naked and forced to parade openly on stage with ten thousand stadium lights burning his skin and a thousand voices of inquiry tearing at his wounded soul.

At home, his brothers fought each other ceaselessly in a manner that far surpassed common sibling rivalry. There were fist-size holes in the every wall in the house.

Ches hurt for his whole family. Could they not see? Did they not hear the still, small voice that bids humankind to healthy mental progress?

From his perspective, the presence of God was inescapable; the Holy Ghost was the solitary answer, the sole source of genuine peace, and the opportunity for all the world to finally speak the same language. So, why did his family only pretend? He wondered if other church members pretended. *Am I all alone? Am I the only true believer?*

Questions began to plague Ches in massive quantities, yielding torpid symptoms. He made no effort at school, laden heavy under the burden of inquisition, staring into nothingness day after day. His teacher was divinely patient and never tried too hard to coax the boy into his schoolwork. She painted a colorful little message and placed it on his desk … *Dreamer.*

The family was moving again. Ches was sitting in the back seat of the jalopy when the mother spotted the "For Rent" sign pointing to the old, beige box with brown, weather-beaten trim.

It was much nicer than the house next door. For a moment the mother and the boy ogled the neighboring grounds. Piles of junk covered every square foot of the next-door-neighbor's yard. Military boxes and car doors leaned against the house; a giant mound of car tires filled the center of the front yard, which served as a privacy barrier between the highway and the old place. The porch spilled over with stacks of empty animal cages and an eclectic mix of filthy furniture and car parts and other stuff. There was a porch swing, though, with a surfboard lying lengthwise beneath a stack of newspapers. The mother stared indignantly. "How could anyone live that way?"

A woman stepped out the front door and waved, but the mother and boy turned back to the prospective rental. The mother peered through windows, gathering information. "It has three bedrooms." The boy didn't respond. He'd already spotted the utility room in a detached wing of the main house.

The place was a few paces from a major highway, so the persistent noise of whizzing traffic and honking horns was inescapable. It was walking distance from Gussie Mae's though, and there was a public library at the main intersection.

Family episodes boiled over frequently, and Ches was growing impressively adept at spotting and plotting escape routes. Any time, day or night, without warning, a new episode or another new provocation resulted in much yelling and screaming, or worse. It was in his best interest to know when, where, and how to retreat. With the passage of time, he developed the ability to move with and within the sphere of sanity. He could employ stealth and mobility at any given moment with little inconvenience. He had discovered how to disappear.

Everyone was home except the dad. The family was all moved in, but most things remained in boxes. The morning was oddly peaceful, and Ches decided to get dressed and explore the outside world while the others slept.

He stepped quietly through the front door into the morning sun and let his eyes adjust to the immense brightness. Cars and trucks whizzed past only fifteen steps from the front door. He stood for a moment next to a sweet viburnum and noticed how the dew remained on the tall grass in the shadow of the bush, while the sunlight revealed the excessive bits of trash that accumulated in a yard so near the main highway.

He picked up A small plastic bag with the public library's emblem as he ambled toward the sidewalk. He could see the corner of the library building one hundred yards away on the opposite side of the road. A tractor trailer roared past with such speed the displaced air nearly knocked the boy off balance. He determined it safer to cross the road before reaching the intersection, which he did, looking both ways before crossing. There wasn't a paved sidewalk on the other side of the street, but a well-worn, narrow path unfolded for the short journey to the corner.

He approached the library entrance and the automatic doors opened as he moved forward, introducing the boy with a rush of air like a thousand sparrows swooshing a spectacular welcome. "I am a king!" Ches laughed to himself.

All the stimulating qualities of a library instantly fired his senses: the smell of the books, the quiet and comfort, and the opportunity for an uninhibited search for anything a boy ever wanted to know. Feeling fresh and stealthy, Ches moved through the entrance half expecting an adult to step into his path, but no one noticed him.

He gazed at the giant towers of books in every direction. In an instant, it occurred to him. It was all there. Everything he needed to alleviate the ever-encroaching anguish. All the answers unfurled before him. He continued between the shelves with a vibrant sense of anonymity and freedom until he spotted the kids' section aptly decorated with colorful themes at the top of each aisle. The first aisle displayed a painting of boy and a wolf behind a variety of books. The boy opened an earth-tone book with a sketch of sled dogs and a man cracking a whip. He whispered the title aloud, "*The Call of the Wild.*"

The boy settled into the story and was immediately whisked away. The hours passed as minutes until the lights flickered, signaling the time. An audible voice over the library intercom announced the library was closing. He'd been there all day, caught in the timeless world of boys and wolves. His stomach growled as he stood to his feet and rolled his head to ease the cramp in his neck. He marked his place in the story, returned the book to the display, and quietly moved toward the entrance.

It was hot and humid outside. The late-afternoon sun was low and as bright as it had been the morning, only hotter. Traffic moved through the carbon-monoxide haze as the boy waited for a lull. He crossed the highway with a dreadful pang—not so much of emptiness and hunger, but for having been gone so long with no one knowing his whereabouts. He passed by the utility room door and stepped inside his small bastion of sanity to collect his thoughts while gathering the sense of having been there all along. He exited the utility room, eased around to the back door, and entered the house.

The mother stood in the kitchen, facing the boy, but she stared motionless at a piece of paper on the counter. The boy eased past without a word and sauntered along the hall to his room. He sat on his bed and silently examined the moment. It was apparent the house was empty except for the mother. He pondered the possibility that he could be so unnoticed. He stayed put for a half hour until he heard the door to his mother's bedroom close, then he tiptoed to the kitchen, poured himself a glass of milk, and contemplated the world of wolves.

The next-door neighbor, a widow, Ms. Snodgrass, had often offered to take the boys to the beach. The mother always refused the invitations because she suffered from an acute fear of water. The boy wondered why, on this day, the mother agreed to let the boys go to the beach.

There was hardly enough room for the four brothers to fit in the widow's small station wagon. One of the brothers scavenged the surfboard from the widow's porch swing and stowed it across the back where Ches sat.

Ches couldn't take his eyes off it. The fiberglass board was an agglomeration of mildew and stale wax on the surface, but beneath the filmy layer he could discern the meticulous creation it once had been. It had a bright, blue-and-white finish with stylish balsam lines from nose to tail that whispered a story of sunny days gone by. It had a single keel the shape of a dorsal fin and a vinyl leash with a Velcro ankle attachment. Ches attached the leash to his ankle and closed his eyes. After twenty minutes of travel, the smell of ocean wafted into the back seat.

The brothers piled out of the car and ran for the water. One of them grabbed the surfboard, but the leash was still attached to the boy's ankle. The brother yelled at the boy for the inconvenience, ripped the anklet free, and stole away.

Ches helped the widow with the towels and bags of food. He noticed a lime-green, plastic sand bucket with a matching shovel for digging. Ms. Snodgrass said she bought them especially for him.

Together they found a nice spot on the beach where she spread a blanket, unfolded her chair, and relaxed with a magazine. Ches took the bucket and halfheartedly began to dig in the sand. Within minutes he'd constructed a fine sand castle with a mote, lookout towers, and a secret tunnel, as if he'd done it a hundred times. Nevertheless, his attention was on the activity of his brothers.

He could see the three fighting over the surfboard amid the pounding waves. One brother tore the board from the grasp of another, and a wave tore the board from his grasp. All three chased the board as it tumbled shoreward. Two brothers fell into a drop-off at the edge of the sandbar, while the other brother seized the opportunity and stole away with the surfboard down the beach, where he proceeded to paddle out alone against the crashing waves.

The other two brothers returned to the blanket and collapsed exhausted. Ten minutes later, the brother appeared, boasting of his magnificent ride on a giant wave. He claimed he'd successfully stood to his feet on his first try. Without disputing the claim, the second eldest brother grabbed the board and motioned for Ches.

As they reached the water's edge, the boy's heart raced. The water was cold at first, but it didn't take long to grow accustomed in the summer heat. They stepped into the water and dropped immediately to their waists. The boy urgently reached for his brother's arm as the drop-off was over his head. In a rare show of attentiveness, the brother held fast to his smaller sibling's arm and guided him to the sandbar, where he could manage on his own. They continued trudging onward to the far side of the sandbar.

The swell wasn't big, but the newness of the environment quickened Ches to a brand-new place within himself. While he was especially aware of the dangers, he was so awash with anticipation of what was to come that his fear was neutralized.

They arrived at the far side of the sandbar, and they could hear the other two brothers calling out excitedly and plodding through the water to where their siblings staged themselves. The three older brothers worked together to hoist the boy onto the surfboard and push him further out. Each brother shouted advice from imaginary stores of knowledge as the boy lay flat on his belly, gripping the buoyant board by the rails.

All at once swells materialized on the horizon. The eldest brother began to panic at the sight of the rising ocean. The approaching waves loomed much larger than anticipated. The eldest screamed and frantically flailed his way in retreat to the safety of the shallows.

The other two brothers assured the boy everything would be fine. As the wave rolled beneath, they spun the nose of the surfboard toward the beach and barked unintelligible instructions into both of the boy's ears. The boy could feel the ocean drop as water began to slide to the back edge of the sandbar. For a moment, Ches thought he was being sucked seaward, but then he rose swiftly skyward, and the brothers gave the surfboard a push, sending him headlong into the unknown.

Ches could feel the immediate velocity of the wave as it doubled up, leaving him wavering at the crest in an accelerated motion to shore. The angle of the surfboard began to tilt to the trough with a surge of downward speed. Instinctively, the boy tightened his grip on the rails of the surfboard and slid his weight backward, but his small frame slipped partially to the side of the board. The tilt to the side changed the direction of the nose, angling the surfboard onto the open face of the growing wall of water. His speed increased rapidly as he traveled parallel to the beach.

He could feel the board rattle as the hard plane of the underside skimmed the ocean surface. His senses sharpened. Rushing wind blew his hair back, and adrenaline shot through his body as he raced down the line of the wave. The board drifted higher on the face of the wave, and he leaned lightly to the downhill rail to correct the upward motion. He was surfing! Time disappeared. The boy had entered a brand-new world.

He could feel a smile stretch the parameters of his face. His gut began to tighten too, not from tension, but from laughter conceived in his bosom, pushing its way out. The wave moved into shallower water, growing steeper and increasing in speed. Immense volumes of sea rolled into form, drawing the surfboard so strongly now to the crest that Ches had to lean with all his body on the downhill side. The stacking wave heaved over, capturing the young surfer in a tunnel.

The sound. The chase. The echo of a collapsing watery cave—dark but free. The light at the end grew smaller and slammed shut.

Searing pain shot through Ches's body as his tender nose slammed viciously into the deck of the surfboard. Saltwater forced its way into his mouth and nose. With his lungs only half filled with air, he sealed his lips tight to prevent the deluge of ocean from entering his body. He clung desperately to his board as it rolled violently over and over, upside down and backward, scraping to a stop on the sandy shore.

All three brothers ran to where the boy lay motionless at the ocean's edge. The eldest brother still screamed in high-pitched panic while the middle two cracked up, laughing. The boy was laughing too. Blood poured from his nose and mouth, and he was laughing.

What does it mean to be willing to die for a cause? Does the will to give one's life for a cause validate the cause? Is there a cause so noble, that it commands its adherents never to kill, but to always give life? The unit cycles off again. The congregation below is silent. A man makes announcements and takes prayer requests from the congregation. I sit in the child-size chair as the service transitions to the choir. The harmonies are soft, beautiful; they shower over me and break down the ego I've work so hard to conceal. Why am I trembling? Why do I always tremble? Why do I weep now?

Chapter 4

"GET HIM," THE mother screamed. She was intoxicated with the sound of her own words and the power she wielded. The mother was small in stature, but the dad, a large man, was subject to the force of her tongue. The mother demanded the dad take issue with the second eldest brother.

The brother shriveled backward into the tiny bedroom as the dad gently closed the door and locked it behind them. The mother was smug and satisfied when she turned to the boy, who sat in the corner, quietly studying her movements. "Go to your room! *Now!*"

Ches ran to his room, closed the door behind, and stared at nothing. He could hear his dad's voice, contaminated and grotesque, through the drywall. He could hear languid whimpers emitting from his brother and the loud crash of things he imagined as lamps or toys. Then, a dull thud, and a human body slid down the wall. Ches wondered why his brother didn't cry out. The dad was barking unintelligible military slang. The room went quiet for a time, but the strangeness started again. More thuds and more whimpers from the brother. Ches wept silently.

An hour later, the door to his brother's room opened and closed again, then the door to his room opened, and suddenly he was staring into the face of his dad. For an endless moment their eyes locked, father and boy without expression, and the boy concealed a deep curiosity as he looked into the eyes of a wild beast before the attack. Without speaking, the dad turned away and closed the door behind him. The boy cried again and pulled the bedsheet over his head.

Time moved at an accelerated rate. The boy was nearing his ninth birthday. Two birthdays had passed unnoticed by the family. They no longer attended church. The mother claimed something awful happened and decided it was better not to associate with hypocrites and fakes. She withdrew the boy from the church school and enrolled him at the nearest elementary school. Soon after, the faculty tried to administer a test for the curriculum compacting program, but Ches wouldn't cooperate.

Most weekdays, on the way home from school, Ches would pass right by the house and head straight to the library, where he spent the bulk of his time. The dad hadn't been able to find work for over a year, and with his idle presence, the atmosphere inside the house turned critical. In the past, the dad had been inclined to shield the boy from certain unpleasantries, but now those considerations were withdrawn. The boy wasn't afraid.

Twice he walked in on the parents in the middle of an intense fight. The dad exploded and pinned the boy to the wall. The boy could look without fear into the eyes of his dad. He could feel the moistness and heat from the large masculine body and smell the chronic halitosis. He could see the red pattern of his dad's eyeballs and the blue veins bulging from his temples. In these moments Ches would placidly bore into his dad's beastly eyes, and wrest the troubled sea into compliance. Ches was never afraid. He had the ability to tranqualize the thing that reduced humans to something else, something lower. And when the primal bomb was diffused, Ches would go to the library.

It was Saturday morning. The boy awakened to the sounds of his dad and eldest brother arguing. He could hear some of the conversation and the mother's effort to intercede on behalf of the brother, which was rare. Laundry was such a trivial reason for conflict, but the ghastly tone in the dad's voice sent a chill through the boy's body. There was something different about the sound and shape of the discourse. The mother negotiated soberly, but the boy could make no sense of her ethereal pleas so soft and eerie. A sense of urgency washed over the boy, and he anxiously thought of ways to neutralize this event as it cascaded into an unknown province.

The back door slammed. Ches stood on the mattress, peeked out the window, and caught the image of his brother escaping between the viburnums. With a sense of relief, he pressed his ear to the bedroom door straining to hear.

It was quiet.

He thought for a moment he'd imagined it all. Maybe the strange sense of emergency was without reason. Maybe he discerned something that wasn't real. He slowly opened the door to another strange sound; that of an animal; a partial bleat of a sheep or the short desperate low of a baby cow. Repugnant shivers rippled over his body. His dad was speaking with a voice of one affected by helium gas but deeper. The mother was now very steady, pleading in a clear, articulate manner the boy had never heard her employ.

Silence.

The boy's mind raced with options. He heard the wet thud of a fist smashing into flesh, followed by a long, drawn-out mew of a cat. Again he heard the punching sound, this time more of a crack.

His mother pleaded. The dad's voice sounded like another human being altogether, neither man nor woman. "Shut … it … shuuit … your … mouth … wooman!"

The boy opened his door and stepped into the hall. He could see two feet dragging the floor, and the dad with the mother's hair wrapped in his fist, sliding her body through a pool of blood, smearing a trail into the kitchen. The boy began screaming in the gruffest voice he could conjure with eight-year-old vocal chords. "I am leaving! I am leaving!" He heard his mother's head slam the kitchen cabinet with sickening force as he ran back to his room with the sound of footsteps behind him. He stepped onto the bed, opened the window, frantically punched out the screen, and slid out headfirst.

Thinking he was being chased, the boy ran along the highway toward the intersection. In bumper-to-bumper traffic, he started to cross at the signal but remembered his mother. He felt moisture and a searing pain shoot through his right foot, and he realized he was barefoot and still wearing pajamas. There was a tree on the corner where he examined his foot, caked with blood and dirt. He quickly dislodged the shard of glass, climbed the tree, and stood there trembling on a branch four feet above the ground.

A minute later, the mother appeared, running through the middle of the highway, frantically waving her arms in a desperate attempt to stop one of the passing cars. Traffic swerved to avoid the woman as she staggered toward the intersection, flailing and screaming. The traffic light turned red, and a line of cars formed in the turning lane. The mother banged on every window as she ran past, begging for help, but the light turned green, and cars began to move forward. A VW bug stopped in the intersection, opened its passenger door, and a pregnant woman appeared and climbed into the back seat as the frantic mother disappeared into the cab.

The boy jumped out of the tree and limped toward the intersection. Car's swerved violently to avoid collision with the boy who stood in the path of the VW with his fingers in his ears. The mother spotted the boy and started wailing, "My baby. That's my baby!" The male driver opened his door and rushed the boy into the back seat, where two adults and a nine-year-old girl made room. The car's tires screeched as it sped away.

The mother's face was bloody and unrecognizable. Her nose was folded to the side, her right eye was shut and puffy like a grapefruit, and her lip was severely lacerated, black and swollen. The male driver said he would take her to the fire station. But the mother directed him to the home of Gussie Mae.

The bloody mother and boy wobbled to the door and knocked. Gussie Mae opened the door, extended her hand unstartled, and ushered them inside as if she expected their arrival.

It had been two years, but the smell of the place had an instant soothing effect. There was a fresh batch of peanut butter cookies on the counter.

While Gussie Mae attended the mother, the boy found his corner behind the chair, lay on his side, and curled into a ball.

The dad called the police on himself, was arrested, and was ultimately committed to a mental hospital. The brothers were dispersed to various takers in the church. The mother and the boy spent the next three weeks with Gussie Mae.

During their stay, Ches awoke every morning to the sounds of Gussie Mae praying fervently. He became acquainted with the rhythm and flow of the old woman's habit, studying the prayerful progression as it moved from recognizable phrases to utterances that he could make no sense of. The boy contemplated the meaning of it all—not the translation of the words, but the realness of the unknowable words that summon such palpable peace and stability.

What has kept me from moving to an island in the South Pacific?—Samoa, Fiji, Micronesia, or the Mentawais in the Indian Ocean. Certainly not fear or lack of desire, or survivability. If I could survive here, I could survive there. Couldn't happiness find me there? Couldn't peace find me there? All I really need is a fishing rod, a garden, and a means to tread upon the waves. While the rest of the world cranked out continuous wars over which human system will save them, I could've lived far from the minds of the mainstream—out of sight, out of mind, with a big, genuine smile. O, how I wanted a place in the wilderness for the wayfaring man. As they squabbled within the confines of their pluralistic merry-go-round, I could've flourished in another world free of fighting and backbiting and conspiracy theories.

Chapter 5

It was the month of October, and Ches had already missed five days of school. He liked his teacher, Mr. Coffee, but after the third week, the man hadn't come to work. The rumor was that Mr. Coffee had lost his mind. Ches's new teacher, Ms. Love, had no patience for the boy's reserved manner. She would comment toxically on his reputation as an exceptional student and openly berate him when he wouldn't respond. The boy thoroughly reverted. None of it mattered anyway, because the mother soon announced the family had to relocate.

The church had purchased a parcel of land, thirty-nine acres on a dead-end service road at the convergence of two major highways. The land was a densely wooded mix of oaks and pines, which buffered the sounds of thoroughfare traffic. There was a large freshwater pond with fish and bullfrogs, alligators and snakes. Plans were underway to build a magnificent edifice on the grounds with facilities for a private school. A twenty-five-foot mobile home with two small rooms came with the deal. The pastor told Gussie Mae the family could stay in the trailer until they found another place.

There was an elementary school within walking distance from the trailer, but because of district boundary issues, Ches would be required to commute several miles away to a school in the adjacent zone. The mother abhorred the fact that the boy had to ride the school bus with the blacks from the neighboring projects, so she submitted a fake address and enrolled Ches at the elementary school in the neighborhood behind the church property.

The fact that Ches had attended three different schools his fourth-grade year was of small consequence. The only things that mattered to him were books and space. He became a fixture in the school library, where he discovered Hemingway and Twain. He'd read most of Jack London, including a short story of the author's experience with the sport of kings: surfing. He read incessantly, pursuing answers to undefined questions, questions that resided dormant, buried among the slow, cementing words of authors past. The more he read, the higher the undefined questions rose, until the rising swell of query increased his need for space. The thirty-nine acres of the church property would accommodate this need.

He found a hatchet beneath the trailer next to a crate of fishing gear and chopped down saplings four inches in diameter. He worked in the woods until his hands were blistered and swollen. He worked until the pain gave way to solace. Then he'd sit for hours at the water's edge, thinking, waiting, and a water moccasin would swim past in an S pattern. He'd study the grasshopper floating on the serene surface, how it struggled, and the circular pulses that aroused predators from the pond's dark depths. Something swooshed the water, and the bug disappeared.

He checked out a book of fishing from the school library and learned the step-by-step method for cleaning a fish and knot tying and using a rod and reel. He returned the book with a smidgen of fish blood inside the cover.

Good calluses had formed on his hands from notching logs. He erected a four-by-six-foot structure four feet high without a door or window. He fastened the smaller saplings crossways over the top with palmetto branches woven through for a roof, and then he dug a hole under the wall for an entrance and covered it with palmettos.

He staged the extra logs along the bank of the pond, where he cut each log in equal lengths of five feet, and then he lashed the logs together. He eased his creation into the water. It floated, though not sufficiently.

The next day after school, Ches retrieved two empty gallon jugs from the school trash. He figured he needed at least six more with lids to complete his raft. Instead of taking the usual route through the woods, he walked the opposite way around through the projects.

The iron-rod turnstile separated the vast complex from the rest of the world, and it creaked eerily as he passed through. He immediately spotted a trash dumpster, and beside it his friend, Tyrone Jackson, teaching a small girl to ride a bicycle.

"Whatup, fool?" Tyrone said, smiling, surprised to see the boy.

Ches smiled back. "I know a trick to teach her to ride."

"Whaaat? White boy, you crazy!"

"I mean it, Tyrone. Do you have a pair of pliers or a small wrench?"

"What you gon do, torture my lil sistah? I'll beat you down, punk!"

Daryl, the maintenance man, approached, driving a golf cart.

"Yo, Daryl, lemme hol a wrench. My lil white friend say he gonna teach Lacrishia how to ride a two-wheel."

Daryl pulled a pair of channel locks from his tool bag and handed them to the boy. The boy turned the bike upside down and began removing the pedals while Tyrone and Daryl cracked jokes directed at Ches's big head and little body.

"Dat honkey got a bobble head!"

"Bettah be careful, dat head gon mess with da gravitational pull of da moon and tweak the planetary alignments."

The boy smiled, righted the bike, and told Lacrishia to forget about the pedals and instead use her feet on the ground to drive herself forward. The boy instructed Tyrone to entice Lacrishia into a chase around the parking lot. The siblings disappeared around the corner, and Ches returned to his search.

He slid the door to the trash dumpster, revealing two gallon-sized milk jugs with lids. He walked around the bin and slid the opposite door open. The stench was suffocating. He moved a bag aside, revealing three more empty bleach jugs and a piece of rope under a TV set. He stretched his torso until his fingers blindly grasped the end of the rope and pulled it aggressively. The rope was too long. He measured the desired length and scraped the rope vigorously on the rusty edge of the dumpster until it was severed, then he threaded the rope through the handles of the five jugs.

The final dumpster was empty but for a solitary detergent jug on the sordid floor. As he slid the door shut, Tyrone and Lacrishia came tearing around the corner, cracking up laughing. Tyrone was running backward, with Lacrishia on her bike in hot pursuit. She chased her brother with gigantic, slow-motion strides. Her right foot would push off, and then she would glide for a considerable distance, and then her left foot would push off. The space between points of contact became the magical world of balance. Ches reattached the bike pedals, gathered his stringer of jugs, and made his way out of the projects with Lacrishia peddling confidently after.

Back at the water's edge, he used the line to secure the jugs to the underside of the raft uniformly. With the final jug in place, he eased the raft onto the water. The jugs significantly increased the raft's buoyancy so that the deck remained two inches above the surface of the water. The boy extended his foot to test whether the raft could hold his weight. He transferred as much of his body as he could without losing his balance and then jumped on with both feet. The raft worthily supported his small frame, and he drifted into the center of the pond without a paddle. He lay on his back with his hands behind his head and gazed skyward.

Ches avoided the cramped family dwelling as much as possible. In school, he made enough effort to advance, but was thoroughly repulsed by extracurricular activities. A rumor spread that an overzealous religious group had purchased the wooded property. And when the boy's classmates discovered he lived on the grounds, a relentless barrage of pestering ensued. Every day at every opportunity, one or another of his classmates would comment on how quiet the boy was, and that his peculiarity must be the mark of some strange religion. They would call him names like Holy Roller and Cult Boy.

Things were changing on the church property. Church membership had increased exponentially and construction of an enormous new building was underway. Bulldozers moved earth, tractors felled trees, and the sounds of heavy equipment now echoed regularly. Ches observed from the periphery. He contemplated the purpose of the construction. He pondered the possibility that this might be an overzealous religious group whose growing numbers could be attributed to people who were disinclined to think critically.

He considered himself impervious to it all. His method of withdrawal afforded innumerable advantages. He could make up his mind about the world beneath the obnoxious bullhorn of a particular group bent on mass-producing itself. He found a freedom and invisibility that enabled him to walk on water without the faintest ripple. And he embraced this power, wielding it with effortless grace as one recruited by indestructible forces from a timeless neighboring dimension.

After two years in the trailer, the stench of rotten carcass hadn't faded, and neither had the fighting within the family. The dad stayed away most of the time. But when the man was home, his presence caused the environment to decline rapidly into a volatile state. The boy tried to avoid any spontaneous family outings. But he was forced to participate now and again.

During one such outing, in the middle of a major thoroughfare, a fight erupted over the choice of which park to visit. At a traffic signal, the eldest brother exited the car, calling on the other two to step out and fight him. The mother put the car in park in the middle of the intersection, and the parents began to fight between themselves. The boy slipped into a fake seizure with loud convulsions that miraculously neutralized the family meltdown. The brother quietly climbed back into the car, and they continued on as though nothing had happened.

Ches often wondered why the parents didn't divorce. The primary character of the family was wildness; every man's hand was against every man. The boy would try to understand. *Doesn't this world have more to offer?* He would think about such things as the price of gold and the news of the Iran hostage crisis, and why, considering the grand scheme of things, why couldn't his family latch hold of the tiniest molecule of peace and cultivate it for dear life.

He thought about the future and about life beyond. He marveled at universal forces beyond human control and how he was never given a choice concerning the event of his own birth. He couldn't say for certain what his response would be had he been given a choice. *What if someone had approached me, before the point of conception, and showed me a movie of this life of uncertainty, pain, and confusion? What if I had been invited to choose? Would I have declined the invitation?*

Ches mastered the skill of gleaning pockets of pleasure from lifeless circumstances in spite of the tangible loneliness asserting itself into the process. He saw family relationships as superficial and unfulfilling, as something one must guard oneself from. At the same time he began to suspect that the burgeoning loneliness did not stem from the absence of people.

He sometimes thought of a girl. Not girls, but a girl, a girl like Becky Thatcher, a girl with whom he could hold hands and explore the inky depths of the darkest cave. He imagined moments of urgent discoveries together, when the rarest air and arcane light would be the secret between them.

The stay on the property was coming to an end. A serious controversy with the pastor had paved the way for a new pastor, an African American man who was polite and firm when he invited the family to find another place to live. And while Ches couldn't remember a longer place of residency, he never felt the trailer on the church property was his home anyway.

An anonymous church member secured a rental for the family: a house along a busy four-lane highway next door to a gas station. The house was plywood with asphalt shingle siding. It had one bedroom and a spacious utility room to be used as a second bedroom.

There was a perfect hole in the roof the size of a large watermelon, straight through the corner of the ceiling and through the floor directly beneath. By the vertical alignment of the holes, the boy imagined the damage had been caused by an experiment gone awry or a gigantic spear hurled from the heavens. One of the brothers found a four-foot-square sheet of plastic and a piece of plywood. He covered the hole and fastened it with nails, but it leaked all the same.

The smell of the place was every bit as awful as the previous dwelling, minus the rotted carcass. There was a pile of urine-saturated clothes in the bedroom and putrid dirty dishes in the kitchen sink, which was filled with black gunk. The fireplace in the living room was a storage place for books, stacked vertically and filling the entire space. There was a stack of old records and a record player with medium-sized speakers in the corner.

The boy flipped through the records of artists he'd never heard of: Herb Alpert and the Tijuana Brass, Gershwin, Bob Dylan, Billy Joel, Rush, Mahler, and Mendelssohn, plus a two classical 45s featuring the cello and the piano.

The mother stuffed the piles of clothes into large trash bags and dragged them to the side of the highway for the trash truck. She yelled at the boy to get to work, and he began in the living room, gathering an armload of records. He didn't want to throw these away, so he quickly ran to the backyard, hoping to find a safe place for the music.

There was an old doghouse in the far corner, hidden among the overgrown weeds. He parted the spiderwebs and gingerly stacked the records on the dirty doghouse floor, then raced back to the house, coordinating his entrance with the mother's exit. He slid the speakers into the back corner of the doghouse with space in the front for the record player.

Next he gathered the books from the fireplace, but instead of throwing the stack of books in the trash, he stuffed them in the car between the piles of stuff to be taken back into the house. Before long, the mother was carrying the books from the car into the house and stacking them nicely in the corner. "What are you staring at? Help me with these stupid books!"

As he carried stuff in and out, he began to strategize for this next phase of life. It was summer, and dark summer clouds gathered overhead. The clouds gave way to rain as a beat-up pickup truck pulled into the driveway, filled to capacity with more of the family's stuff.

Why is conflict, with the prospect of death, a force that gives us meaning? What would the masses do without war? And yet haven't I found something worth dying for? —the only thing worth dying for; the one thing so powerful that it doesn't require a sword to force faith upon the world. Or has it found me?—that thing that too few find worth living for. I stand to stretch in the small dark space and unintentionally kick the vent just as the unit cycles off. I am sure the people below heard the sound. If I get caught, I will comply at first, but then run, far away. But I will not get caught. I will go through with this. I am committed.

Chapter 6

CHES SPENT THE hottest days of summer in the backyard under the oak tree, reading the books in his collection. By August he'd read a book of essays and poems by Ralph Waldo Emerson and a book of short stories by Fyodor Dostoyevsky, including *The Dream of the Ridiculous Man*. He read the story several times but couldn't understand why it made him laugh and made him feel gross all at once.

There was also a complete set of Hardy Boys mysteries, which he read through as if sugar were pouring from the pages. The Hardy Boys weren't as deeply layered and gut punchy as Dostoyevsky, but he liked the two equally.

The book he found most captivating, by far the thickest book, was a book of Greek mythology. The cover and title had been torn away. The pages were laden with three-in-one doctrines, triadic groupings of fickle gods and goddesses roiled in steamy conspiracy, jockeying and competing to self-serving ends.

He found the idea of a pluralized deity intriguing. He'd been taught to believe rigidly in only one God as opposed to any archaic triad—a solitary one as opposed to a pluralized or composite god. In fact Gussie Mae was quick to differentiate between the different types of monotheism. There is the trimorphos monotheism of the post-Nicene era, giving rise to the Crusades and worse. But before Nicaea there was the pure monotheism represented in the much-persecuted pretrinitarian church. "They made it a capital punishment to deny the Trinity, but a double-minded or a triple-minded anything is unstable and impure," Gussie Mae would say with a wrinkly chuckle. "When the Trinity became law, the church became corrupt and violent!"

Ches recalled that the overwhelming majority of modern Christians worship a triune god, but there have always been a minority of Christians who reject the plural explanation of God on pain of persecution. Anyway, the idea of a pantheon was refreshing, expressed in deities such as the three judges of the underworld, Rhadamanthys, Minos and Aiakos, and Hecate in her special role at three-way crossroads, all erotic and unabashed, manipulating the affairs of mortal man.

It was the week of his birthday. He would be eleven years old. He decided to celebrate by repairing an old bicycle he'd found in the weeds behind the doghouse. It was a BMX-style bike with a nickel-plated chain.

The bike's frame was constructed of composite aluminum and had very little rust. Most of the mildew washed away with the steady stream of the water hose, and a soapy rag struck an effortless swath clean through the sap and dirt, revealing the brightness of a nearly new machine. He squeezed the sparkling blue hand brakes, and the alloy calipers functioned perfectly. The bike had a much nicer setup than the average bike from a department store.

Both tires were completely flat, but the frame was incredibly light, so he carried it to the neighboring gas station to use a public air compressor. He listened for leaks by pressing his ear to the inflated tires but there were none.

Ches leaned against the gas pump, staring awestruck at the BMX bike perfectly suited to a boy his size. The colors were what he would've chosen if he'd had the luxury of choice.

A car coasted to the gas pump, and a woman stepped out and asked the boy if he was okay. Ches stared straight at the ground without a word, wheeled the bike into the open parking lot, and rode away. He passed the family shack and kept riding.

The highway was busy, and he hadn't noticed how big a highway it was until then. Cars whizzed by in pulses, wafting carbon monoxide swirls into his nostrils. He passed shopping centers, grocery stores, and beauty shops until he came to a four-lane intersection. He pressed the pedestrian button and waited for the signal. A city bus rumbled in the turning lane, and the boy shrank beneath the noisy grill. In the distance he could see a familiar sign.

The new library was an enormous, multilevel construction of white coquina with floor-to-ceiling windows on three sides. It was set in a manicured landscape of tropical plants and St. Augustine grass. Sprawling concrete steps wrapped the compound, with a ramp on each corner.

Ches rolled his bike up the ramp and lifted it into the bike rack in the breezeway. He notice a ten-speed secured to the rack with a lock and chain and wondered if it was unwise to leave his bike unsecured, but he decided to make a quick inspection of the library and check on his bike every few minutes.

He passed through the automatic doors and received the welcoming woosh of air and familiar smell he'd come to associate with all public libraries. The interior was open from floor to ceiling with an atrium and spiral staircase in the center of the facility. A giant display posted dates of conferences and lectures, and a signboard pointed to the various departments.

The calendar listed a classic film night on Tuesdays and karate classes on Thursday nights, about which he immediately inquired. The librarian smiled and gave the boy a form that required the signature of a parent or guardian. He filled in the form with a fake phone number and address and then forged a signature.

Ches ambled in a random direction toward a towering aisle of books labeled "Philosophy." The book at eye level caught his attention and seemed a good enough place to start.

It had a classic binding with gold letters: *The Origin and Goal of History,* Karl Jaspers. The boy slid the book from its place and quietly moved beneath the towers to the children's section, where he was greeted with colorful décor celebrating famous authors. At the center was a giant animated painting of a steam locomotive with Mark Twain as the conductor and train cars filled with characters from literary classics such as *Oliver Twist*, *White Fang*, and *Alice in Wonderland*. He walked to the back corner to a desk beside a giant beanbag.

The kids' section was stone quiet. Ches had the entire place to himself on a hot afternoon. He plopped onto the beanbag and opened the book. It was different from anything he'd read to that point. He would read a section and ponder and stumble on the meaning of a word. By the second page, he found it necessary to leave his station and retrieve a dictionary from the main library, keeping it handy for words such as *empirical* and *existential* and *paradigm*.

Ches read about humanity's origin, which gave birth to four rivers of civilization, each splitting into a multiplicity of cultures until the Axial Age, when philosophical and religious thought blossomed, enlightening humankind with its spread. The rise of vast empires gave rise to modernity and world war until globalization forced humankind to re-join as a whole. "That which is experienced in the loftiest flights of the spirit as a coming-to-oneself within Being, or as *unio mystica*, as becoming one with the Godhead, or as becoming a tool for the will of God is expressed in an ambiguous form."

The boy searched the dictionary for the meaning of the word *ambiguous* and came first to the word *aboriginal:* "inhabiting or existing in a land from the earliest times; indigenous." This presented another thought. He hurried to the card catalog and searched for books about aborigines. There was the *Encyclopedia on Aboriginal Cultures* and, skimming through, he stopped at an article on oppressed and devalued indigenous worldviews: "Any culture not in line with the Western Judeo-Christian paradigm was deemed to be either backward and inferior, or altogether obsolete. Nevertheless, there are viable alternatives to the Judeo-Christian paradigm, as the aboriginal worldview is extremely relevant today."

According to the writers, aboriginal wisdom is rooted in ancient relations to the world and must be accepted as equal to Western scientific knowledge, precisely because it is inherently holistic and cyclical. The boy pondered this idea, recalling his first-grade teacher's preoccupation with the perfect peace and harmony of the Native Americans—peace and harmony that, she claimed, was disrupted by the Europeans.

Ches shook himself from this tangent and returned to the definition of *ambiguity*. He concluded that having a double or triple meaning with respect to spiritual matters could well explain the world's colossal level of confusion. *If the final destination is ambiguity, if heaven itself is unresolved mystique, why should I aspire to it?*

Ches stood to stretch and realized the sun had set. He gasped as he remembered his unsecured bicycle. He hadn't checked on it. He quickly squeezed the book between two giant children's picture books on the bottom shelf and hurried through the empty library, craning his neck, scanning the breezeway. As he passed through the sliding glass door, his heart sank. The rack was empty.

He stood there shaking his head, dumbfounded. It was almost nine, and he was miles from home. Perplexed, he turned his head, and out of the corner of his eye he caught sight of another bike rack at the other end of the breezeway. His heart raced as he rounded the corner by the main entrance. There it was, right where he had left it. He stood shaking his head again, staring at his birthday present.

The return ride was dark and unsettling. The roads were no less busy than they had been that afternoon; cars whizzed by with blinding speed under the dim light of the pole-mounted street lamps. The night was warm and humid, and beads of perspiration formed on his lip and forehead. His mind buzzed with the theories of Karl Jaspers. He felt sick to his stomach as gluttonous portions of alien information swelled in his virgin mind. A defined question arose as a result, or maybe a symptom: *So many religions, culturally unrelated, and geographically disconnected, yet they hold so many things in common. How is it that ancient aborigines in the Southern Hemisphere share similar cyclical views as an ancient culture in the Northern Hemisphere?*

Ches stopped at the traffic light, pressed the button, and waited for the walk signal. Car tires screech in the distance, followed by sounding horns, and another sound, which he determined definitely to be a crash. Noisy tractor-trailers made it impossible to perceive in what direction the calamity was.

The walk signal changed, and he cautiously rode his bike before the waiting cars. Screams echoed in the distance. A man sat on the corner sidewalk, gulping the contents from a bottle hidden in a brown paper bag. He garbled something sinister and unintelligible, and the boy accelerated with a burst of fear and adrenalin. He peddled furiously into the growing night. He could see that beyond the next block, it was pitch black with no streetlights. He would have to travel the final portion of his journey by the light of the passing cars, now growing fewer.

The night air cooled his overheating body as he peddled cautiously onward until his eyes acclimated to the darkness and his confidence pushed him to maintain his pace. His T-shirt was drenched with sweat, and he continued the sprint ten minutes more, stealthily negotiating obstacles until he arrived at his destination.

The boy's heart pounded all the way to his temples, and his legs trembled as he coasted by an unfamiliar car next to the family jalopy. He stood in the dark kitchen for a moment, preparing an alibi of hide-and-seek with neighborhood kids. He could hear strange voices coming from the lighted living room, and he hoped to pass through without a word. As he entered, he saw two of the brothers and the mother sitting with youth workers from the church, a young man and a woman.

The couple was clean and heavyset. The man had short, unparted hair slicked straight back, reminiscent of the Roaring Twenties. His modern-fit polyester suit matched his patent-leather, square-toe boots. The roll of flesh below his chin barely moved when he smiled. The woman wore her hair piled on top of her head, with long strands left out to accentuate her plain, round face.

The mother introduced the man and his wife. Ches nodded politely, and the hefty man winked as though he and Ches were longtime friends. "Boy, yer sweat'n like a long-tail cat in a room full of rock'n chairs!" Ches nodded again and made his way into the back.

After a shower, he tucked into his bed, closed his eyes, and whispered, "*Happy birthday.*"

He awoke the following morning and sat in his bed, assessing the new information that took awkward residence in his brain. The Greek mythology seemed harmless in light of common consensus that it was indeed myth. Karl Jasper's theory, however, was not presented as myth but as theory, derived through empirical methods. Until now the boy had never been so directly challenged to take inventory of what he believed.

After breakfast, Ches returned to the doghouse and transferred the old records and record player into his bedroom. He found an electrical outlet behind his bunk and neatly assembled the player so it could slide under the bed and back out again conveniently. The head of the bunk bed was already eight inches from the wall, so he inserted the speakers into the space between, out of sight of the doorway.

He flipped through the albums and found one that bore no artwork, only handwriting in sloppy cursive, *cello.* He gingerly placed the swing arm on the edge of the turning disk until the needle rested on the outermost edge. A crackling sound echoed in the dusty space below as the boy squeezed his body under the bed next to the speakers.

Ches relaxed and closed his eyes. The crackling sound gave way to roaring applause, then silence again. Another sound in five beats gently pierced the darkness and flowed into his ears like a human voice, deep and lonely. One note sounded—low, long, and slow—then a half step to the next note with a vibrato. Then, from a great distance, with rising intensity, the high note of a viola swooped in and swirled around the long, sad notes of the cello simultaneously cascading from the stereo speakers into the dark beneath the bed.

Ches's heart rate increased. He hadn't known such things existed. He felt his facial expressions torque to the flow of emotion emitting from these incredible instruments. Then a third instrument, a violin, drew a large arc over and around the yearning flutter of the string dual. It all stopped abruptly with a repetitive skip over the scratched vinyl. The boy then listened to the Rush album until he had every lyric memorized.

Ches's visits to the library became routine. Everything was there, and it was all free. He packed food and water into a backpack he'd found in the bathroom closet. Tuesday nights he would view reel-to-reel classics, such as *House of Usher* or Marx Brothers films. On Thursdays he participated in a karate class with two other students: a red-haired, pale-skinned boy of fourteen who was extremely overweight and a twelve-year-old girl, tall, with a popular hairstyle and trendy neon clothes.

The mustachioed instructor wore a gold necklace with a 3D yin-yang snug around his neck. He smelled of cigarettes and cat. His gi pants were white and bore the visual evidence of his pet on the seat. The top portion of his gi was sleeveless, exposing a fresh tattoo of a dragon on his flabby right shoulder. A black belt with white stripes double-wrapped his waist, underlapping a bulging gut.

The man handed each student a leaflet with hand-drawn oriental symbols accentuating the rules of the dojo, copied in scratchy Xerox. A coffee stain the size of an egg seeped through each copy, blurring the first five rules. The paragraph at the center of the leaflet with the underlined words *Mission Statement* read: "Anger is your enemy. Wing Chun practitioners believe the person with superior structure will win. A correct Wing Chun stance is like a piece of bamboo, firm but flexible, rooted but yielding. This structure is used to either deflect external forces or redirect them, emphasizing movement economics. No wild, wasted movement!"

The instructor ordered the three students to stand shoulder to shoulder facing the dojo banner draped over the library conference table. He walked around the students with militant swagger, back and forth, thumbs hooked into his belt, head cocked to one side, as he eyed his disciples. His high-pitched voice was an odd match with his rotund physique, and as he spoke, his accent shifted from Southern draw to slightly oriental, depending on eye contact.

"You will be introduced to powers not known to the common man. Wing Chun teaches practitioners to advance quickly and strike at close range. This means, theoretically, if the correct techniques are applied, a shorter person with a shorter range can defeat a larger person by getting inside his range and attacking him close to his body."

The instructor stopped directly in front of the boy, who happened to be the shortest in the group. Ches stared straight ahead, motionless, giving the instructor all due respect. The instructor cocked his head inward with squinting eyes and an affirmative nod.

Ches practiced obsessively in the backyard on an army-green duffle partially filled with stuffed animals and old clothes. He used a dog chain to hang the duffle to a low limb of the oak tree. He perfected his roundhouse and forward kicks by kicking the bag one hundred times a day, twenty-five for each type of kick, left and right. He would repeat the instructor's words over and over in his mind as he practiced, "Every kick is both attack and defense; legs are used to check incoming kicks and take the initiative in striking through before a more circular kick can land. Kicks are delivered in one movement directly from the stance without chambering or cocking. Chinese philosophy: Greet what arrives, escort what leaves, and rush upon loss of contact. Yip Man."

The first day of school was merely five days away. The very thought of it made Ches sick to his stomach. He packed his backpack, including a book of poems and essays, and embarked on his final trip to the library.

A significant wind was blowing. Ches had ridden in the wind before, but he felt queasy and out of sync as a solitary raindrop stung his cheek. He pedaled a notch slower, and a gust nearly forced him off the sidewalk. Traffic emerged from an ominous background with bright headlights and windshield wipers operating. He increased his effort straight toward the blackness. The harder the wind blew, the harder he pedaled until he felt a surge of anger rip through his being in response to the gathering storm. He could see the wall of rain two blocks in front of him. He spit into the wind and pedaled fast toward the charging torrent. Lightning flashed. His shirt was already soaked through with sweat, and when he felt himself slowing, he pressed harder to stay on pace as huge raindrops peppered his eyelids.

At the crosswalk he pedaled full speed into traffic, tearing through the streams of water that flooded either side of the highway. Another bolt of lightning struck with a simultaneous deafening clap as a car whizzed past, leaning on its horn, sending a muddy shower into the boy's face and torso.

The library came into view, a dull white exterior against a backdrop of black. He coasted into the empty parking lot. He could see only darkness inside as he rolled his bike up the ramp. The sign on the door read, "Due to the section-wide power outage, the library will be closed for the remainder of the day. We will reopen tomorrow at 10 p.m. Thank you."

Ches leaned his bike on the bike rack and sat on the library steps, then lay on his back, staring straight into the falling rain. The rain looked different from this position. The wind subsided, but the residual gusts bent the direction of the sheets. Millions of droplets curved together, falling as one into the memory of when he was a little boy waking his mother in the night. But he shook himself, stood to his feet, and rode away.

Rush-hour traffic was at its peak. Ches took his time, wet and melancholy, weaving through the puddles, much more at ease than during the ride over. He wondered why he'd felt so anxious—probably the prospect of a new school. He'd heard there were twelve hundred students registered.

At the intersection, he eyed the extra-long lines of impatient commuters in every lane and coasted to the side, finding comfort in traveling alternative to the mainstream. He smiled in appreciation of the freedom his bicycle afforded.

He coasted to the crosswalk and pressed the button. Glancing to the right he noticed a gang of teenagers, also on BMX bikes, riding toward the signal. He rolled politely backward a couple of feet to allow the group to pass. The leader of the gang looked to be in his latter teens, with months of peach fuzz on his chin and sideburns. A cigarette dangled from his lips.

Ches backed behind the power pole as the teenager approached. The gang leader pretended at first not to notice the boy, but as he passed, he kicked the front tire of Ches's bike with brute force, knocking him to the ground. Ches righted his bike, and another teenager kicked the handlebars, jerking the bike from the boy's grasp and to the ground again. Again Ches quickly righted his bike and made a valiant effort to pedal away.

The gang surrounded the boy. One teenager had a hold of his back tire so Ches couldn't move, while another unscrewed the chrome caps from the valve stems. Ches was defenseless. They ripped the backpack from his shoulders as the leader and his sidekick bolted across the highway, laughing deliriously. From the middle of the crosswalk, the two antagonists turned to the rest of the gang just as the tractor-trailer in the turning lane responded to the signal. One of the gang members started yelling and pointing frantically, followed by collective screams from the rest of the gang. The boy turned and witnessed the two teenagers rolling from underneath the tail end of the tractor-trailer just in time for the tires to miss their bodies but totally flatten their bicycles. The entire gang gasped.

With all the attention on the narrowly averted tragedy, the boy quietly eased his bike to the periphery. The two gang members whose bikes were destroyed paired with other members of the gang, and the leader led them away utterly shaken.

The boy was stunned. He kept his eyes on the gang until it was decidedly safe to cross the road. Then he pedaled past the shocking image of two crumpled bicycles in the middle of the crosswalk. The handlebars, cranks, forks, and frame had all been flattened by the crushing force of the tractor-trailer.

Up ahead, he caught sight of one straggling gang members, who disappeared behind the barbershop, then a moment later, the straggler reappeared in a hurry to catch up with the rest of the gang. The boy rode slow enough to let the entire gang move well out of sight.

As he passed the barbershop, he glanced to the right. There was a giant trash bin in the alley. Compelled to investigate, he turned along the alley, approached the trash bin, and opened the lid. Right on top in plain view was his backpack. He opened the pack and saw that his book was dry and undamaged.

The boy stared listlessly into space, at once keenly aware of that uncanny, familiar presence. An involuntary movement of his mouth began to pronounce that name, *Jesu*—, but he held his hand to his mouth, turned his back to the rusty trash bin, and slid to the ground, trembling. An upsurge from untenanted depths transported Ches instantly again to the little boy longing for a place he'd never seen. "I want to go home"—the words poured forth in his earthly tongue. He tried to summon anger with which he might absolve or dissipate this moment, but this only stirred the deeper place of evaporated questions and dissolved bitterness. He closed his eyes to a vision: thousands of mazes, varying in color and design, drifted together on one mighty river. He sat on its banks alone, weeping.

How is it, a solitary human soul far exceeds the value of all earthly wealth combined? What am I to Him? Brother Brown has no idea that I am here, looking down on him. If only I could see his expression through the louvers?—that man of color who expelled me from this place, thwarting my preferred lot in life. It is seven in the evening. Brother Brown is praying over the congregation in the familiar apostolic way. He is asking God to speak through him.

My heart races as I hear masculine voices from the other side of the door. I frantically return the chair to the corner and squeeze my body into the tiny space between the opposing wall and the air unit, and wait for the door to open. Music resumes.

Chapter 7

CHES GAZED OUT the window of the Greyhound bus and smiled. He'd traveled this highway before, headed east with his family, and the journey was acrid and affecting. He had endured that six-hundred-mile jaunt crammed into the back of the family jalopy between plastic bags filled with clothes, dishes, and bric-à-brac of little or no value. The mother and three brothers occupied the front seat and yelled at one another into the wee hours. The Greyhound was much more comfortable than that previous ride. He had the whole row to himself.

Gussie Mae had passed away two days earlier, but Ches wouldn't be attending her funeral. There were issues in his family. So, instead of beginning his sixth-grade school year, he found himself aboard a Greyhound bus destined for Berwick, Louisiana, to stay with his grandmother.

The grandmother lived below the Atchafalaya River, a tributary of the Mississippi and Red Rivers. The river is an industrial shipping channel for the state of Louisiana. Tugboats push jumbo barges filled with cargo to be distributed north to various ports along the Mississippi. It was the heart of Cajun Country, where the old-timers walked the line between humility and pride, and thick French accents spoke of a world far different from the boy's experience.

As the bus pulled into the station, Ches tucked his reading material into his backpack. He stepped off the bus and spotted Mawmaw sitting on a stone bench amid the azaleas. She wore a modest floral dress, her hair was in a bun, and her angst-free countenance contrasted with the collage of waiting faces. She greeted the boy, "Sha, bae," and gave hime a hug and kiss. Together they retrieved his small suitcase and began the walk to her place.

The street was noticeably quiet. They ambled side by side along the winding path through cypress trees and fragrant magnolias. The enormous live oaks stood as noble monuments to the South, soft, brooding towers laden wistfully with Spanish moss.

They approached a French bakery, where a woman wearing a bead necklace of the Virgin Mary sat before a hand-crafted table, tatting in the sunshine. The grandmother smiled, and the two old women chattered ceaselessly. The boy found irresistible the sweet French words flowing between them, mixed with an odd word or two in English.

The lazy neighborhood had been settled below sea level, and the scent of the river spilled over the levy to lay claim on the inhabitants of the land. Quaint white houses, each with a porch and at least one rocking chair, bore visual evidence of a past flood; the permanent water mark were twenty inches high.

Mawmaw's tiny shotgun house was freshly painted though—blue and gray with white trim. She spoke appreciatively of the men of her church who had recently contributed to the upkeep. The boy followed his grandmother across the threshold, and the aroma of a simmering pot of okra gumbo welcomed them.

Her place was immaculate and peaceful. It was twenty-four feet long by twelve feet wide with a bedroom and one small bathroom. The kitchen, dining room, and living room combined as one open area consisting of a small, round table with two chairs in the kitchen, and a wood rocking chair. A burgundy, vinyl love seat, with white, embroidered linen neatly placed on one end, would be the boy's bed.

His mawmaw spooned some rice into two small bowls, ladled the slimy, green okra gumbo over the rice, and plopped an ample helping of yellow potato salad on top. The grandmother gave thanks, and the two dined sumptuously together. The boy washed his meal down with a glass of tea as his grandmother sifted through the mail.

"Watt dat one read, hon?"

The boy's cheeks turned red. He was embarrassed that he'd forgotten she couldn't read or write.

"Sha, bae," she said compassionately, "yoo mawmaw doon't read. Das whey da good Lowad brought yoo! Now, watt dat one read?" She waved a large, glittery envelope with a five-inch gold star stamped on the front.

"It says you qualify for a chance to win a hundred-thousand-dollar sweepstake."

She hissed and tossed the unopened envelope in the trash and waved another. "Now, watt dat one syez?"

The boy was momentarily stuck in a blank stare.

"Hey, couyon! Dem cat got yoo tongue? Watt dat one syez?"

Ches shook himself. "It's from the Houma Tribal Council—Kirby Verret."

"Watt dat nex one syez?"

"It's a utility bill."

"Dat's dem elixtristy and dem watar beel. Yoo mawmaw don't have de moneys to pay dem. But yool see. Da Lowad takes care of yoo mawmaw! Heem always provides."

The woman relied totally on an odd babysitting job and prayer. Her husband had died two decades earlier while working a row of barges; an over-taut cable gave way and struck his head. The grieving widow refused to seek compensation.

She also avoided talk concerning the Houma Indian Nation tribal leaders and its legal fight for recognition by the federal government.

"Yoo mawmaw doon't need dem fadril govment to tell me who I am. I am a child of da Lowad Jesus! Dat Catoliks Church tried to change avrybody neem, but dey doon't even baptawze in Jesus

Neem. I am baptawzed in Jesus neem. And I got dat Hooly Ghoost. Das awl dat matters!"

After filling his belly, the boy was exhausted. His grandmother wiped his face clean with a warm wash cloth and laid out his pajamas. He laid his head on the fresh-scented pillow, and his grandmother began to pray over him. "Lowad Jesus, bless dis lil child. Heal hees tenda heart in da night hour. Tank yoo, Jesus, dat heem had dat safe jurnee all da way to my hoom by heemseff." The boy's eyes grew heavy as her loving words flowed above the darkness, doing their work to clarify and heal. He felt exceptionally comfortable far from his usual place of residence. She continued her prayer as he drifted off.

Hours later, Ches awakened to sounds coming from the tiny bathroom. He tiptoed to the kitchen and saw the clock next to the stove. A quarter past five. A small light from his grandmother's room softly illuminated the tiny quarters. Ches could hear the sounds of her getting dressed and fixing her hair. Then the light switched off, and again silence. He wondered why she would've gotten dressed for the purpose of returning to bed, so he tiptoed curiously to the edge of his grandmother's room.

A faint whimper gave him a strange feeling, and he craned his neck in an effort to make sense of what he heard. He squinted, and images took recognizable shape: a clock on the wall, a lamp next to a bed, and the silhouette of his grandmother, kneeling at the foot of the bed, davening in prayer, with a handkerchief to her face.

He tiptoed back to his perch, pulled the soft blankets to his chin, and listened attentively as her intense prayer underscored the ambiance of the tiny shotgun house. There was much confidence in her voice as it quivered with urgencies from the deep. "Lowad, keep you hand on dat lil child. Anoint hees life, protect hees mind, brought heem tru all dem dawrkness and confusion, Lowad Jeesus, dat he might serve Yoo awl da days of hees life."

Her prayer had a clear, potent quality that intensified as she slipped into another language, a language that he couldn't comprehend, though he recognized it certainly. He remembered an earlier time when those words had flowed from his tongue with a militant thrust, forcing back the flanks of ambiguity.

The image of his mawmaw davening in the dark filled the boy with confidence and a desire to do good. He felt the inclination to pray but quickly pushed it back. This belonged to his mawmaw. This was her way. His way was different now. His experience had expanded into a more plausible reality that encompassed a plurality of ways. All at once the boy became agitated and displaced. The room felt stuffy and small. He rolled out of bed and slipped through the door into the humid morning.

The boy spent the following days exploring his new surroundings. He was pretty sure it hadn't occurred to his grandmother that she should enroll him in school. The value of formal education was casually dismissed by her kind. As the eldest of eighteen children, she and her siblings had grown up working the land as trappers and shrimpers. But the modern world had emerged, rendering the old ways less than meaningful. Nevertheless, the boy practiced extreme discretion in his coming and going, just in case an anonymous member of the community would be so thoughtful as to see to the boy's school attendance.

He was anxious to explore the behemoth levee, which unfurled along the river. It was at least fifty vertical feet from its base, and he climbed to the top energetically. It seemed strange, walking along the top, that the water level to his left was considerably higher than the houses at the levee's base—a sobering reminder of the ever-present flood held back by a manmade earthen wall.

A bend in the river revealed rows of rusted old barges and riverboats, mostly dead hunks of steel, with functional ships anchored alongside the remains. With close inspection, the boy could determine which boats were currently active, though there was hardly a new thing about any of them. A bright-orange buoy or smoke trickling from a smoke stack or the unfaded color of fishing gear aboard a particular wretched craft were sure indicators of life. Ches wondered if Mark Twain ever navigated the Atchafalaya.

He could see the Long Allen Bridge and the sporadic commuters to Morgan City and the enormous Roman Catholic edifice that towered over St. Mary parish. He scanned 180 degrees to the town of Berwick and spotted another tiny church tucked into a hammock of live oaks. Beyond the little church, he could see a building with the markings of a public library. He counted the number of blocks from Levee Road to the library and set out to investigate. He passed modest mobile homes and houses of Victorian architecture side by side with humble shotgun houses, and then he took a left turn that led him to the building on the next block. The sign confirmed it was the public library.

The place was older than it appeared from a distance, with its cypress clapboard with fresh white paint covering aged weather cracks. A wraparound veranda and windows encased the building. Ches sauntered between two rocking chairs, opened the French door, and stepped onto the dark-stained hardwood floor. Every step was loud and would have announced his presence if the building had not been so empty.

The main area was furnished with an antique French secretary desk atop a well-worn Savonnerie carpet and a Toulon chair on either side of the desk. Compared to the libraries he had frequented in Florida, this was much smaller, smelled of old house, and had a fraction of the books. Ches immediately scanned the place for pockets of privacy. He had started toward thc leading row when the lone librarian, a little women of dark complexion, bifocals, and salt-and-pepper hair, caught his attention. "Can I halp yoo, suhr?" she said with an accent slightly different from his grandmother's: more reserved and genteel. He asked for the card catalog, and she pointed to where it stood two feet from him. He smiled sheepishly, and she smiled back.

Ches was curious as to whether Karl Jaspers had written other books, but Jaspers was nowhere in the card catalog and neither was the title of his book. The boy searched a related subject, the R section, for a book on religion. He thumbed through the file until he came to a book that caught his eye regarding Christian martyrs and heretics. He took a mental note of the call number and made his way to the appropriate shelf.

He settled into a mahogany chair in an obscure corner along the back. The first chapter began with illustrations of the first followers of Christ who were killed for their faith. Beginning with Stephen, the gruesome accounts detailed crucifixion, stoning, and various forms of torture, ending with death for nearly every original follower of Christ but one, John the beloved, who survived the horror of being exiled to an island.

Ches marveled at the will of these men who died for their faith. Were they mad? Or did they know something the rest of the world didn't know? The book documented the opening centuries of Christian persecution at the hands of the Roman government. *How brutal Roman policy must have been*, the boy thought. He was puzzled, though. He had always believed that ancient Rome was a free and open society, a place that fostered tolerance and acceptance of religion and culture. He wondered too why anyone in his or her right mind would convert to Christianity in such an adverse climate. The potential convert would be forced to weigh the realities of conversion. Did the value of the spiritual experience outweigh the horrifying earthly consequence?

He read about Christianity's acquisition of earthly power at Nicaea, the enforcement of laws against heresy, and the gruesome methods of interrogation. It was as though Rome donned the cloche of Christianity only to preserve the core of Roman values. The boy's heart sank as he pondered the images depicting heretics being burned at the stake and, worse, all at the hands of church enforcers.

Who were those church enforcers? Who were the heretics? Were heretics really nothing more than troublemakers, too ignorant to conform to belief in the Trinity? When did the church fathers abandon dying for the sinner and take up killing the sinner?

The following Sunday morning, the boy awoke to the usual sound of prayer followed by the squeaks of the ironing board as the grandmother ironed clothes for Sunday service. She laid his clothes neatly across the rocking chair and placed a plate of toast with homemade blackberry jelly and a glass of milk on the endtable.

The morning was cool, and together they walked four blocks to the tiny church. The building was a humble picture freshly painted the same color as the grandmother's shotgun house but larger. It was in stark contrast to Morgan City's Catholic Cathedral with its gothic stone carvings.

The sign out front was a simple four-by-eight sheet of plywood with large, blue, hand-painted letters in cursive: *Apostolic Lighthouse.* The background was light-blue with a black-and-blue shrimp boat in the distance. The lighthouse in the foreground shone, and a white beam of light was painted across the length of dark clouds. Two scriptures were posted on the bottom right of the sign: Deuteronomy 6:4 and Acts 2:38.

As they stepped to the door, the boy became increasingly unsettled. Beads of sweat dripped from his forehead. "Mawmaw, I don't feel so good," he said. Then he tiptoed across the veranda and took off for the levee.

Hours later, Ches stepped into his mawmaw's place to the aroma of red beans and rice with his appetite sufficiently intact. He started to apologize to her, but didn't. They dined sumptuously, and her sweetness diffused all pangs of guilt. "Sha, dat whole church prayed for yoo, and da Lowad heeld yoo body. I tol dem yoo gon be at dat night meetin."

Ches knew that if there is anything unsettling about oneness Pentecostalism, it's the Sunday-night service. At six that evening, he wanted to turn again and run, and he would've, but he felt a hand gently grip his arm. He turned to look into the eyes of a man of his midforties. He had natural, jet-black hair with a hint of gray, slickly parted on the side. His suit was of considerable quality, which didn't jive with the boy's idea of Cajun culture. Such exuberant attire seemed an odd contrast to the raw sincerity in the preacher's eyes.

The man grabbed the boy's hand and shook it vigorously. "I am Pastor Etienne Melancon." He spoke with a French accent similar to the grandmother's. "Anythin I can do … you jus seh da word."

Music began to play. A piano, drums, an upright bass, trumpet, and flügelhorn worked together with skills exceeding even the preacher's impeccable style. Melody and harmony and extraordinary musical collaboration seemed one more strange fit considering the backwater essence of the place.

The pastor eased to the platform and began to pace reverently to and fro. He turned his face upward, clapping his hands and wagging his head in awe of something moving across the sky. An aged feminine voice sounded through the loud speakers. Her quavering, darksome notes found a perfect place within the beat and melody of the music.

"There shall be light in the evening time … a path to glory you will surely find … it is the water way … it is the light today … baptized in Jesus name …"

People poured into the already overfilled sanctuary.

"Young and old repent of all your sins … and the Holy Ghost will enter in …"

Young men sporting slick suits sat side by side with elder gentlemen in overalls and plaid shirts. Beautiful girls in modern modest dresses walked arm in arm with aged women with approving smiles, wearing humble, hand-sewn dresses.

"The evening time has come … it is a fact that God and Christ are One."

The boy's grandmother nudged him into the second-to-last row. He knew she would rather sit toward the front, so he tapped her on the shoulder. Her eyes were already filled with tears. "Mawmaw, you can go sit by the front if you want." She smile and kissed him on top of his head and continued to clap her hands and sing. Ches eyed the back door and scanned the parameter for other exit routes.

People continued to file in and stand along the back and side walls. The pastor began to address the crowd in decibels exceeding the jazz melody. "As fowah me and mah house, we are goin to exalt da name of Jesus! Da oonleh Name undah heaven! And somebodeh … in dis house needs to know who dey really are. If yoo would acknowledge who He is … He will show yoo who yoo really are!"

The entire crowd moved together. A woman across the aisle swayed back and forth with her arms stretched skyward. Both of her hands fluttered as though extended from a car window doing sixty.

The preacher grinned ear to ear. "The stadium at LSU is filled wit faithful fans … wit painted faces … goin crazeh ovah a man … because he can kick a piece o leathah filled wit air! But we … give our praise and adoration … to the one who speaks worlds into existence! Our God … is infinitely more talented … dan a man who can kick a ball! Da moost intalligent ting you and I can do tonight … is praise *His Name*!"

There was a surge through the congregation as people stood and pointed skyward. A man ran toward the altar and across the front and up the opposite aisle shouting and praising his God.

The boy sat on the pew, leaned forward with his face in his hands, and pretended to sleep. His mind was racing. He was familiar with this type of worship, yet the ceasing of it all couldn't come quickly enough. He wanted to excuse himself to find the restroom, but he was trapped. An arm draped over his shoulder, and a man's voice began speaking into his ear.

"Da Lowad knows watt yoo are goin through, mah friend. Yoo are of da fortified camp! And you have a gift … here." The boy felt a hand pressing on his chest. "God still has dat work for yoo, mah friend. God has not forgotten yoo. He still desiahs to use yoo hands and yoo feet, and dar is no greatah honor!"

The boy wanted to wrench away from the man and run. He would run until his heart stopped beating, if only he could break the power of the words spoken into his ear, his soul. He opened his eyes, but only his grandmother stood next to him. He heard the pastor's voice again, adoring his God through the loudspeakers. The entire congregation swayed in unison with tear-stained faces exposed to the rushing ethereal breeze. The boy seized the opportunity and slipped through the exit into the night air to sweet relief.

His ears rang from the extreme loudness and the disarming atmosphere inside. His mind buzzed from the tug-of-war between two opposing worlds. The church building pulsed from within, rattling the windows and loose hinges. He moved a significant distance away from the building, pressed his way into a row of azalea bushes, and stood there staring objectively into the night.

Ches respected his grandmother immensely. He adored her accent and the way she doted on total strangers as though they were dear friends. She would talk for hours, telling stories of different times—times of injustice, times of joy—and of the freedom of life in the wetlands. She retold the tale of extortion in the Houma Delta, an enormous swath of land had been swindled from the family by big oil. Two of her brothers, men who were more in step with the changing times, had incurred substantial gambling debts. Somewhere amid the fray, the land that had sustained the family for generations had slipped away.

It was all rather confusing to Ches. How does land slip away?

Most members of the family were caught in the middle world between sustenance and modernity, content to pass their bitterness and alcoholism to succeeding generations. The grandmother protested the attitudes of the disaffected members. "Noobodeh owes me any ting, no," she would say, defying the psychological mantra of her angry kin. "Sha, don't waste yoo whole life thinkin dat da whorld owes yoo! Da Lowad gives and da Lowad takes aweh! Yoo sool is worth more dan awl dem gold and seelver en da whorld. Awl dat oyall dat dem oyall rigs pull from de ground … das ges dirt, sha! But yoo sool … dats de trazure of da Lowad."

Ches was at once shaken by the abrasive sound of the preaching. He could hear it plainly. He wondered if the neighbors ever complained.

"Somebody in dis house hears da voice of da One True Livin God! If yoo will believe on Him … not just any ol way … but believe on Him as *da scripture* sayeth … somethin gonna happen! Yoo got to believe on Jesus … as dat *Shema* scripture say … because there is no other!"

The boy felt as though the preacher was speaking to him specifically, from the podium, straight through the wall, zeroing in on his crumpled form hidden in the bushes. He reasoned this to be scientifically impossible, as he was thoroughly out of sight and out of mind of the preacher. He reasoned too that other individuals amid such an attentive, noncritical crowd may feel that the same preached words were specifically for them as well, and that particular feeling was inherent or predesigned in the preacher/audience dynamic.

"You must believe dat Jesus is da oonly truth … because Rome wants yoo to believe dat Jesus is merely a way among many ways. Yoo bettah believe dat Jesus is da oonly weh, da oonly truth, da oonly life! Because if yoo reject da true Prince of Peace, yoo gonna get what yoo ask for!"

After everything, how could this man's words touch me so? I breathe in the air that flows from the sanctuary through the vent and concentrate of the opening remarks of Brother Brown as he tells how he came to be a preacher: "I forfeited a lucrative civilian career as a military consultant to do what I do now. And in all honesty, there have been times when I've asked myself, 'What … in the world … are you doing?' In these moments, questions tend to pour in like a flood, but let me be clear. Without a doubt, I saw the light, and it turned my world upside down. That's one thing. But it's something else entirely to make it one's life mission to boldly bring that unique light to the world at large, because we live in a time of myriad possible sources of light emitting from all directions—all coexisting, coequal lights."

Chapter 8

The second half of the school year was well underway. Ches avoided the truancy officer by coordinating his routine with the schedule of Berwick Middle School. His mode was efficient and smooth as he navigated beneath the attention of the adult world. He would do extra chores for his grandmother to assuage the guilt of exploiting her innocence. He considered telling her that he should be attending school, but as far as he was concerned, the intelligence of his illiterate grandmother transcended the cookie-cutter intellect of any teacher at any school he had ever attended. And these happened to be special family circumstances under which noble sacrifices must be made. Besides, school was school, no matter the grade, and the daily subjection to government-employed academicians greatly undermined anything beneficial.

Now that Ches had his own library card, he could check out books in the afternoon as the streets filled with school buses. He'd read at night and the next day from breakfast to noon. After lunch, he'd make his way to the levee to explore until two thirty, and then head to the library to return books and check out more for the following day. His daily movements flowed beautifully with that of his mainstream peers. And the librarian always greeted the boy with a wise nod, as if she were a co-conspirator in his secret plot to fool the world. Ches smiled back sweetly, but he never made conversation with her.

As a way to manage inventory, once a year the library gave away books for a small donation. New books replaced old or redundant books donated to the library by members of the community. It was an opportunity for the boy to add to his collection at minimal or no expense.

Ches casually sifted through the selection of old hardcover books and soon discovered a peculiar artifact shelved next a set of encyclopedias. It was a box disguised as a book: black and faded, with all the markings of a conventional book. At a glance, it appeared to be an outdated college dictionary or an old classic, such as Moby Dick, with gothic stitching. The title was stamped on the front cover in medieval, block, gold letters inside a triangle of serpents: *Magique*.

He carried the box to his usual table and slowly opened the lid to a horrifying sight. He immediately closed his eyes, chilled by the image of a human finger trapped in his mind. As the chill receded, he slowly opened the box. The finger rested within another little box lined with purple velvet. After a moment, his frozen lips broke into a warm smile. It was a fake.

Inside the box, beneath the rubber thumb, he found a red silk handkerchief, three walnut shells painted sky blue, and three brass serpent triangles linked together. A miniature instruction book lay on the bottom. The writing was in French, but the illustrations were numbered and had easy-to-follow lines and arrows.

The first illustration depicted a pair of hands showing themselves front and back. The fake finger on the right index finger was hardly discernible. In the next window, the left hand formed a fist and the right hand poked each of its fingers into the fist as though attempting to ferret something out. This was a means of sliding the fake finger off undetected. The final illustration showed the thumb and index finger of the right hand pinching the corner of the red hanky inside the fake finger and pulling it from the left fist. Brilliant!

He walked toward the checkout desk under the watchful eye of the librarian and placed the box before the smiling woman. She pulled the box toward her, turned it slowly, and then pushed it toward the boy again with her head cocked to the side in a slow, forward nod. The boy mimicked her expression exactly, and pulled the box to his torso. With his head tilted to one side in a reverse nod, He slowly turned and made a wordless exit.

He couldn't believe his luck. On the walk home, he planned a night of magical entertainment for his mawmaw. He stepped into the shotgun house to the aroma of shrimp jambalaya and apple beignets.

"Kyaw, sha! Did I toll ya? See, I toll yoo! Avri time da Lowad provides! Avri time!"

The boy stood there smiling at his mawmaw's sweet expressions.

"Da sweet ladies done brought two pounds of dem shrimps. Tank yoo Lowad Jesus! Now I done made shrimp jumbalayas, yeah. What did I toll ya?! And dats not awl. Dahr was a lil white envelope wit more dan enough monehs for dem elixtricity beel. See, sha! Yoo bettah trust da Lowad. Always, sha!"

The boy gazed at his glowing grandmother. She was unshakably convinced that the shrimp and the money had been sent from heaven. He listened with great affection for her sweet voice as she lavished praise on her God with sentences of gleeful Cajun chatter mixed with the unintelligible spirit language. Her fascination with such fantastic coincidences was adorable. And whatever his reservations, Ches saw no benefit in calling her claim to question. And what did it matter anyway? It was the best shrimp jambalaya in the world. Of course it came from heaven. And to top it off, the "'elixtricity beel'" was paid, and the lights were on. Life was good.

They finished their meal, and the boy helped his grandmother with the dishes. She washed, he rinsed, and together they dried and stored the dishes in the appropriate place. As her chatter subsided, the boy told her of his plans for after-dinner entertainment.

She poured two glasses of milk and removed the apple beignets from the oven. She placed them on a separate plate to cool and lightly dusted them with sugar. While Ches wasn't big on sweets, this was the one treat he would certainly partake of again and again. He finished his beignet before his grandmother and washed down the abundant sweetness with the last of his milk.

He turned his back to his grandmother and stuffed the red hanky into the artificial finger. After sliding the prop over his righ thumb, he held his hands together for inspection. Perfect. He closed the box so it appeared as a book again and placed it on the table before his grandmother.

The boy made a bow with exaggerated hand motions, mimicking his best magician's voice, overdramatized facial expressions, and large arching movements. He showed both sides of both hands. "Behold! There is nothing in my hands."

His grandmother was at once noticeably agitated. Ches began to make funny faces and scary looks with rolling eyes. He brought his hands together, closed his left hand into a fist, and stuffed his thumb into his fist as if searching. He slid the fake thumb into his fist and then slowly began to pull the red hanky from his fist.

The old woman exploded. "In da neem of da Lowad *Jesus!* You get dat out of dis house!"

"Mawmaw, it's fake! It's not real! See." He held the fake thumb in plain view.

"Ooooh! I tol yoo git dat aweh!"

"Mawmaw, it's only a trick … look." He opened the book and began to place the contents one by one on the table: the miniature book, the walnut shells, and the triangular snakes.

The woman began weeping and speaking in tongues. "Oh, Lowad, send yoo ahngels to dis house."

Ches urgently scraped the artifacts into the box, stuffed the box into his backpack, and placed the backpack in the corner.

"Oh no! You get dem tings out of dis house! You get rid of dem davil tings!" Her voice ratcheted another octave, high and soft. "Dem tings don't balong in yoo bag! Tro dem davil tings out, shaa … awl da way." The frustrated boy pulled on his tennis shoes and his backpack and hurried out the door.

The night air was cold, and the fog was as thick as it gets in the Atchafalaya basin. It was past ten o'clock. Ches didn't know where to begin. He walked toward the bakery but could see no lights, so he turned toward the levee, trying to process the ordeal as he climbed the steep embankment. The dew on the tall brown grass soaked cold through his shoes.

He thought of how quickly the atmosphere had changed within the sanctified space of the little shotgun house. Weren't they having a nice time? What happened? Clearly an undetected malignancy had surfaced. Could the toys in his backpack really be so evil? The odd thing was, his grandmother wasn't afraid. Her countenance projected no fear, but a peculiar blend of defiance and compassion. Isn't fear fostered in the unknown and confidence in the known? How could something as trivial as a magic trick sour an ambiance otherwise so permeated in peace? Isn't it plausible that his grandmother's *interpretation* of the fakery disrupted the harmony? This had to be the solution, because after all, it was nothing more than a childish box of illusions. Its value, if there be any value, was human amusement.

He reached the top of the levee and walked the muddy path into the palpable blackness. His pant legs were soaked through and frigid. In this moment he was coming to terms with something that, until then, he'd been able to manage, or suppress—a feeling that loomed as an ever-present cynical reminder of his personal estate. He had no friends and no family with whom he could connect. *Is life worth living alone? I am just breathing, and nothing more. Is merely breathing sufficient in and of itself? Does experience alone have value, absent another human with whom one can share space and experience?*

Ches turned his face to the sky, but the sky was as dense as the path before him. He turned toward the houses below, identifiable by the odd porch light that intermittently cracked the thickness of the fog.

"What if I stopped breathing?" he said aloud, acutely aware of the river but a step away, serene yet foreboding. He remembered when he first learned of the uncanny power of water: power to impart the secret of weightlessness and flight, power to silence instantly the uninvited voices that prod ceaselessly at the human soul. *Water has the power to silence everything.*

He walked slowly along the edge and could hear the seductive flow as it collided with an obstruction. In that moment he remembered why he would never take his own life. With a flash of light, he reasoned how quickly time passes. It seemed that yesterday he was just a little boy, sitting before that peculiar Sunday school man, the man with a light bulb in his mouth who forced out the lesson that would take permanent residence within a five-year-old mind.

Ches shook his head contemptuously. It all passes as quickly as vapor. No, he would never commit suicide. *It would've been nice if someone could have asked first, before so rudely pushing me into this world.* He angrily slung his magic box into the black Atchafalaya River.

THE FOLLOWING MORNING, Ches woke to the sounds of his grandmother praying. "Lowad, keep yoo hand on heem … protect his good ground from evil seeds. Encamp yoo anhgels roun heem … open hees lil eyes dat hee might see, and know da truth, and walk da right patway."

Ches was becoming adept at recognizing her recurrent prayerful words. He pondered the possibility that this was a notable event that took place every morning of this woman's life—a conversation event of colossal proportions, when the soul of a human communes with its creator. *But shouldn't the occasion be joyous? After all, the answer to the big question has come, and the weary soul rests in the absolution of a very present God. God now speaks to and through the participant, so why all the seriousness and weeping?* He closed his eyes and drifted off again.

His grandmother woke him with oatmeal and blackberries. She glowed upon the boy as he quietly ate his breakfast.

"Ded yoo tro dems magique aweh?"

"Yes."

"Where?"

"In the Atchafalaya."

"Yoo tro dem davl tings en de Atchafalaya? Sha, for true?" The pitch of her voice was rising, almost girly and hysterical.

"Yes."

"And yoo don't even know why yoo mawmaw don't want dat stuff in dis house?"

"No."

"Das why yoo anointed, yaa! Yoo obey de Hooly Ghost even when yoo don't unduhstand. Das why the Lowad has got a vahry special calling for yoo, sha. Alwehs talk to Heem, even when it feels like He's not dar. Say His name wit yoo mout and yoo voice, and He will guide yoo and protek yoo. Sha, if yoo mawmaw nevah did pray, yoo mawmaw would, lil by lil, stop believn. If yoo mawmaw nevah did pray, how would I know watt to do? Yoo mawmaw would be loss and loonly."

She stopped speaking for a moment. The boy studied her affluent face. How could this illiterate woman from a forgotten swampland possess such a diplomatic edge in a parallel kingdom?

The grandmother stared into the boy's face. After a full minute, she broke the silence. "Dar is peace in my hoom because I shun da vahry appearance of evil, and I enjoy de presence of de Lowad in dis lil house."

She was silent again. Her head dropped affectionately to one side and cupped his face in her hands. She spoke barely above a whisper, "Sha … bae … I know dem magiques is just pretend. But da Lowad Jesus is not pretend magique, no! Da Lowad Jesus is not even real magiques. Da Lowad Jesus is holy."

I reposition my body in this dark loft and can almost see the preachers swarthy face as he begins his sermon. "I want to preach for just a few minutes on this subject: At evening time it shall be light."

Brother Brown: "There are verses in the book of Zechariah regarding this phenomenon that I find very interesting. The prophet said, "It shall come to pass in that day, that the light shall not be clear, nor dark: But it shall be one day which shall be known to the LORD, NOT DAY, NOR NIGHT: BUT IT SHALL COME TO PASS, THAT AT EVENING TIME IT SHALL BE LIGHT."

Chapter 9

Ches pondered the concept of windows. His nose bumped the glass as he tried to focus on the rows of sugarcane ticking through the frame. Now and again the Greyhound bus would slow enough so that he could peer into the uniform tunnels formed by the tall green stalks. The passenger across the aisle slid his window open, and a warm draft filled the cabin.

His fellow travelers were mostly quiet as the world outside sped past in a vexing blur. Now and again the swamp along Highway 90 could be seen, sometimes with a row of power poles running through it or an oil derrick dipping its giant beak for a murky drink.

Ches questioned his own confident sense that his destination would be no different than when he left. The boy wasn't cynical. He simply understood that he was changing. He was returning to the familiar world of his family, and he was fully prepared for whatever challenges lay ahead.

Ches was small for his age, but he was entering that particular stage of physical transformation. Coarse hair replaced soft fuzz on his legs. The hair on his head was changing too. He wondered how he would comb it if it continued to grow curly. He would keep it short, but not too short—the perfect length to maintain the inconspicuous mobility he so enjoyed. He'd vested much thought and planning into the art of blending in. It would be necessary to keep tabs on his inevitable exterior changes.

Ten hours into the journey, he'd visited the restroom ten times, staring into the mirror, grappling with an objective opinion of his persona. He peeled his lips back and stuck out his tongue to contrast a normal expression. He placed his hand on his forehead and wiped his hair back, isolating the image of his face. He clearly appeared younger than twelve. This was a good thing, not because he dreaded growing older—his birthday was his favorite day of the year—but because, at this juncture, appearing a touch younger would simply be useful.

As he buckled his seatbelt, he noticed the couple seated in the next row. The man sported bleach-blond, spiky hair, wire-rim glasses, and a cigarette behind his ear. His T-shirt was splattered with neon colors around black block letters: *Police*. The woman's hair was thickly gelled into a meticulous messy style with a matching makeup scheme. She held a boombox on her lap. Ches could hear the music through the openings between the seats. It was a three-piece band different from RUSH, with high vocals like Geddie Lee, but raspy and jazzy. The drummer was good. He played with an elliptical, less-is-more style in contrast to the drummer for RUSH, who approached his craft with extreme detail.

The cigarette smoke billowed into the boy's space as he strained to understand the psychology of his fellow travelers. Were they deliberately trying to be noticed? Or were they being their genuine selves, with no thought of making themselves a spectacle? Was the "I don't care what you think' message carefully orchestrated? The boy laid his head on the armrest and tried to breathe as the New Wave tunes transported him into the smokey future.

Ches awoke to a groggy voice over the intercom announcing their arrival. He gathered his book bag, disembarked, and claimed his small suitcase. He exited the building and sat in the row of seats along the sidewalk as people loaded luggage into cars and taxis. The parking lot slowly emptied. It was five in the morning. Ches had laid his head on his book bag and closed his eyes when a green station wagon pulled into the loading area. All four doors opened, and the five members of his family exited and greeted the boy in the first light of the morning.

"There he is." The dad was the first. Ches felt awkward, squeezed into his dad's chest with dangling legs. He felt his mother's soft, cold hands wrap around his neck and head. "That's my baby," she said, with a perfected motherly tone. All three brothers were there too, scuffing the boy's hair and patting him on the back. The boy returned the affection with similar intrigue. The family was together and happy. Ches was happy too with their ability to eke a slither of genuine functionality. He had no fear. Neither was he cynical. He was happy.

The ride was quiet. The family car sped along the four-lane highway as the sun cracked the horizon. They passed the familiar gas station, and Ches craned his neck to get a glimpse of the squalid former dwelling. It was gone. Nothing remained but a vacant lot, a small pile of debris, and a large sign on the tree: *Lot for sale.*

After ten minutes of travel, the boy reckoned with the quietness. He supposed that if it were another family, he might have asked lots of questions about the different car, the house—the harmony? The dad turned the car into the driveway, and Ches grinned at the faint quality of these questions as they entered his mind and vaporized, made neutral by past experience in an environment not conducive to curiosity. The family ambled single file to the front door of the house, and the boy noted of the utility room adjacent to the carport.

The house was a thousand square feet with three bedrooms. The mother and the dad retired to their room, and the two eldest brothers disappeared into the room they would share. The boy surveyed the room he would share with the brother closest to his age. The brother fastly staked his claim on the bottom bunk as though such things mattered to the boy. Ches made his way into the kitchen, poured himself a cup of water from the tap, and stepped out the front door.

A quick tour of the backyard presented nothing of interest. He made his way to the front and opened the utility-room door, hoping to find his bike. But it was gone. There was an old lawn mower with an empty gallon-sized metal gas can tied to the handle.

The morning was nice, and the neighborhood was normal. An old man across the street worked his garden as the rising sun did its work on the collected dew. All the houses in the neighborhood were identical: concrete block structures with varied colors and landscapes. A woman with hair curlers stood on her driveway dressed in a pink robe with matching fluffy slippers. She spilled her coffee while stooping for the daily newspaper, which was stuffed in a wet plastic bag.

The boy walked along the road until he came upon a blue-and-white 1957 Chevy with racks on the roof. Two boys in their late teens, both overly tanned with peeling noses and sun-bleached hair, loaded gear into the trunk. One of the teenagers closed the trunk while the other gingerly placed a lime-green surfboard on the roof racks and fastened bungee straps across it. The other surfer retrieved a red-and-white surfboard and reverently strapped it to the racks in the same fashion. The driver noticed the boy standing at the edge, staring.

"What's up, brah? Where's your board?"

The boy shrugged.

"Ooh, painful!" The surfer held one hand on his heart and the other on his head, demonstrating the great mental anguish experienced by anyone who didn't have a board.

The other surfer raised his eyes, utterly astonished. "Dude! Are you serious? No board? What will you do?" He dramatized the dilemma by banging his head into the side of the car, literally.

The boy smiled. The two surfers walked to the end of the drive.

"My name is Chever, this is Thomas, but his real name is Caveman. They both extended their hands, which the boy shook the traditional way.

Caveman laughed. "Shh, let me show you, brah. Hold your hand straight." Caveman held the boy by the wrist and slapped his hand. "Now curl your fingers." Caveman curled his fingers and pulled them forcedly against the boy's curled fingers. "Now push your thumb against my thumb to a snap." The boy did as he was instructed, and his four fingers gave way to a full-handed snap.

"Sweet! It's a foot overhead … a board and a little gas money, and you're in."

The boy was hesitant.

"Your call, brah."

Both surfers piled into the Chevy. The boy impulsively started for the car but caught himself as the engine rumbled to life. He stood to the side. The car rolled backward then stopped at the end of the driveway. The driver's window lowered, and the two surfers motioned to the boy. "Come up with fifty bucks, and I'll get you a board," Chever said.

Caveman extended his arm in front of Chever's face, his pinky and thumb fully extended while his three middle fingers closed to form a shaka sign. Chever made a sheep-bleeting sound and extended his hand in a shaka too. Ches looked down at his own hand and formed it accordingly. Both surfers reverently nodded. "Indeed." And the Chevy rumbled out of sight.

The boy's thoughts flowed immediately into the special place that got things done in the most expeditious manner; a zone that didn't require deductive reasoning; it came from a place in the mind different from the one for chewing food or holding one's breath before diving into a lake. This particular cerebral plane yields actions comparable to when one has unwittingly sat in an ant bed. Upon discovering one is covered with fiery insects, it doesn't take several days to devise a plan that most efficiently removes them. One simply begins to remove the ants with hardly a thought, quickly, efficiently, and with no wasted movement.

Ches knocked on the door where he'd seen the old man working in his garden a short time earlier. There was no answer. He returned to his own house, then went to the house next door and rang the doorbell. A woman answered. She had excessively long, red fingernails, giant hoop earrings, and a gaudy necklace with a diamond-studded crucifix. Her unnatural red hair was a peculiar salon creation that resembled a feather mantelpiece.

"May I help you?"

"Yes, ma'am, I would like to rake your leaves for five dollars."

"Really? Okay."

The boy stood there for a few seconds and then slowly started to turn.

"The rake is stored by the trash can in the tool shed out back," she explained with a glint of pride behind her thickly painted eyes.

The boy nodded graciously and bolted for the back. As he opened the shed door, he wondered if his face seemed familiar to the woman.

He used the jumbo rake to clear the yard methodically into four sections, beginning with one long section straight through the middle. He crossed that line, then walked to the corner of the first quarter and raked a line to the center, and another. He did this all the way around the square until all the leaves were piled in the center of the square. He repeated this pattern three more times while thinking of what job he could do next, until he had four large piles of leaves.

He carried the large plastic can to the first pile and laid it on its side with the opening against the pile. He straddled the can, and with one swoop with the rake, the majority of the pile was raked into the can. He dragged the full can to the back corner of the yard and dumped the leaves over the fence into his own yard.

He repeated this action feverishly five more times. Then, with rake in hand, he eyed the woman's house, scaled the fence, and quickly spread the pile of leaves to blend into his own unraked yard.

He knocked on the woman's front door and waited nonchalantly, staring at his hands. In the short span of time, blisters had formed; both hands were red and raw. He knocked again and rang the doorbell. After several minutes, he returned to his own house.

He pulled the old lawn mower out of the utility room onto the carport and unscrewed the cap. There was a minimal level of fuel in the reservoir. He found the choke, turned it, and gave the pull chord a vigorous tug.

Nothing.

His hands were painfully blistered. He pulled twice more with no response. He adjusted the choke, pulled again, and the mower roared to life. He switched the engine off again, retied the empty gas can to the handle, and was underway.

As he passed each house, he searched for lawns that needed maintenance. A few lawns were perfectly manicured with trimmed hedges and sharp edging along the driveway. Others were not so cared for. Two adjacent houses were empty altogether with thoroughly overgrown grass and unkempt shrubbery. One of the houses had a For Rent sign, and the neighboring house had another sign reading, "For Sale: Ponce de Leon Properties."

He decided to try the neighbor of the man he'd seen earlier, working in his garden. As he approached the front door, he could hear dogs barking inside. The door swung open, startling the boy. "What?!" A bearded man in a wheelchair wearing a Vietnam cap and a half-buttoned flannel shirt grimaced at the boy. Ches stood motionless. "What's yer problem, boy?" The old man craned his neck and spotted the red mower. "How much?"

"Five dollars."

"By god, it better look like a golf course when yer done!"

In a half hour, the man paid Ches for the job. As the boy made his way out the drive, a woman across the street motioned to him. "How much?"

"Five."

"Five dollars? For the whole thing? How long have you been doing this?"

"Since this morning."

"You are not charging enough. I'll give you ten dollars, but you have to rake and bag the grass. The rake and bags are inside the utility room," She handed the boy a ten-dollar bill and got into her car and drove away.

By midmorning the boy was soaked to the bone, and the gas reservoir was bone dry. He pushed the mower to the side of the house between two azalea bushes and headed for the gas station.

The woman behind the counter stood motionless, hypnotized by a soap opera blaring from a black-and-white portable T.V.

"Did you say a dollar's worth of gas?"

"Yes."

She rang the register without breaking her stare from the television and counted a five and four ones onto the countertop.

The next yard was less than a week uncut. As the boy dragged the final bag to the end of the drive, a white Monte Carlo with a magnetic sign, "Ponce de Leon Property Management," pulled to the curb. A woman wearing high heels and a blue, pinstripe business suit got out of the car. Her perfume contrasted the scent of freshly mowed lawn. Her makeup was heavy purple fading to blue with finely tweezed eyebrows and long, artificial eyelashes. She smiled with her mouth but not at with her eyes. The boy had come to notice these things. People can smile with their eyes, or with their mouth, but rarely did both.

"I am the property manager for Ponce de Leon Property, and I wonder if I can interest you in a job?" The boy just stared at her. "There are two empty houses right there that need lawn maintenance. I will pay you forty dollars once a week to mow and rake both lawns beginning today."

"Who decides that the identity of God must never be definitively resolved? Where does the idea come from, that any specific truth regarding God, with a single, clear meaning, intention, and interpretation shall be reexamined and refitted with a pluralized interpretation, explanation, and meaning? Because there is a theme woven in these ancient verses. And Zechariah brilliantly captures the social, political, and religious climate of this present day. It is now, not clear, exactly what is light. We pass by the light and mock it and spit on it and cannot understand why everything is blurry. It is now, not clear, exactly what is dark. We wallow in dark stuff, and we can't figure out why we are sick. This is how we know it is evening. And, of course, when the ancient prophet uses the phrase 'evening time,' this is a reference to the era coming to a close."

Chapter 10

"Let's go, Grommet!"

The boy clambered into the back of the '57 Chevy while Caveman secured the surfboards to the racks. Both surfers slammed their doors, and Chever accelerated, but then slammed on the brakes in the middle of the lane.

"Get The Clash!"

"Oh yeah! This is the Grommet's theme song."

Chever and Caveman sang, "Should I stay or should I go now," simultaneously, but Caveman sang with an exaggerated baby voice. Chever curled his lips back and cackled like a chimpanzee, and then he held his hand in a stark motion for silence and turned to Cave. "Dude, do your baby cry."

"Should I stay or should I go nooooo?" Caveman's protest was a perfect Mick Jones impersonation.

Chever parked the car in the middle of the road. "We go no further."

Silence.

Ches stared contentedly out the window.

Chever fumbled under the seat for a surfing magazine, rolled his window down, and propped his feet out. "Dude, Wes Lane is, like, six foot twelveteen inches in stature. How in the world does he surf small waves?"

Silence.

A delivery van sped past with its horn blaring.

"Do you think Mark Richards is rich?"

"Chever, you know I don't acknowledge names," Caveman replied as he increased the volume for the next Clash tune.

Chever looked back at the boy. "Cave is serious! He actively protests the name-concept! So we're at the art museum, masterpiece paintings, and Cave decided to make a statement by attempting to sign his own name on the bottom of a Jackson Pollack original. Can you imagine? Jackson Pollack, *No. 5,* by … Caveman. Armed guards escorted us to the door as Cave threatened to scratch out the signature at the bottom of every painting. He insists that signing a name to a masterpiece is offensive to those with lesser abilities. Cave has got serious issues."

"Shut it, Chever! You believe your God is the supreme artist, but do you know His name? I don't think so!"

A car screeched past. The driver laid on the horn and shouted expletives as the surfers bickered in the middle of traffic.

Ches was no stranger to such middle-of-the-road antics. He quietly smiled and surveyed the back seat. There was a Rip Curl duffel bag on the floor, a stack of books on the seat, and two custom Alpine stereo speakers by the back window. The car was clean and vintage. The boy stretched out on the original teal-and-white vinyl and rested his head on a book titled *Thus Spoke Zarathustra.*

After half a dozen cars whizzed past, Caveman finally raised his arm with his index finger extended stiffly upward, quivering, as a sign of capitulation. Chever muted the music and giddily turned to Cave, who gathered his composure. After a brief silence, the boy couldn't believe his ears. "Buuaaaaghahagh … Buuaaaaaghaghaghga … aa … a!"

It was an eerily perfect sound of a newborn baby, complete with pause for deep, baby gasps and a quivering tail to a deep silent draw for another breath.

"Buuaaaaghahagh … Buuaaaghaghagha … a … a …!"

Chever grinned knowingly. His countenance was full of wisdom as he pressed his fist to the dashboard and turned to make eye contact with the boy. The boy nodded. Chever put the car in gear, and the two surfers snickered as they drove onward. The boy stared straight ahead without a word.

Within minutes they pulled into a business park. The sign read, "Beaches Public Storage." They drove slowly along numerous rows of garage units used as facilities for various startup businesses, garage bands, and basic public storage.

They parked in front of a unit with a vintage airbrushed surfboard: Zanzibar Board Factory. It was an eight-by-ten unit with the roll-up door removed and a glass double door installed. An interior door connected the small space to a neighboring twelve-by-twelve unit. The smaller unit was furnished with two chairs and a small desk next to a wall covered with surfing posters. Opposite the desk was a row of new surfboards displayed in protective vertical racks. The strong smell of resin filled the air as they stepped through the door into the factory.

The dim, waist-high lighting was designed to accommodate a board shaper's eye. It illuminated the center where two vertical iron beams stood three feet apart and bolted to the concrete floor. Thick padding atop each beam buffered the latest creation as it lay horizontal—a beautiful, hand-shaped surfboard freshly airbrushed and waiting for fiberglass.

Ches was immediately taken by its lines and subtle curves. The floor lighting accentuated the gentle taper on either side of the stringer along the board's length. Ches admired the smooth transition of the rocker to the nose and tail. He wondered how hand-shaped boards could be perfectly uniform on both sides of the stringer.

A man of his midtwenties pulled a respirator from his face and greeted them. "What's up, bros?" The shaper presented himself to Chever and Caveman as though he was their understudy. He gave them the surfer shake with a four-finger snap, and he turned to the boy. The boy nodded upward without a word and shyly worked through the hand greeting as though he'd done it a hundred times before. The man's hands were flecked with paint, and his hair and eyebrows were white with dust from shaping the foam blanks. He pointed to a rack in the corner that was filled with used surfboards

"Your board is there, brah. Take your pick."

The boy walked to the corner while the three bantered over the latest surfing news. Seven used boards of various design, size, and color lined the wall. He studied each board. Two had a leg rope attached, and one had "Minutemen-Paranoid Time" spray-painted on the bottom. The boy felt his face flush with a concurrent rush of excitement and humility. He knew nothing about surfboards or hydrodynamics. He tried not to smile.

"You can't have all of them, Grommet." Chever and Caveman stepped over to give Ches a hand while the shaper turned on the overhead lighting. Ches eyed the boards as the other three discussed which one would best suit him. They considered his size, weight, and projected growth. They agreed on two plausible choices. The shaper told the boy to try out both. "You can pay when you return the unchosen board." The surfers expressed their appreciation, and they parted ways.

Caveman unstrapped his board and bolted for the water before Ches had even exited the back seat. Chever stayed behind. "The idea is to get to your feet early, while you're at the top of the wave." Chever handed the boy one of the surfboards and handily carried the other two under his arm. "If you merely go straight to the bottom, the wave will break, and you'll get stuck in the whitewash."

Chever eyed a sand dune in the identical shape of a wave and placed his board atop it to demonstrate his instructions. "Once you drop in, you want to point the nose of your board at an angle with the wave, not straight toward shore." Chever lay on his stomach on the surfboard and simulated a paddling motion. "Don't paddle with both arms at the same time with a butterfly stroke, or you will look like a kook. Arch your back to raise your chest off the deck, and use a smooth, overhand front-crawl stroke, one at a time, without rocking side to side."

Chever demonstrated the paddle method with his eyes on the horizon. Then he made three vigorous strokes and stood to his feet, left foot forward, knees slightly bent. "Go straight to your feet without your knees touching the board. Left foot forward stance means 'I am a natural-foot.' Caveman surfs right foot forward. Right foot forward is called goofyfoot. But don't let the term fool you. Caveman rips."

The boy lay on his board exactly as he was instructed. With three quick strokes, he stood straight to his feet, left foot forward.

"If you're a natural-foot, wear your leash on your right ankle, your back leg." Chever attached the Velcro strap to the boy's right ankle. The boy was wearing jeans and a T-shirt, but Chever pretended not to notice.

"Two more things." Chever pointed to the ocean. "Notice that the swells begin breaking along the same line. That line is the impact zone. You must paddle through and then beyond the impact zone." Chever repositioned his board with the nose pointed toward the sand dune as if it were an oncoming wave. He lay on his board and simulated a paddle-out against the breaking surf.

"You must learn to duckdive, or you'll never make it to the lineup. Water is one of the most powerful forces on the planet. Don't fight it! When a wave breaks toward you, as you paddle out, you must time it perfectly. As the whitewash rushes toward you, push your board under the surface this way." Chever paddled vigorously with his eye on the approaching sand dune. He brought his knees under his torso to a doggie position and simulated pushing his board beneath the surface.

"Once your board is thoroughly under the surface, flatten your body against the board as the wave passes over top. If you time it right, you will avoid the breaking wave dragging you backward. Most people who are interested in surfing end up quitting because they never learn how to manage the impact zone. You cannot be afraid to take a beating, and you cannot let yourself get frustrated when you've mistimed your duckdive."

As they made their way through the sand dunes, Ches vividly recalled the day he rode his first wave, the sensation of sliding with the wave, and how the wall of water unfurled as he angled to keep the board in the sweet spot pointed down the line.

When they arrived at the water's edge, Chever pointed to the line of debris and tiny seashells marking the tide. "It's low tide now, but in a few hours, the water will reach that line. Always leave your gear on the land side of that line, or the tide will carry it away."

Ches stationed the longer surfboard on the high side of the tide line in the sand. Chever hurried off, but then turned back to the boy. "Also, find a landmark on the shore, a condo, high-rise building, lifeguard chair, whatever, and make sure to maintain positioning with that mark. There is a current that flows parallel to the beach, and you will drift a mile down the beach unless you pay attention to where you paddle out, so try to stay in that general area. The waves are chest to head high. Doesn't sound like much, but it'll clean your clock, so pay attention. Good luck, brah."

Chever departed as if he were late for a very important meeting. Ches watched as he paddled out. He studied as the experienced surfer pushed his buoyant board beneath the breaking waves with perfect timing. After several minutes negotiating a few good-size breakers, Chever punched through the violent zone into the deeper water of the lineup.

Ches refastened the leash to his right ankle, tucked his surfboard under his arm, and stepped into the ocean. It was a comfortable temperature. He trudged steadily forward until the water was to his waist, then he slid onto his board and began paddling. At once he discovered the difficulty of staying centered on the surfboard. Chever made it look easy, but the boy found himself slipping side to side.

He paddled onward, determined to find balance while drawing ever closer to the impact zone. Chever was right. Waist- to chest-high swells didn't sound big, but as Ches approached the impact zone, the increasing loudness of a four-foot wall of water colliding violently with the ocean floor quickened his regard. The boy was now floating above the sandbar as immense volumes of water slid to the back end of the sandy floor toward the open ocean.

A small wave began to stack. The boy readied himself to duck-dive while eyeing the oncoming whitewater. The board was impossibly buoyant. He pulled his knees to his torso, extended his arms with a wobbly effort to push the board beneath the surface. The whitewater came fast, and Ches urgently hugged the board, hoping the wave would pass right over. The wave slammed into the boy full force, dragging him backward.

He regained his composure in the shallows, coughing and clearing his sinuses with a newfound respect for the ocean. After several disastrous attempts, the ocean offered a lull, and Ches was able to scratch his way through.

The boy sat upright and drew deep, steady breaths. It was serene and beautiful beyond the violence of the impact zone. The waves rolled majestically beneath the line of floating surfers, a satisfying token to all who fought for this position in the lineup. No amount of insider privilege, nepotism, or injustice could lay partial claim to his victory. With a quick survey, he counted eight surfers at various positions to the north and an equal number to the south. He spotted Chever pushing through the impact zone, having just surfed a wave to completion.

The boy copied the movements of the other surfers, who scanned the horizon for oncoming waves. He heard hoots and whistles from Chever's direction and turned to see his friend yelling frantically, "Outside, outside!" The boy turned as the sea's vast horizon came to life. The approaching set of waves caused the ocean to heave and rise, and the line of surfers paddled frantically for deeper water.

The boy did likewise, paddling toward the rising swells that rolled gracefully toward the sandbar. Hoping he was in the proper place, Ches used his arms and legs to turn the surfboard to the beach.

The first wave of the set approached, rising higher as it stacked on the shallows. Ches paddled with all his might. He felt the water moving beneath and then the unforgettable sensation of being whisked upward and forward. Seconds later he found himself speeding down the face of a wave, and he could only hold fast to his board as the menacing curl rose behind. It slammed with such force that the boy was blown up by the physics. The explosion knocked him forward and sideways, ripping the board from his grasp midair, and driving his small frame straight to the sandy bottom.

He felt as though a giant's foot had stomped his body, pressing his face and upper torso to the ocean floor, while his legs peeled over his back as if he were a ragdoll in the enormous turbulence. The wave rolled the boy several times, and he felt as though his lungs would burst.

His legs rolled beneath his torso, and his feet contacted the ocean floor. He catapulted immediately upward with all his might, breaking the surface with a deep breath seconds before another wave drilled him down again. He felt the leg rope straining his hamstring. This time he relaxed and waited for the pressure on his leash to ease. He turned his body to face the open ocean and pushed for the surface while anticipating another breaking wave.

With a deep breath, he opened his eyes to another surfer crouched in the pocket of a right peeling curl. The boy stood awestruck at the speed of the approaching surfer. He came to his senses in time to take another deep breath before diving to safety as the surfer skimmed past at breakneck speed. The boy resurfaced to a lull and immediately pointed his board out to sea for another wave. He heard another surfer paddling behind him, hooting and shouting. It was Chever.

"Grommet … Grommet … yeeeewww! Did you see that tube? Yeeeww!"

The boy paddled harder with a surge of adrenaline and an impossible smile. Chever paddled beside with experienced strides and passed the boy, stoking his young friend with cheers and jibes. "Come on, Grommet. Paddle! Another set is coming!"

The boy could see the ocean rising, and he paddled with increased fury to avoid being caught inside. His shoulders burned, and his chest was raw from contact with the sticky wax on the surfboard's deck. Chever was already safely beyond the impact zone, scanning the horizon and positioning himself for the oncoming set. The boy made the lineup and sat upright for a quick breather.

He had begun to pivot his board toward the beach when Chever paddled next to him. "Stand to your feet while you are at the top of the wave, and ride it at an angle the way I showed you." Ches felt his board moving backward as Chever latched hold of his leash and dragged him to a proper position relative to the sandbar. "I am going to give you a push to help you get into the wave early. You will feel the energy transfer from your paddle power to the power of the wave moving forward. Stand while you are at the top, not too soon, but the moment you feel your forward speed increase with the wave's power, stand up. Get ready … paddle, paddle, paddle!"

Chever gave a rhythmic push. The boy stood to his feet, bypassing his knees as instructed. He instantly realized the advantage of planting his feet before the board made its slide down the face of the wave.

He crouched instinctually, lowering his center of gravity. This stance was not aesthetically pleasing, but it was functional. The wave began to stack against the sandbar, adding verticality to the angular momentum. These combined forces exponentially increase the speed of the surfer. Ches leaned slightly to his right-hand rail.

The line unfurled, and Ches was suddenly aware of the hydrodynamics at work beneath his feet. The surfboards shape accommodated the movement and bend of the morphing wall of water. A slight shift of weight allowed the fins and inside rail to grab. He held his position in the critical portion of the wave, but the face of the wave began to grow beyond vertical, drawing his board downward. Ches allowed his legs to extend and at the same time put all his weight on the inside rail. The board responded to this pressure with a dramatic drift up the face like a horse responding to the slightest tug of the reigns to one side.

As the board drifted speedily toward the top, the boy again bent his knees to a crouch position, in full command of the converging forces. He relished the increasing speed, knees bent, driving forward. He turned down the face of the wave and realized another surfer was directly in the path. The boy wasn't sure what he should do, so he tried to turn into the wave. The inertia catapulted his body over the back of the wave ten feet into the sky. He rotated midair into a dive, and emerged to the hoots of the surfer with whom he'd avoided collision. It was Caveman. "Holy wow, Grommet! You are totally surfing! Nobody surfs their first day!" The boy smiled and continued paddling.

Hours later, Ches made his way back to the car. Chever and Caveman were there, changing into dry clothes, using their towels in a haphazard attempt at modesty. The boy stood in his wet jeans and T-shirt, smiling. Chever handed him his towel. "Sit on that, Grommet … please."

The boy nodded graciously and wrapped the towel around his wet jeans at the waist.

Caveman stared at the boy. "You are a thoroughbred freak of nature! Nobody … nobody surfs their first time. For that matter, nobody even learns to paddle out, duckdive, or negotiate the impact zone their first session … nobody!"

Chever chimed in, "I have never seen it. It is impossible to leapfrog the prerequisites. I mean, he didn't even care he couldn't duckdive. I watched him get absolutely drilled, grade-A beat-down, on the inside. The next thing I know, he bobs to the surface and flounders his way through, then scratches with all his might for another wave. The size of the waves should've scared the freebird out of him in the first place. Dude, you are in there! Deep!"

Caveman kept shaking his head. "Thoroughbred freaker. Did you ever try the longboard?"

The boy shook his head and remembered the money in his pocket. He forced his hand into his jeans, pulled out the folded bills, and handed the saturated money to Chever: a ten and two twenties.

"Whoa, Bill was only asking forty." Chever waved the ten and stuffed the wet bill into the back of the boy's damp T-shirt."

On the ride home, Ches subtly placed the ten-dollar bill on the front seat between Chever and Caveman. He smiled and stretched out in the back seat, damp and exhausted, and explored the pages of *Thus Spake Zarathustra*.

"This has become the unspoken, official procedure and system of rules governing affairs of state, religion, and diplomatic occasion. Such an ethos suggests, in fact, that there is a solitary, human embodiment of truth! It further indicate a diabolical, opposing force which employs myriad means of emulating that truth for the sole purpose of creating a colossal distraction! But this era begs the question, with all the possible coexisting, coequal lights, why so much darkness? Here is a time not unlike that of ancient Rome. In ancient Rome, the citizen is free—even encouraged—to worship whatever God he chooses. But he, or she, is not free to declare one particular god the only valid God, because in Rome there are many coexisting, coequal gods. Such policies facilitated the execution Jesus Christ. Awe, but somebody say it with me: at evening time—" the crowd responded loudly in perfect unison, "At evening time."

Chapter 11

CHES GLIDED THROUGH the dark hallway, clutching his surfboard with both hands. He was to rendezvous with Chever at the corner of Normandy and Granville at five thirty in the morning. He entered the bedroom and turned on the lamp. There was an envelope by the alarm clock with a message scrawled on the face: "Five dollars from the next-door neighbor and five from the old man down the road. I borrowed five. Pay you back later, Mom." The boy leaned his surfboard at the head of his bunk, admiring its fluid rails and fin placement as he gathered clothes from the dresser and headed to the shower.

He stood under the bright light and stared into the mirror. His eyes were beet red and scratched by the sand and salt. His forehead was raw and bruised from contact with the ocean floor. His entire face was burned from overexposure to the ultraviolet rays. Ches smiled at this brutal visage, a brilliant contrast to a countenance free of woe. He embraced the image as a mark of privilege. He had become one of the few who'd obtained the secret to the sport of kings.

After a quick shower, he found a pair of scissors, which he used to cut off the legs of his wet jeans. He folded the cutoffs into a plastic bag and packed them into his backpack with a towel, an extra change of clothes, a peanut butter sandwich, and a jug of water. He placed the backpack by the door, climbed into his bunk, and closed his eyes.

Bright visions of the day's adventure flashed to the forefront. His leg jerked involuntarily to the image of a wave closing overhead.

He smiled again and reached through the spindles to touch his board as he drifted off.

At 5:25 a.m., Ches crouched under an oak tree with his board and backpack. The '57 Chevy pulled to the curb right on time. In mere seconds, the board was strapped to the racks, and they were underway. They passed the house where the three surfers had first met, and Ches wondered why Chever didn't stop.

"Keep your eyes open for Caveman. He had an incident last night."

"Is he not home?"

"Yeah, actually, I think he's at his place. He doesn't live in the house where we first met. Those people are social workers, temporary guardians, since Caveman was a ward of the state. But he lives over there now, behind the shopping center."

They turned into an alley, and Ches could barely detect the outline of a small camper-trailer through the trees. Chever turned off the motor, and the two stared silently. The boy rolled his window open to the sounds of morning songbirds. Within a minute they discerned the faint cry of a baby. Chever slowly lifted his head and nodded. "That's gotta be Caveman." The cries grew louder as the image of a young man carrying a surfboard emerged from the mist.

Caveman strapped his board to the rack while reciting poetry in a British accent. "Once upon a midnight dreary … you found my castle, no? O, to spark a dreadful query … if only you too were poor."

Chever turned back to the boy, shaking his head. "Cave, what happened last night?"

Caveman pulled a piece of paper from his pocket. "I got a warning. They gave me ten days to move my castle."

Chever examined the ticket. "Dude, your mail has been going to my uncle's house … in Ponte Vedra Beach."

Caveman turned to the boy. "I am a baaad goy. I got cherished Chever dirty all dirty. Cherished Chever's doctor daddy will not permit cherished Chever to mix with the bad goy." Caveman scrunched his eyebrows to the center of his forehead in a sincere expression and continued with the British accent. "Cherished Chever opened my mail, no?"

Chever grinned. "You gotta find a different mailing address."

Cave switched to his usual surf jargon. "Dude, your uncle owns, like, every appliance store from here to Miami. And his house is gigantacious. I could live there, and no one would even notice."

"Thomas, you *have* attempted to live there, and they *did* notice. Bubbe caught you making water behind the greenhouse!"

"Chever, where's my mail?"

"Two envelopes. Your report card. All A's, one A minus, and a letter from UF. You're in. Full ride!"

Caveman turned to the boy with a wry grin. "See what I mean? There is a conspiracy! UF, huh? No waves in Gainesville, Chever."

"That's right, Cave. No waves in Gainesville."

Ches understood anxiety as a generalized mood that can occur without an apparent stimulus. He also understood that anxiety was different from fear. Fear was an appropriate cognitive response to a perceived threat. For Ches, increased anxiety triggered increased vigilance regarding potential threats. He was not confused over the matter. He had come to accept that a certain stimulus, no matter how irrational it might appear to a third party, must be avoided at all cost. He'd precisely pinpointed the specific source of discomfort and had devised various means of avoidance.

The first day of seventh grade would begin in five days. Chever had gone away for his senior year to attend a private school. Caveman had moved his camper to a lot near the Intracoastal Waterway, deciding to forgo UF and instead attend the local community college. So Ches lost contact with his friends. It had been an incredible summer, the best of his life, but now he was forced to come to terms with the daily commute aboard a noisy bus to attend an overcrowded seventh-grade center on the opposite side of town.

The boy moved through the bustling halls without looking into the eyes of the other students, but the faces turned toward him as he passed. His books were heavy and ill suited to his stature. Beads of sweat burst from his forehead as he wished himself invisible. He imagined his exterior, his whole body, to be a mechanical apparatus with him is the operator's seat, strapped into the head, peering through blinking oculus windows. He maintained a forward gaze while gathering information from right to left at lightning speed.

To his right, three girls with frizzy, bleach-blond hair jumped up and down in a fit of giggles. A wild scuffle between two larger boys fluttered violently from the left, drawing a bulk of inquisitors. He heard the sound of their bodies crashing into steel lockers and the thud of a human head on the resilient tile floor, followed by gasps of the crowd as the logical end of their attraction became real. The sound instantly summoned gross memories, the bludgeoned faces of his brothers and mother, but he pushed the awful memory back and pushed through the exit door before him.

He marched forward into the courtyard without acknowledging the teacher's aid as she wielded her walky-talky with authority. He aimed for the far end of the barbed-wire boundary. There was an unlocked gate. He passed through the opening, merged with the convoy of yellow school buses, and escaped into the unfamiliar neighborhood.

The streets were littered with cigarette butts and broken booze bottles. A car axle had been stuck vertically into the ground with a sign at the top pointing to the main highway. He walked three miles through the seedy environs to the highway and turned onto the parallel service road, which he followed east for eight miles.

As the landmarks became familiar, he scouted places that might accommodate his plan for the coming school year. There was a patch of woods behind the barbecue restaurant on Normandy Boulevard and another larger section of woods near the bowling alley adjacent to the public library. He passed the bank, which had a digital sign that flashed the time and temperature. It was 11:46 a.m.

He could see the library a half block beyond the bowling alley. He passed the bowling alley and spotted a familiar image exiting the building. It was his brother, the one closest to his age. He slowed his pace, hoping to avoid a confrontation, and then ducked behind a parked delivery van, but it was too late.

"What have we here? Is somebody trying to skip school at the bowling alley? You are so *busted*!"

"I'm going to the library."

"Yeah, right! And I just came from the library after completing my invention on the pathagatheorom theorom. Don't be an idiot. It's not like I'm gonna rat on you. Come on over to my turf. There are pool tables and video games."

"I'm headed to the library, honest!" The boy was smiling, well aware of the absurdity of a twelve-year-old truant hiding out at the public library. His sheepish grin further encouraged the skeptical brother.

"Okay! I'll come with you to the library, and we can memorize the dictionary together; we can bond." The brother grabbed Ches by the back of the shirt and pulled the direction of the bowling alley. The boy tried to wrench free until his shirt tore. After a futile protest, Ches decided to appease his brother.

The boy darted glances in every direction as they stepped into the bowling alley. There was a girl in her late teens working behind the counter, but none of the patrons appeared to care that two school-age kids were in such a place. It smelled of cigarettes and beer and burnt pizza. The jukebox played a continuous loop of Duran Duran. Right away the brother gravitated to the girl behind the counter. The boy sat in the corner with a *Reader's Digest*.

Ches established a daily routine of waking early for school and taking great care to appear to be the compliant and studious type—the type who wouldn't dare be tardy, much less miss an entire day of school. He was always impeccably groomed, with a pressed shirt tucked into Levi's.

En route to the bus stop, twenty yards before the corner, he ducked into the woods behind the substation. His routine had formed a well-worn path along a drainage ditch for a half mile to the main road. The library was on the other side of the road, but a small bridge provided adequate cover under which the boy made stealthy passage. He exited the path among the manicured shrubs bordering the library maintenance room.

Ches traveled the entire area under cover of various patches of woods between the shopping centers, apartment complexes, restaurants, and residential housing. Proper body language and timing became well considered tools that afforded safe passage from one concealment to the next.

He would always allow a few hours to pass before entering the library, and he was careful to avoid becoming a fixture recognized by the staff. He'd sit in the back corner near the large glass wall, through which he could see the shrubs, drainage ditch, and bridge.

He read *Zarathustra* and a biography of the author. A lump formed in his throat as he pondered the words "God is dead" and the idea that humans are no longer the image of God but merely a chance product of a nature uninterested in purpose or value. Could the values common to both Jewish and Christian traditions really be obsolete? He wondered.

As Ches read Nietzsche's philosophies he felt at once captivated and naughty. Nietzsche's mission in life had distanced him from the pursuits and interests of his fellow students. Loneliness and physical pain had been the constant background of his existence.

The boy questioned his own ability to effectively process such potent material. *Should I be reading this? Do I agree? Why don't I lay it down? Why do I feel as though I am hurting someone?*

The Birth of Tragedy gave an imaginative account of the forces that led to the rise and fall of Greek tragedy. Ches gained some insight into the Greek mythology he once loved, as he realized the book was not a simple commentary of Greek mythology but a complex theory, possibly above his level of comprehension.

> Either through the influence of the narcotic drink, of which the hymns of all aboriginal humans and peoples speak, or with the invigorating springtime's awakening that fills all nature with passion, these Dionysian impulses find their source, and as they grow in intensity everything subjective vanishes into complete loss of self-recognition. Even in the German Middle Ages singing and dancing crowds, ever increasing in number, moved from place to place under this same Dionysian impulse. There are people who, from the lack of experience or thick-headedness, turn away from such manifestations as from "folk-diseases," mocking or with pity derived from their own sense of a superior health. But of course these poor people have no idea how corpse-like and ghostly their so-called "health" looks when the glowing life of the Dionysian swarm buzzes past them.

Ches shook his head as he read how Nietzsche collapsed on a street, lost his sanity, and sent peculiar letters to strangers, signed, "Dionysus the Crucified," as he sank further from the real world until his death.

The boy felt an intense compassion for this man who had long since passed. He couldn't help but wonder if Nietzsche had misappropriated a veritable premonition. Maybe Nietzsche had a valid repulsion for mainstream Christianity. Ches contemplated the idea that Nietzsche's pain could've been a symptom of this misappropriation, and his fate the logical effect: a plight akin to pouring sugar into the tank of a Mercedes Benz 380SL, but a more sinister malfunction when pouring the wrong substance into the human mind. *Is it possible that the human mind is not designed to follow every thought to its logical conclusion? Could Nietzsche's own thoughts, brilliant as they were, have made him sick?*

Ches imagined himself living during Nietzsche's time, consoling the disenfranchised genius, righting his wayward course. He would have affirmed Nietzsche's alien plight, but for other, more glorious reasons than realized. But it was too late.

Ches believed his own behaviors stemmed from repulsion from both the Dionysians and the thick-headed. From his perspective, all sides appeared unwittingly influenced by deadly poisonous philosophical substances. Suddenly, he heard a loud knock on the glass.

He turned to find his brother at the window, pointing and jeering. He turned back to his book, but he knew it was no use. His brother would persist and possibly ruin his hideaway permanently.

He swiftly returned the books and made his way to the exit, where his brother held the door with military posture. As Ches passed through, the brother saluted, a hand above his eye, and his cheeks puffed full of air, ready to explode. The door closed behind them, and the brother burst out, "Oh … my … you really do skip school at the library! What kind of a moron are you? It's matinée time, and you're at the library."

"What's matinée time?" The boy inquired indignantly.

"M-A-T-I-N-A-Y!" The brother spelled the word slowly and concisely so the boy could understand. "The first showing of the day—we're going to the movies."

The boy didn't bother correcting his brother's spelling. "I have no money." He lied. He had forty dollars excess from the summer's lawn work. He'd purchased a pair of Sperrys, two pairs of Levi's jeans, and two shirts; otherwise, he would've saved over one hundred dollars.

"You don't need money, genius. Follow me."

The two made their way across the street and through the woods to the next block, where they exited the woods behind a shopping mall. "That's the back door of the theater. Stand there and wait." The boy did as instructed. After a few minutes, the back door swung open. "Shhh! The previews have started. There are only five people in the theater. It's called *Scarface*."

The state-of-the-art sound system rumbled in stereo as they stood for a moment, allowing their eyes to adjust to the darkness. Then they clambered down the single flight of concrete stairs behind the movie screen. High-tech sounds blasted the boy's ears. "In the third millennium, two adventurers came upon a city imprisoned in silence." He stood gazing up at the reverse side of the giant screen until his brother grabbed him by the shirt and led him to another set of stairs, which emptied into the forward seats of the theater. The final preview faded, and they quickly settled in the third row.

The movie was raw and violent. The boy felt sodden throughout the viewing, adding to the previous, self-inflicted breach of Nietzsche to his twelve-year-old mind.

In a final cocaine-fueled fury, the main character, Tony, stood on the balcony inside his mansion with a grenade launcher. Bleeding profusely from multiple gunshot wounds, Tony continued to fight until shot in the back. His flaccid corpse tumbled from the balcony into a fountain at the foot of a statue of a female triad, which read, "The World is Yours."

As the final credits rolled, the brothers bolted for the exit and the paralyzing light beyond. Ches was speechless, shocked by the graphic images. He had never experienced anything so seedy. As they walked through the woods, the receding shock was replaced by a sense of awe for the main character, a man who would rather die than relinquish control of his own destiny.

"Whatever your opinion of Jesus Christ, whether you think of Him as a raving lunatic, or you believe He is the definitive embodiment of truth, either way, we can all agree to His boldness. We have all witnessed Jesus standing alone, like a criminal in the courts of earthly power, before a Roman ruler whose creed

is: what is truth! What is wrong with this man Pilate? He's got the truth, standing right in front of him, speaking words directly to him … the answer to the big question. What more can the man want? Indeed a founding principle of Rome is that abstruse concept of innumerable coexisting, coequal truths. Aw, but somebody say it with me again: at evening time."

"At evening time!"

Brother Brown slapped the pulpit with his hand. "There shall be light!"

"There shall be light!"

Chapter 12

O man, take care!
What does the deep midnight declare?
"I was asleep—
From a deep dream I woke and swear:—
The world is deep,
Deeper than day had been aware.
Deep is its woe—
Joy—deeper yet than agony:
Woe implores: Go!
But all joy wants eternity—
Wants deep, wants deep eternity.
—Zarathustra's *Roundelay*

"GET IN THERE, you little brat! You will do what *I* say, you spoiled-rotten brat!"

Ches winced at the sharp pain as a familiar hand violently smacked the back of his head again and again. The eldest brother was having one of his episodes. This time he would be committing suicide for real, and he aimed to force the boy to witness the event. They entered the living room, and the troubled brother shoved Ches into a chair with extreme force, tipping the chair backward, smashing Ches's head to the floor. "Get up, you fake! You're a fake! *I* am real and *you* are going to face reality now!"

The eldest brother held the sharp end of a steak knife to his own throat. The boy watched as the point of the knife began to push the skin of his brother's neck inward. The troubled brother reacted to the pain with long, drawn-out grunts. "Ughhhh, ughhhh." He paused a moment and bent dramatically forward with his hands on his knees, blowing forcefully through tightened lips three times, psyching himself for the deed that must be done.

The boy slouched in the chair, the back of his head stinging from the blows he'd received. He waited for the knife to puncture, but it would not. Whispers and giggles could be heard from the adjoining room. The boy turned to see his other brothers craning their necks, their faces filled with glee, disbelieving their eldest brother would finally do it.

"Get in here!" The troubled brother held the steak knife as he bobbed and weaved like a boxer signaling he might jump bad at any moment. "You don't know the real me! You are all just a bunch a wannabe nothings! But in reality you *know* nothing!" He took a deep breath and made another attempt to stab his own throat.

The second-to-eldest lost his patience. "You're an idiot! Why would you do such a thing in front of him? Let's leave, guys. Don't give him an audience."

The two middle brothers walked toward the front door, and the boy bolted after them, leaving the troubled one with the knife to his throat. All three parted ways at the end of the driveway.

I will be prepared to live on my own when I am eighteen—no, before I am eighteen. Ches thought about Chever. Chever would graduate at sixteen. At seventeen, he would attend college. Caveman was seventeen, on his own, and doing fine. The boy desperately wanted to go surfing. He had no car, and he was too young to hold a real job.

He picked up a beer bottle from the side of the road, hurled it at the stop sign, and watched it explode. He wondered if his brother could really do it. He pondered a world where troubled souls had never been born. Would there be no questions or answers or pain or confusion? Ches believed himself to be one who would never deliberately hurt another person. Suicide hurts others, but still he empathized with his brother.

Over the months, Ches constructed a makeshift shelter in the woods for a hideout during school hours. He acquired building material from the surrounding area: four wooden freight pallets from behind the neighboring shopping center, a half sheet of plywood pulled from a nearby dumpster, and a frayed piece of tarp. The pallets formed the walls through which he weaved pine boughs and various other branches and vines. The plywood lay nicely on the pallets as a slanted roof, allowing a four-foot ceiling. The interior was furnished with a child-size chair he'd found outside the grounds of a nearby elementary school. A five-gallon plastic bucket protected his books and surfing magazines. It wasn't a perfect shelter, but it kept him dry on rainy days.

It was a blustery winter morning. As soon as the school bus passed, the boy casually stepped into the woods several yards shy of his normal entry point. His foot sunk to the calf in the soft ground. He kicked a tree stump several times to dislodge the mud from his Sperrys and Levi's.

As he approached the hideout, he noticed that the small chair had been placed on the roof. He cautiously opened the door and started to step inside when a blood-curdling scream came from within. Ches fell back on his rear end. His heart pounded as he scrambled to his feet and started to run. Just then his brother exited the hut, roaring with laughter.

"You're an idiot!" the boy screamed. He was visibly shaken. "I hate you!" He felt an instant twinge of remorse for the latter words.

"No, you're an idiot!" The brother was clearly impressed with himself having discovered the boy's hideout. "I like what you've done with the place. It's really nice. The blue tarp enhances the camo look, and the kiddie chair really gives it a nice personal touch."

"What do you want?"

"Whatta ya waaaant? Let's go to the bowling alley. Or would you rather sit in your cold playhouse all day and stare at your surf magazines … like, totally, dude."

Without reply, the boy tore off in the direction of the bowling alley. His brother chased after, cackling like a hyena. They exited the woods behind the bowling alley, walked around to the front entrance, and immediately noticed the police car parked in the handicap space. Both boys paused for a moment. The boy shook his head and turned back to the woods.

"Where are you going?"

The boy continued walking.

"You baby!" The brother caught up with him. "Come on, where's your sense of adventure? If anybody says anything, we'll say our mom is in the hospital and our uncle dropped us off to cheer us up. But if you're a quitter, I understand. Just quit and leave. Quitting doesn't make you any less of a man, no matter what they say. It's okay. I'll go in by myself."

The boy paused for a moment and stared at the ground. "I'm not a quitter."

The brother laughed. "You were gonna to quit."

The boy grinned and hustled to the entrance, with the brother racing after. They burst through the front and made their way past the trophy case. Both boys at once spotted the officer in uniform, leaning over the counter, flirting with the teenage girl while she polished the bowling balls. The brothers immediately turned and hurried out the door, laughing.

"You scared little quitter!"

The boy shook his head. "This is stupid."

They walked by the police car, and the brother stopped to peer into the cab. "Holy cow, there's a mini TV in the back seat."

"What?"

"A miniature, portable TV-radio. Brand-new!" The brother tried the back door of the cruiser. It was unlocked. He eyed the policeman's standard Duval County winter patrol coat with removable faux-fur collar. The officer's official badge was attached to the breast of the coat. The brother tried it on, zipped it, and admired his reflection in the window of the cruiser. It was several sizes too big.

"Are you crazy?" The boy hissed. "Let's get out of here."

"I'm not leaving without payment from that pervert." The older brother slung the coat in the back seat, grabbed the TV, and slammed the door.

"Why are you doing this?"

"The girl is only eighteen. Officer Friendly is gonna pay!"

They stepped off the end of the walkway, and the boy stumbled on a small boulder, tearing a hole in his brand-new Levi's. He sat on the ground for a moment, holding his knee, then stood with the rock in his hand, turning it over and over.

"Let's go genius," the brother said. "We're gonna get busted."

"I'll be right back."

The brother started giggling. "You won't do it. You're too chicken … no way … you're not gonna do it."

Ches rounded the corner to within five yards of the cruiser and without hesitation slung the boulder directly at the police car, crushing the blue beacon on top. Both boys bolted for the woods.

In an all-out-sprint, their heart and lungs pumped to peak capacity. They were surrounded by sirens, barking dogs, and the helicopter overhead. They ran to the end of a dried-up creek, and then they separated. The brother ran for the viaduct, and Ches ran for the far edge of the neighborhood. He followed the rear lot line and decided to enter a tool shed behind a house that appeared empty.

Dogs barked in the distance as he shivered in the darkness, crouched next to a faded Christmas box. He fiddled with a broken hammer handle and imagined himself getting caught. "I'd rather die than go to juvenile shelter." He closed his eyes and tried to calm himself with the memory of his first time surfing. He wondered what Chever might be doing. He imagined himself living in an oceanside home where he could check the morning surf conditions from the comfort of his bed. His muscles ached, his adrenaline levels crashed, and the dream of new beginnings billowed to the floor.

Ches forcibly repressed the tendency to pray as the world outside closed in. At some point, somewhere in his experience, in a place that could not be defined, he supposed there must be alternatives to his original religious experience. He sat frail and toneless in that strange enclosure until his thoughts became a confluence of sad conclusions, reminders of how long he'd been suspended. He'd had nothing firm under his feet from as far back as he could remember. A foundationless beginning could only lead to this hiding in a cold, dark, confined space.

He heard footsteps outside the shed. The door slid open, and his brother appeared. "Come on. This guy is going to help us."

The brothers made their way to the front, where multiple police cruisers were parked in the driveway. Ches started to make a run toward the road, but another police car screeched to a halt directly in front of the boy. Minutes later, the two were in handcuffs, sitting in the backseat of a car with a metal cage.

The team of officers congratulated one another with smiles and handshakes. The boy could see their egos clearly, as physical things. Each man had a visible, boorish knob that protruded from his forehead. One officer nodded with peer approval and approached the captured boys. The man conjured the most intimidating countenance possible and scowled through the glass at the delinquents. The boy studied the face of the officer, who pumped his fist into the cruiser window, shouting expletives, and spewing tiny droplets of saliva into the glass.

"How does this person who carries a gun with an official badge see himself? Is he filled with a genuine desire to see us afraid?" Ches tapped his brother on the leg. "Do you see this?" He pointed to a particular area on the officer's face as though the man were a specimen on an examination table. The boy used two upright fingers to frame the little droplets of spit on the window and on the officer's bottom lip. "I think this creature would really like to hurt us."

The boy's gestures enraged the officer. He began cursing and slamming his fist atop of the police car. The brothers turned to one another and burst into a suppressed fit of giggles. The officer opened the door. "You think this is funny? I will beat you to within an inch of your faggot little life!"

Ches didn't doubt the officer's words, but the man's reaction pushed him to a state of glee so intense that he had to bite down on his bottom lip to the point of tears, and then he attempted to appear remorseful. The other officers restrained the angry man and slammed the cruiser door closed. The boy's sobs were now as real as his laughter. He marveled at the place from which all emotions spring. "Could laughter and tears share the same roots?" he asked his older brother. "Do they come from the same place as anger and folly?"

"What in the world are you talking about?" the brother scoffed.

Another officer slid into the driver's seat and read the brothers the Miranda rights.

Ches tapped his brother on the leg again. "Do you think this nice man always aspired to be a policeman?"

"Why are you talking?" the brother retorted. "You never talk!

The officer was silent as he drove the boys across town to the juvenile center for processing. The brothers were cuffed together and led through a maze of cubicles while headquarters personnel stole glances. The onlookers were baffled, not only by how young the boy was but also by his clean-cut and innocent appearance.

The booking office was a small room with a metal desk, three metal chairs, a scale, a height chart, and a wall-mounted camera for snapping mug shots. The officer uncuffed the brothers and asked for basic information, address, and birthdates, and so on. He took their prints and placed an old coffee can and a stack of paper towels on the desk. "There's soap in the can. Dispose of the used paper towels in the trash can."

They sat on metal chairs for over an hour. The brother grew restless and began opening the desk drawers and taking out small things such as paper clips and erasures. He dropped the items into the can of soap and pushing them beneath the creamy surface with a pencil. He then ordered the boy to stand against the screen for another mug shot. At first the boy resisted, but he ultimately warmed to the idea.

He stood straight-faced, staring into the camera while his brother snapped photos. After a few clicks, he began to pose with exaggerated criminal expressions. They traded positions, and the boy snapped several shots of his brother in various creative poses and muscle flexes until the camera quit working.

Eventually an officer came in and escorted both boys to a cell and closed the door behind them. When the mother arrived, she tried to convince the police to keep the boys.

The two boys were found guilty of petty theft and tampering with a police cruiser. Truancy was never mentioned. The judge sentenced the teenage brother to twenty hours of community service: janitorial work at the nearest public school. Because of Ches's age, the judge couldn't give him community hours, so he was ordered to write a 1,500-word essay expressing remorse for his behavior. Ches was also ordered to complete eight weeks of state-funded counseling.

The Beacon of Hope Mental Health Center was walking distance from Granville Road. The resident psychiatrist introduced himself as Don. He was tall with hawkish features and stylish blond hair, short on the sides, curly on top. He wore large, trendy eyeglasses with red rims. His office was a blend of posh Zen and low-end comfort. There was a mandala on the wall next to an oversized photo of Carl Jung. The boy suppressed the urge to compliment Doctor Don on his nice perm.

As he surveyed the office, he mulled over the ways he might present himself. *Should I present a manufactured plight in a humble way, as one in need, longing for help? If so, the need should have a simple solution that would allow the counselor a sense of accomplishment.* He pondered another possibility: the counselor might offer something beneficial.

Ches considered his own perpetual feeling of being suspended between two places with no foundation and his ever-present yearning for home. He considered that persistent feeling of being invisible yet always seen, as though on a stage in a different dimension. He rather enjoyed the feeling of being invisible but loathed the notion of always being watched. *No!* he concluded, *I must keep the process quick and simple.*

The first meeting was an introductory mix of small talk and lightly administered questions. Such introductions are designed to give the helping professional a feel for the client's surface before proceeding to the deeper issues. At first, the boy couldn't get a bead on Don's neutral personality, so he pulled back, forcing Don to work at engaging him. This was a much better position from which the boy could guide the process.

"How would you describe your home life?"

Ches stared downward and fiddled with his fingers, and after a brief silence, made as though he would speak, but stared down again and shifted in his chair to a less comfortable position.

Don responded sensitively, "Did you want to say something? Because it is nice to be in a place where there are no wrong answers. You can say whatever you wish. And do you know what makes this a fun place? It's okay to say nothing at all."

The boy felt the stirrings of laughter tugging at the corner of his mouth, which he immediately pushed back lest he be discovered. He was impressed with himself. Why shouldn't he be? He'd anticipated this scenario precisely, without a reference point, without the slightest personal experience with such an awkward dynamic.

Ches noted Don's subtle glance at the clock, and the way Don concealed his darting eyes and how careful he was not to send the client the message that the session was timed. Don was a consummate professional, a rigorous social scientist; it was his duty to be fully engaged with a client six times daily.

"Let me tell you a story," Don said sweetly. "Would that be all right?"

The boy gradually lifted his head with a slight tilt to the side, deliberately and slowly, exposing his countenance the way a budding flower responds to the sunlight.

"In India, there are a lot of monkeys. And when the locals want to catch one, they take a bottle with a neck barely large enough for a monkey's hand to fit, and they anchor the bottle in the ground. Next, the locals put a small banana in the bottle. Then they sit back and wait. Before long a monkey saunters by, and seeing the banana, the monkey pokes his hand into the bottle and grabs the banana. The monkey is trapped because his fist around the banana is larger than the opening of the bottle. The monkey chatters and squeals as a local trapper places a burlap sack over the poor creature. In the darkness, the monkey releases the banana, but it's too late.

The monkey could, of course, let go of the banana and run before getting caught. Some do. But many of the monkeys hold fast to the banana until they are captured. Why? Because the banana has value to the monkey, and the monkey is unwilling to let go of that value—so much so, that he is willing to trade his life for it."

The boy sat attentively and searched Don's words for recognizable cues. Ches was familiar with the closed-fist-trap metaphor from the book *Where the Red Fern Grows,* which he read when he was ten; the author used raccoons instead of monkeys.

Don continued. "People get trapped by their thoughts the same way monkeys get trapped by bananas. The philosopher Friedrich Nietzsche wrote, 'I get through many a bad night with the thought of suicide.'"

Ches started to lift his eyes at the cue but held his humble stare without letting on that he recognized the subject matter.

"Friedrich Nietzsche saw value in certain thoughts that comforted him when he felt down and depressed, easing the pain of his sadness. Unfortunately, these thoughts trapped him in the depression, like the monkey trapped by the banana."

Don expertly utilized all the proper tools as he'd been trained by his alma mater. Years of clinical experience allowed him to do his work confidently and methodically. As Don spoke, the boy slowly inched a sincere gaze upward. And without staring directly at the face of the clock, he used his peripheral vision as he'd been trained in Wing Chun. It was less than ten minutes to the hour.

Don was quiet for a moment before slowly and audibly exhaling in the manner that exudes boundless stores of patience. He used this identical expression every session at ten minutes before the hour.

"I'll bet you have thoughts that you would be willing to share, if only you could trust that sharing those thoughts would set you free."

This was the boy's cue. He started again, pretending his words wouldn't come out, and then he brought his hands to his face and pretended to break down. "It's … just … that …" Ches's words were beautifully muddled with the sobbing. It was a great stall tactic for being slightly unprepared with what to say. The tears were real though. He was experiencing the same sensation as when he walked through the halls of the seventh-grade center on the first day of school. It was as though he were the little man sitting in the seat of control inside the body of a growing boy, pulling the levers of superficial sadness and perplexity, pretending to grasp for ways to express himself. "I … just … feel … nobody … understands me." The boy's sobs followed the client script to the letter.

Don uncrossed his legs, clasped his hands pristinely in his lap, and drew another longsuffering breath. As Ches calmed, Don tilted slightly to the side, and his eyebrows scrunched together in the upward slope to convey empathy as he gazed upon the boy.

"First of all, you need to know that everything … really is … okay. You are feeling something that every human being who has ever been your age goes through." The counselor paused for a moment and waited for the boy to lift his head, which he did, with an impeccably choreographed motion until his own empathetic expression could be perceived by Don. The boy wiped the tear from his forlorn eye, and Don darted his eyes to the clock on the wall. The counselor stood to his feet, bobbling his head in an effort to transfer amusement to the boy.

"There is a name for what you are experiencing … if it makes you feel any better … two actually. The first is personal fable. It's what we silly psychologists call a cognitive distortion. It's when a young person perceives his self as extraordinarily special and unique, believing no one can relate to his personal experiences." Don paused for a moment until the boy again lifted his eyes. "The second is described as imaginary audience. This is another cognitive distortion that relates to the adolescent living life believing he is constantly being watched and judged by others. And those others, he thinks, are as concerned with his appearance and behavior as he himself. But you need to know, though there might be a million ways to be a human, the fact is, we do understand you, and we can relate, if only you … would give us … a chance."

At two minutes to the hour, Don stooped before the boy with a knowing grin. His chin moved in a circular motion as he extended his hand. The boy slowly reached for the counselor until their hands clasped. "This week, instead of watching television, I want you to write down at least five positive things and five negative things about life, and we'll explore your thoughts at your next appointment. Can you do that for me?" The boy nodded and smiled as he made his way out the door.

He pondered the concept of freedom as he trampled through the impeccably groomed garden that bordered the Beacon of Hope offices. He kicked over plastic Buddha and smashed the budding chamomile, giggling as he walked past the reserved parking between the black Mercedes Benz and navy-blue Jaguar. He wondered which one belonged to Doctor Don and then noticed the personalized plates on the blue car: DONJUNG. He smiled again and resisted the urge to pick the largest rock in the pile and toss it through the Jaguar's window—a self-affirming demonstration of his own uniqueness in the presence of the imaginary audience. He rounded the corner and whispered, "I never watch the stupid television."

Brother Brown's preaching has progressed in rhythm with the response of the congregation. "Many Christians give Pilate a free pass while laying the execution of Jesus squarely on the shoulders of the Jews. But there are three statements Pilate makes that we must take note of. First, when Pilate says, 'What is truth?' This might be more a statement than a rhetorical question. Pilate is not playing the humble underling seeking wisdom of the bloody, beaten Jew standing before him. Pilate is not capitulating before this Jesus who claims to be the definitive embodiment of truth. The statement 'What is truth' says, I am Roman. Pilate is validating his position of authority over Jesus by demonstrating that he does not believe in truth in a singular, solitary sense. Florida is hot. But is it really? Relative to the surface of Venus, nearly nine hundred degrees Fahrenheit, what is truth? Brothers and sisters, it is evening time!"

Chapter 13

When Ches discovered the public transportation system, everything changed. For a minimum fare, he could ride the city bus ten miles east to Kathryn Abbey Hanna Park—a national park frequented by local surfers for its camping facilities and uncrowded beach breaks. Ches had stashed his surfboard on the grounds in a clump of palmettos covered with branches and leaves. Because of public transit, he could spend as much time in the water as any local surfer. The winter ocean temperatures in northeast Florida can dip to the low fifties, sometimes colder, which is dangerous without proper equipment. The hot showers at Hanna Park had kicked hypothermia on numerous occasions. But his new wetsuit greatly improved his time in the water.

By the end of the school year, Ches had studied Freud and Sternberg and a long, disheartening list of cognitive distortions. He had a good grasp on European and American history too. But, more importantly, he had honed formidable skills as a surfer.

He purchased a two-man tent, a sleeping bag, and a surf duffle. On the weekends he'd concoct believable stories, such as helping his friend with overdue house maintenance for his widowed grandmother, Hanna. His mother was none the wiser. The only truth to the story was the elderly woman's name, as in Hanna Park.

The third hurricane of the season churned the mid-Atlantic, and Ches decided to celebrate his thirteenth birthday with five days of camping. The surf report called for five- to seven-foot waves with larger sets and light offshore winds. Ches made a quick pass through the grocery store for bottled water, a jar of peanut butter, two loaves of wheat bread, and some fruit. He made it to the bus stop right on time, and within a half hour he walked through the gate at Hanna Park.

He staged his gear at the usual campsite and climbed the dune to check the surf. He could see an enormous break on the outside and another smaller break closer to shore. The swell had begun to fill in. He peeled off his outer layer of clothing to a long-sleeved rashy and a pair of knee-length surf trunks, then grabbed his board and bolted.

The intervals between pulses of swell allowed for a relatively easy paddle-out. However, after merely seconds of making the lineup, the ocean began to rise.

Ches was no longer a simple, down-the-line surfer. He was a rail surfer, setting his edge in the flats, relaxed and stylish, releasing to a vertical turn off the top with explosive flare.

He paddled north, eyeing the shape of the oncoming lines as they appeared from the deep. The first wave rolled beneath, and he scratched vigorously, positioning himself for the larger wave of the set. As the wave approached, he spun around, and with three slick strokes, he stood to his feet and slid adeptly into the oily face. He pointed the nose of his surfboard straight to the bottom and accelerated with a natural sense of how much forward pressure the rocker would allow without pearling. Using the fins and rail as torque against immense hydraulic forces, he leaned hard until his fingertips graced the surface as he charged at a forty-five-degree angle over the flats.

With his hair blowing back, his eyes focused on the crumbling section of wave before him. He approached the section at breakneck speed, unweighted, and placed the bottom of his board flat on the downward chunk of water. A cubic area of water weighs a ton, and Ches used the downward fluid force to whip his board, generating an exponential increase of velocity to the bottom again.

From the flats, another seamless transition to the shoulder allowed him to lean back and divert the energy into the tail and rail in a reverse carve on the open face of the wave, gouging out a ten-foot fan of water. He pumped the wall of the wave twice more before kicking out.

"Hey, Grommet!"

The boy kept paddling.

"Hey, *Grommet*!"

The boy paddled clear of the impact zone and then turned to see who was calling.

"Yo, you little phoonbot. You're ripping like Tom Curren." It was Caveman. The boy grinned and paddled for another wave, shredding it to completion. As he paddled back out, an involuntary hoot burst from his lips as Caveman obliterated a section and transitioned into a powerful cutback, showering the boy with spray. Both surfers cackled in full appreciation of the rich bounty of perfect groundswell. They surfed until the setting sun brought the session to a close.

At the water's edge, the two friends clasped hands and laughed at one another. Caveman shook his head. "Man, I knew you had it bad, you little styler."

Two college-age surfers joined them on the shore, producing a quartet of giggles. Caveman introduced them. "Guys, this is the Grommet I told you about. He's a thoroughbred freaker, hardcore to the bone marrow. He likely surfed all winter without a wetsuit." Caveman patted Ches on the back. "Grom, this is Trey and Matt."

Matt snapped hands with the boy. "Man, my arms feel like two noodles. Was that you doing those Curren turns on the inside? Dude, you are in there!"

The boy smiled and bowed his head.

Caveman gave Ches another high five. "How are you getting home, brah?"

"I have a tent," the boy replied with a partial grin. "I'm staying till the end."

"*Whaaat*? See, I told you guys, Grom is eaten up with the affliction. Better get his autograph while you can."

"Grom, are you surfing the contest Saturday?" Trey asked.

The boy just stared at Trey.

Caveman grabbed him by the shoulders. "Grommet, you're in. I'll get you registered, boys division. The winner gets a free custom-shaped surfboard, with prizes for anyone who makes the final."

Ches still didn't reply. The idea of surfing before a panel of judges and a crowd of spectators was hardly appealing.

"Guys, we gotta go," Trey said, pointing to the setting sun. "It's gotta be seven or better. The show is at nine."

Caveman and the others followed the boy to his campsite. They commented on the hurried pile and unpitched tent as obvious signs of a wave-starved surf addict. Trey helped the boy set up his tent while Caveman scavenged firewood from neighboring campsite. The boy spread the food out, started making himself a peanut-butter sandwich, and motioned for the guys to help themselves.

"What's up now? Yeeaahhaahaa!" Caveman made a sandwich, and the two others followed suit. They passed the water around and rehashed the insane surfing session while stoking the fire. "Where do you guys wanna surf tomorrow?" Matt asked. "High tide is at noon."

"Dude, I am surfing right here tomorrow. There is enough swell to hold right through high tide. Besides, the pier and every other spot will be packed with weekend-warrior goombayahs. The freaker-grom is dialed in. No sense letting him have it all."

Everyone agreed and turned to the boy, who quietly enjoyed a banana. Trey pinched an end piece of bread and thumped it in the boy's direction. "Dude, how old are you anyway?"

"Thirteen … today."

"*Whaaaat*? Your birthday … today? No way! You can't be human." All three surfers cracked up. "Grom, yer comin with us tonight. Summer concert. On campus! The Ramones, brah!"

The boy flashed a nervous glance.

"Grommm, don't worry," Cave said. "I've got you covered, trust me."

Ches retrieved a pair of Levi's and an Oxford shirt from his bag and joined the other surfers, who wore only their wet, salty clothes. They drove into the college parking area to the sounds of the Ramones echoing throughout the campus. Caveman handed the boy a latex Halloween mask of President Ronald Reagan. "Wear this. Do not take it off! You'll blend with the college crazies."

Matt protested. "Dude, the Grommet is barely five feet tall."

"Trust me. If he's a politician, no one will know the difference. They'll think he's a Spaniard."

Ches stuck close to Caveman as they moved through a grassy field littered with plastic beer cups. They trudged closer to the center of the activity, but the group began to separate. Throngs of students pushed and staggered in every direction. A guy and a girl faced one another, surrounded by a mob chanting, "Sell the Buick. Sell the Buick," as the two vomited the excesses of their revelry.

The boy worked hard to keep his friends in sight. They walked past an enormous tower of lights and approached the giant stage. The extreme loudness made it impossible for the boy to make sense of the music. The other surfers yelled something and started to run. Ches tried to follow, but the latex mask obstructed his view. He breathed heavily and fought the urge to peel off the mask as he struggled to see through the slits.

"Grommet!" Caveman yelled. The boy stopped in his tracks and slowly scanned a large swath in the general direction of the voice. Caveman grabbed the boy by the arm. "Easy now … don't freak on me … gotcha covered!"

"I can't exactly see the world through the eyes of a politician," Ches retorted.

"I don't doubt that," Caveman shouted. "Come on, I want to introduce you to the clan."

The two approached the rest of the group, where two additional surfers were huddled together with Matt and Trey and an equal number of girls.

"Guys, this is the grom we told you about."

"What's up, brah? I'm Aaron. This is Dave, Candice, Carson, Suzanna, Liz, and … her weird sister … uhhh."

"Hi, Ches, I'm Sarah. Liz is my friend, but Aaron is my deranged brother. Nice to meet you."

The boy shyly extended his hand. Sarah defied her brother with a subtle wag of her head, grabbed the boy by the wrist, and curled her fingers into his. "Soo … you're a politician?"

The boy's forehead burst with beads of sweat as Sarah held his wrist while moving her head back and forth, inches from his face, searching for his eyes inside the tiny peepholes. The hokey façade adequately concealed his lack of confidence, yet he could see all of her. He'd never seen such radiant beauty. There wasn't a drop of makeup on her face. He stared at the miniscule pearls of feminine perspiration on her upper lip. Her prominent nose was dusted with the faintest splay of freckles—exquisite complements to her bright hazel eyes.

Sarah fit in with the group, each of whom was physically exceptional: perfect teeth, perfect complexions, and healthy, uncolored hair. Ches recalled the words of Mark Twain, "Good breeding consists in concealing how much we think of ourselves, and how little we think of others." He felt notably at ease.

Caveman was the only one of the group who exhibited unsavory stock, with a huge scar under his eye and a chipped tooth. He wore raggedy clothes, but not as a deliberate statement; his cutoff army pants and an undersized T-shirt were the clothes he could afford.

Cave seemed to be the star of the group, though, as he made jokes of the passersby: "Look, it's Simon Le Bon!" An extremely tall guy had stumbled past; he was wearing a white zoot suit with a skinny, neon tie, and bleach-blond hair professionally coiffed. The guy stopped in his tracks.

"Hey, I love your hair, brah," Caveman proclaimed, sincerely.

The guy turned, cocked his head, squinted, and then wobbled menacingly toward the group with a bowed chest and balled fists. Caveman stood flat until the guy's nose nestled against the top of his forehead.

"No, I am perfectly serious," Cave said, wincing under the brute's putrid breath. "I really wish I had your hair. See, my hair is pathetic."

It was true. Caveman's hair was most unattractive. And the fact he was his own barber didn't help matters. He turned and pointed to the back of his imperfect cut. The Simon Le Bon guy cocked his chin and inspected Caveman's hair. Cave smiled and extended his hand, but the guy grunted an unintelligible insult and walked away.

While the attention shifted to Caveman, Aaron noticed that the boy had slipped quietly into the inebriated swarms. "Cave, where'd your politician friend go?"

"Dude, I can't believe he let me talk him into coming. He rarely speaks. But if you can get him to talk, he'll blow your mind. Moreover, he is crazy hardcore for surfing. He keeps a campsite at Hanna … by himself. He'll surf from sunup to sundown … by himself."

"How old is he?"

"Thirteen. Today is his birthday."

"*Whaaat*? Seriously? Let's blow this bag of hammered fiends and go to Hanna and celebrate by the campfire!"

They found the boy, still wearing the Ronald Reagan mask, leaning cross-legged on the hood of the car.

"I'm voting for you!" Sarah laughed as she tugged at the mask, revealing his young face.

"Me too," Aaron said, squinting to get a glimpse of the boy, "There's like twenty thousand drunken boneheads under the spotlights, and Grommet's like, 'I'll just do my thing over here in the shadows, thank you.'"

On the ride back, someone lit a joint and began to pass it around. Sarah let it pass, and Ches stared straight ahead as she inspected him closely as though he were a newly discovered treat from the bakery. "You are so sweaty," she pointed her index finger and swiped the boy on the nose. He acted as though he would bite her finger with a click of his teeth. Her eyes lit up, and she snatched her finger back. "You're crazy, aren't you?"

When they arrived at the campsite, the group gathered around the fire. Ches eased shyly into his tent and closed his eyes to the image of Sarah touching his nose.

On Saturday morning Ches stood on the beach as the announcer introduced the competitors. He felt dumb wearing a tight, neon-green Spandex jersey. *How do I let people talk me into these things?* It was not a rhetorical question. He made a mental note to address it at a more convenient time. The colored jerseys were assigned to the competitors for identification by the judges and the spectators. Ches had always fantasized of surfing as his livelihood, but he had never considered competing. But somehow, on this day, with Caveman as his coach, he'd earned a spot in the final.

The other three competitors already sported logos of varying sponsors on the decks of their surfboards. Ches recognized the kid with the blue jersey from surfing magazines; he was a prodigy who held numerous amateur titles with the Eastern Surfing Association. Ches didn't feel as nervous as he felt awkward. He wanted to escape somehow; up the beach to surf without the bullhorns and neon jerseys and hoopla. He would've been content, on this occasion, to be a spectator, studying and applauding the skills of the other three competitors.

The horn sounded, and the other three surfers bolted to the lineup. The boy followed. He tried to muster the competitive fire of the other three surfers, who broke through the impact zone effortlessly. Ches got caught in a series of ruthless poundings. He finally broke through in time to witness the surfer wearing blue in a blistering bottom-turn, releasing to a vertical smash off the top, followed by a seamless series of lightning fast maneuvers.

Ches was awestruck. He rested in the lineup as another set approached and the competitors in white and red jockeyed for position. The surfer in white was up and riding, and Ches paddled furiously out of the way. The wave passed by and he craned his neck as the surfer's head disappeared, followed by a huge fan of spray out the back of the wave as the speeding surfboard gouged into the wave. The surfer in red followed with a series of roundhouse cutbacks all the way to the inside.

Ches had the lineup to himself. He felt like a fish in a bowl and tried to ignore the colorful flags, judges' tower, and hordes of spectators on the beach. A set approached, and instantly all the hubbub disappeared. He allowed the first wave to pass, opting for the larger, more powerful wave that followed.

His positioning was perfect. He paddled, stood to his feet and faded, and then charged forward. A faint hum vibrated from fins pushed to the limit. The wave was three feet overhead as it stacked on the sandbar, forming a steep, heaving wall. The boy leaned nonchalantly into the wall, dropped his back knee, and stalled as the wave barreled overtop.

The hoots from the other competitors echoed inside the watery cave. The surfer in blue held his hands to his mouth and shouted his approval before duckdiving the behemoth. Ches drifted deeper into the darkness but released his fins, slid down the face, and pumped for speed in a race for the light at the end. After a fraction of a second, the wave offered an opening. He seized the moment, angled his board toward the beach, and made for the exit out the front. His board planed into the flats, but a heaving section of water clipped him on the back of the head, swatting the boy from his board like a bug.

He felt himself blacking out. His lungs were burning. He hadn't taken a full breath of air before being violently smacked beneath the surface and shaken like a ragdoll. The wave dragged the boy along the sandbar and fizzled into the depths. When he finally surfaced, the horn sounded the completion of the heat. He gained his composure and paddled to shore as the other three competitors gathered on the beach, shaking hands.

The three walked toward the boy, smiling. He was still rattled but couldn't help smiling with them. They gathered around, patting Ches on the back. The surfer in blue gave the boy an extended surfer snap. "Dude, you … are a madman! I heard this is your first contest ever. Insane!"

At the end of the day, Ches walked the trail to his campsite with a brand T-shirt and a fourth-place trophy. He gazed across the dunes and spotted the other three finalists well beyond the path.

"If I believe in a plural God I become a dangerous person. These are vain and deadly philosophies, and here is Jesus's response to that pluralistic society: 'ye are from beneath; I am from above: ye are of this world; I am not of this world.' Common earthly reasoning is not applicable to the word of Jesus Christ. And when Pilate says, 'I find no fault in Him,' this statement is in the same vein as 'what is truth,' because one truth is just as good as another; it is all relative. Do you wish for me to release Jesus or Barabbas, because it's all the same to me, I am Roman! One man's murderer is another man's messiah! Awe, somebody tell me what time it is."

Now, I am mouthing the words, "Evening time!"

Chapter 14

The pastor had spoken to the mother about Ches. As a result, the mother aimed to see the boy more involved with the church. He'd been far too reclusive. "It ain't healthy! Hurry up, we're late already!" Unbeknown to Ches, he'd been enrolled as a student at the church's private school.

The pastor, Brother Brown, was a black man in his midfifties who also served as the school principal and student evaluator. Each student was given a set of diagnostic tests to determine academic level. The evaluator would decide the student's needs regarding each subject and prescribe appropriate gap PACEs to specific weaknesses. Ches tested to the highest level in each category with the exception of math and biblical studies, in which he tested average. The principal scheduled an orientation with the mother and the boy to discuss the parameters of student expectations.

The school facility was a World War II–era portable purchased by the church and installed behind the sanctuary on a new foundation of concrete blocks. The mother and boy sat in the waiting room outside the office. It smelled old and stuffy but with a hint of fresh paint. After a few minutes, a man with graying eyebrows and a stern demeanor motioned for Ches and the mother to enter the office.

There was a massive deer head high on the wall and two stuffed mallards above a small bookshelf with a stack of fishing magazines and religious pamphlets. The principal greeted them from behind a giant oak desk. The boy detected a smattering of freckles over the principal's dark skin as the man briefly shared his background as an army retiree and how he came to be a minister. Brother Brown expressed a deep passion for the school, explaining in detail how much planning and hard work went into the success of such an establishment.

He pressed a button on the telephone, and seconds later a woman entered. She wore a brown-and-yellow plaid jumper dress with a yellow Oxford blouse and no jewelry. Her hair was pulled back in a bun. She didn't wear makeup, but her complexion was radiant, not unlike the boy's beach friend, Sarah, except this woman was clearly in her forties.

"This is Sister Petrosh. She is our lead monitor."

The boy tried not to stare. But there was something familiar, something comforting and trustworthy about the woman—a peculiar air that transcended style or trends or convention. She presented two freshly starched uniforms and hung them on a hook on the wall: brown trousers with a yellow button-down. She bid a warm welcome and exited the office.

Principal Brown continued. "If you have issues with wearing a uniform, this is not the school for you. Each of our students is assigned a personal cubicle in the learning center with privacy dividers between each cubicle. You may not speak to your neighbor during study time. You will be expected to set your own study goals daily. If each goal is not achieved, there will be a penalty. You will be expected to score and correct your daily work. However, a learning center monitor will score your tests. This is an honor system … which brings me to a very important question."

There was a lengthy pause. Brother Brown put on a pair of reading glasses and examined some papers, and the boy reasoned such moments were orchestrated to draw attention to the obvious power differential. To this point the pastor hadn't acknowledge him, but suddenly he stared authoritatively into the boy's eyes. Ches rarely made eye contact with anyone but felt obligated to return the stare.

He did so without squirming. The pastor searched the boy's face like he was a hardened criminal before an interrogator.

"Have you ever cheated on a test?"

The blood drained from the boy's face as he searched frantically for a proper response. *Does this man know something? What does he see?* Truthfully, the boy couldn't recall cheating on a test. But at that moment he was guilty. Consternation tweaked his facial expression.

"At this establishment we don't follow the mainstream," the pastor declared indignantly. "We don't do what *they* do. We don't go the places *they* go. We are not entertained by what the mainstream is entertained by. It is our position that obedience to the Word of God fosters genuine freedom and liberty. Thus, we don't mark our bodies with tattoos per Leviticus 19:28. We don't pierce our ears, as it is a mark of slavery, and we don't dye our hair." The man moved around his desk and stared directly at the boy's hair. Ches became painfully self-conscious. His hair had streaks of blond from extreme exposure to the summer sun.

"Our boys behave as gentlemen, and our girls behave as ladies." Brother Brown turned his attention to the mother, who was smiling and nodding as if she'd always agreed with such standards. "And we encourage our families to separate themselves from the inhibitory and unhealthy behavior of the mainstream. I do not have a television in my home. And I would encourage you to not keep a TV in your home. It is our position that television greatly decreases quality of life and learning. We ask our students to refrain from television. If any student cannot comply with these simple standards, he or she will be disenrolled … permanently." He turned to the boy, but directed his words to the mother. "Ma'am, Sister Petrosh will have you sign for the uniforms while I have a word with our newest student."

Brother Brown opened the door for the mother without taking his eyes off the boy. When the door closed, he paused, smiled, and took a deep breath. "Apparently, you scored exceptionally high on our diagnostic test."

The boy stared at the man's chin without blinking.

"So … apparently you are a very … smart fellow? Hmm. I must inform you that we have a zero-tolerance policy for cheating. Do we understand one another?" The principal extended his hand. "I think we can be friends, don't you?" The boy shook the man's hand and made his exit without a word.

Ches adjusted nicely to his new school environs, including the required Bible memorization. He discovered the richness of the book, its style; the beauty of the writings of Solomon, and Job, and Isaiah was captivating. He'd commit to memory whole chapters in Ecclesiastes.

He found himself content with the church school, the uniforms, the structure. And while he tried to suppress the nagging need for a father figure, he couldn't help wondering whether the pastor was to be such a one. Deep down, he felt a slight sting of guilt having skipped exorbitant portions of his schooling, presumably undetected. But on the other hand, he couldn't believe his luck. He wouldn't have to repeat the missed grades.

Sometimes after school, when the surf report was favorable, Ches would hop the city bus to the beach. He could be in the water by half past three, surf for two hours, and be home again by half past six. Other days he would rake yards after school and do various odd jobs for pocket money. Studying was done mostly during school hours. With two breaks per day plus lunch, the schedule and curriculum were very convenient.

A biography of Isaac Newton caused an old question to resurface, which required him to resume visits to the library for a spell. It wasn't the widely known scientific contributions of Newton's life that triggered his curiosity, but one little-known fact: The Bible was Sir Isaac's greatest passion. In fact, Newton's passion for the Bible exceeded his love for mathematics and science. He was a believer who obsessed over proper interpretations. He grappled with Christian theology with intense fervor, he learned Hebrew as a means of strengthening his theological position, but his notes overflowed with disturbing submissions.

The topic that most absorbed Newton's interest was the relationship of God and Christ, and the reality of first-century, uncorrupt Christian doctrines. Newton's greatest source of discomfort became the *trinitate*, which he categorically renounced. He secretly embroiled himself in the great controversy at Nicaea and Constantinople and the official declaration of the plurality of God.

With further investigation Ches learned that the doctrine of worshiping the plurality of God ultimately became law, and denying the Trinity became a capital offense. The boy felt as though he had stumbled upon a conspiracy of profound global significance. Ambiguity had been institutionalized during this pivotal era, with disturbing implications into modern times.

It wasn't so much Newton's rejection of the Trinity that bothered Ches. The boy was quite familiar with such objections. But why did Newton have to hide his views? Newton was a Protestant. And yet denying the Trinity led to life-threatening consequences. Nevertheless, through decades of study, Newton crafted a perfect argument. His discoveries simultaneously solidified his faith and ensured his place among so-called heretics. By documenting his position, Newton became a criminal.

The boy began to study the history of heresy. He uncovered a disturbing historical fact: when a person denied the Trinity, that specific crime became an occasion for both the Catholic and the Protestant church to come together on common ground. Protestant leaders, otherwise eternally opposed to the Catholic Church, would corroborate one with the other, and then collaborate on the cruel and inhumane means of dealing specifically with deniers of the Trinity.

Ches read the account of Michael Servetus, with its extraordinary imagery of Catholics and Protestants together at last, discussing the fate of that "troublemaker" Christian. He imagined Servetus chained to a stake and the copious supply of kindling strategically bound round about his body, and the hooded trinitarian applying the flame that unified Catholics and Protestants for all eternity.

The boy poured sorrowfully over the pages depicting the tortuous methods used to enforce the Trinity, losing heart altogether after reading of a despicable gadget called "the Holy Trinity": an iron mask heated until glowing red and then applied to the face of the heretic and allowed to simmer. Red-hot pincers were used to remove the heretic's tongue. The boy thought of his grandmother and her crime of speaking in tongues.

Ultimately Ches decided to return to more secular literary interests. Eventually Brother Brown reprimanded him for reading Dostoevsky's *Crime and Punishment* on school property. Brother Brown gently pulled the reading from the boy's grasp, flipped through the pages, and confiscated the book with the promise to return it at the end of the year.

Brother Brown was a sincere man. The boy often heard him weeping in prayer from his office, calling aloud various church members and the student body at large. Ches wondered if Brother Brown had knowledge of his previous years of truancy. This question was answered when Sister Petrosh was assigned to monitor the boy's every move throughout the day.

"I believe you have a gift," she would say in an effort to encourage the boy, even though he expressed no injury. "You understand the meaning of a word based solely on syllable and sound." The woman's demeanor betrayed the wedge between her and the rest of the faculty. "I have a master's in English literature from Duke," she commented nonchalantly, as if the boy understood the difference between knowledge acquired at a university and knowledge acquired at the local library. "I am studying for my PhD."

The boy enjoyed Sister Petrosh's constant attention. She monitored him even as he studied during break time, working through the Paces with executive-level efficiency. By November, the boy was near high school completion in both English and social studies. But the fact that he rarely socialized with the other students caused rumors to fly.

One student had heard that the boy was one of the best surfers in Florida. Another claimed the boy had a genius IQ. Ches pondered the sources of such information. Where did it come from? Whose was the first mouth to speak it? He noticed his classmates exhibiting things stereotypical of surfers, including sentences with abundant use of the words *like* and *totally*. They wore little neon neoprene bracelets against school policy. Ches was certain he hadn't mentioned his secret passion to any of the sheltered darlings of the learning center. Still he couldn't hide his fascination with how trends are transferred from external forces.

The following Monday, he awoke five minutes late. The electricity had been turned off due to nonpayment. He hated being late, as it attracted unnecessary attention. When he stepped into the learning center, Sister Petrosh was there, solemnly waiting, and the learning center was noticeably quiet. Students stole glances at Ches from behind cubicle dividers. Sister Petrosh met the boy at his desk, and she whispered, "Brother and Sister Brown wish to speak with you immediately in the main office."

His mind raced with questions. Surely they weren't calling him up for being tardy; it was his first. Maybe they intended to make reconciliation for having false suspicions of him cheating. But why all the whispers? Why was Sister Petrosh so concerned?

As he stepped into the waiting area, Brother Brown stood by the office door and motioned him to enter. Sister Brown was sitting in chair at an angle behind the desk. The boy stared at the small bookshelf, half conscious of his copy of *Crime and Punishment* being used as a bookend to a pack of religious pamphlets.

"Have a seat, please."

The boy sat in the same seat as the day of orientation. He sat there feeling smaller and smaller as the room took a different shape. The awkward angles drew emphasis to the depleted levels of comfort, placing the boy as the subject within the center of the frame.

Brother Brown began, "I think you know … we think you are an intelligent young man."

The man and his wife nodded with identical expressions; tight lips, upside-down, U-shapes, protruding lower lip; and furrowed brows with forced concern in the upward-turned eyes.

Sister Brown approved the statement with a wobble of her head. "I said it from the very beginning … he's a smart fellow."

The couple turned to each other again with affirming orbital nods.

Sister Brown spoke with extreme pauses between phrases, "Maybe … you've noticed. What you do … and … what you say … the other students do … and say." She paused again, and the silence lasted an eternity. The boy thought for a moment that Sister Brown had nothing more to say, but she continued. "You … are not … a leader. But maybe … eventually … you can be … a leader."

After another short pause, Brother Brown said, "We would like for you … to live for Jesus. Because if you … live for Jesus … the others will follow."

The boy studied the faces and words of Brother and Sister Brown. He pondered the plausibility of possessing such powers over his classmates. *Is it possible? Can I influence them to live for Jesus? Why would I want to? Brother and Sister Brown are suggesting that, from my position within an enclosed place of study, I influence the behavior of a group of individuals outside, literally, considerable distances away.*

And this assertion wasn't a joke. Ches searched their faces for the smallest hint of humor, possibly sealed behind the tightened corners of their mouths, but he found none. They were serious. He felt his own sense of humor stirring, which he ignored, lest the slightest attention fan the flames within until his body collapsed to the floor kicking, screaming, and foaming at the mouth under cascades of endorphin-induced laughter.

No, he thought, *it is not humanly possible to possess such power. While I recognize the various factors present that might contribute to their theory, clearly Brother and Sister Brown do not have access to the same information. The fact is, I have been thoroughly compliant with their standards of conduct.*

But why do I bother these people so? We agree on much of the same things. I am not a television hypnotic. I wouldn't think of dying my hair. I would never waste precious gems of creative expression on a tattoo or piercings. Maybe I have cheated, in some way, but not here. I haven't cheated here, in this place.

The meeting dissolved without a handshake. Ches returned to the learning center feeling as though he had missed an opportunity. And yet he had no idea what the opportunity might've been.

"Pilate finally says, 'Crucify Him.' Pilate believed he had the power to release Jesus, and he offered to release Jesus, but he ultimately executed Jesus. Why? Because Pilate was dyed-in-the-wool Roman, and Pilate was obligated to send the message—both to Jesus and the world at large—that there are a lot of things tolerated in Rome, but there is one thing Rome will not tolerate. A person simply cannot go around saying, I Am the Truth, the definitive; I Am the—and there is no other—Truth. 'What is truth' and 'I find no fault in Him' sound inoffensive and benign, if only we could disentangle these two phrases from the sinister third phrase 'Crucify Him.' These three are inextricably bound in one more pagan triad. Now we see that the crucifixion of Jesus Christ is dynamically Roman. Rome's pluralized god was appeased when they thought they had terminated that sole manifestation of deity. Does anybody here know what time it is?"

"Evening time!"

Chapter 15

It was the long weekend of Thanksgiving. No school Thursday and Friday. The boy informed the mother that he'd be at his friend's place until Saturday evening. Wednesday after school he packed his camping gear and caught the bus to Hanna.

The ocean conditions were abysmal, but a Hatteras low had churned the open water three hundred nautical miles northeast. The ground swell was expected to arrive through the long weekend.

After a short session, the boy took advantage of the campground showers. Other campers rarely used the shower facilities, probably because they were at the far corner of the boundary in a wooded area void of activity. He took his time to peel away his wetsuit under the endless supply of hot water.

An hour later he made a fire, leaned back, and enjoyed a banana. Just as the sun dipped below the horizon, a late-model BMW with tinted windows pulled into the parking space by the campsite. The motor went quiet, the driver door opened, and the swirling breeze carried a familiar scent. Ches's heart rate increased. It was Sarah.

"How did I know I would find you here? I am sooo impressed with myself."

She wore a Burberry silk scarf, a burgundy cashmere sweater, and a denim skirt with Italian leather sandals.

He gazed appreciatively as she held her hands to the fire and then sat beside him. Her long, natural hair was tied back, but a few unrestrained strands framed her flawless complexion. How could natural coloring be so exquisitely coordinated? Auburn hair untainted by artificial chemicals and the untouched hue of her lips were a perfect contrast to her healthy ginger complexion dusted with barely discernible freckles beneath lustrous, brilliant eyes.

Most girls her age wouldn't be seen in public without first smearing a factory-concocted color wheel over an otherwise perfect skin tone. Girls in the surfing community viewed such vanities as shallow and uninformed. Even the whites of Sarah's eyes were extraordinarily white—especially compared to his eyes, so red and suffering from exposure to salt, sand, and sun.

Sarah was flawless. With a perfect smile, she kicked off her sandals and casually lifted her delicate feet to the crackling fire. Even her hands exuded affluence. Such pleasant femininity amid the sea oats and sand dunes was an exquisite fit for firelight in the autumn.

"I'll be spending Thanksgiving alone too. My family is scattered all over the world. Aaron is surfing Australia, my mother is covering the Middle East, and my father is teaching in Europe."

Sarah and Ches sat side by side, staring into the flames. Ches enjoyed listening to her talk, the way she pronounced her words without an accent.

"I enjoy college, except it gets lonesome; I am not even seventeen yet, probably the youngest student on campus so …"

He studied Sarah's mannerisms as she spoke. She let him.

"Will you go to college, Ches?"

He furrowed his brow and shrugged his shoulders. She crossed her leg and lightly kicked the boy's knee. "Sorry, I forget you are *only* fourteeen."

Ches didn't correct her. He was only thirteen. The waning fire prompted him to move from his spot and search for more wood.

"Let's douse it altogether and go to my house," Sarah suggested. She stood, stretched, and unpinned her hair, shaking it free. "Come! You can meet Sister Fuentes, our house lady from El Salvador. She's awesome, and her sons surf Punta Roca." Sarah helped herself to the jug of water by the boy's tent and poured it over the fire. The boy stood there, smiling.

Ches had never ridden in an automobile of such exquisite engineering. He inhaled the new-car smell as he slid into the blue leather seat and closed the door with an effortless click. The engine purred with the slightest turn of the ignition. The state-of-the-art equalizer blinked blue and red to the beat of faint progressive sounds from hi-def tweeters and woofers. He craned his neck politely, trying to hear the transcendent music.

"Ooh ... somebody likes The Cure," she said, flittering her hand as she turned up the volume. "This song is called 'The Drowning Man.'"

Ches was mesmerized. He stared out the window and allowed the heady music to do its work as they journeyed to Sarah's world.

They approached the guard gate and slowed for clearance. The guard stepped from the shack and waved them through once he recognized Sarah. She stopped anyway. "What, you too good to say hi?"

A man of his midseventies approached. He wore a uniform, a badge, and Glock on his hip, and he spoke with a slight accent. "How's the big-time college girl doing?"

"So-so. Did Anjelo get into Harvard?"

"Sure did! And I haven't heard from the little stinker for two weeks."

"Well, I can't imagine why. It's not as if we college kids have nothing better to do than make phone calls."

"I hear ya, little Miss Smartypants. You can go now," he said, smiling, as he pressed a button that lifted the black-and-white striped gate. Sarah waved. "He's a retired detective. His wife died last year; their youngest son was recently accepted into Harvard."

The boy gasped as they motored beneath an ivy-laden archway that opened to a sprawling gardenscape. They passed between two giant ponds with extravagant water fountains bursting from the center of each. The road was lined with elegant, acorn-shaped light fixtures that created interesting shadows beneath the ornamental trees.

The homes were enormous. Ches was too embarrassed to ask whether or not people actually lived in them. Each driveway spoke of excessive luxury—some paved with brick, others with stone. Sarah confidently turned into an understated entrance paved with asymmetrically patterned blue slate. They followed the low-profile lighting until it opened to a pristine landscape designed to draw the eyes to the centerpiece of the property: a ten-thousand-square-foot, multilevel home constructed of stone and cedar.

Sarah parked her car behind an SUV before the slate steps. Ches remained in the front seat, unsure of what to do. Sarah ascended the steps halfway, but came back to the car and opened the passenger door. "Are you coming, you phoonbot?" The boy nonchalantly rolled out of the car and followed Sarah up the stone steps to a lighted entryway.

"Sister Fuentes?"

The boy felt himself shrinking as he crossed the threshold and realized his ragged Sperry's made tracks across the marble floor.

"Sister Fuentes?" Sarah called excitedly after the house lady.

The boy thought it odd that Sarah addressed the woman as Sister Fuentes. *Maybe it's a Salvadorian expression, or Catholic, or both.* Sarah walked ahead. Ches closed the heavy oak door; it latched with barely a touch. He quickly used his shirt to wipe the sweat from his forehead.

Cheerful foreign chatter echoed through the hall. Ches waited in the foyer next to a desk with a lamp beside a giant mirror. He evaluated his reflection. His image contradicted the extreme quality of the surrounding material. He wondered at the collaborative effort it took to produce such a dwelling: generations of inheritances of educated stock, doctors, lawyers, and familial support. Ches determined his reflection unsuitable for such a world. He wanted to return to Hanna Park.

"Hey, weirdy, are you going to set up camp in the foyer or what?" Sarah poked her head around the corner and switched on the sophisticated lighting. The boy grew increasingly uncomfortable as he moved Sarah's direction. He peeked into a kitchen, which was considerably larger than anyplace he had ever lived. Sarah grabbed him by the hand. "I want you to meet Sister Fuentes."

They walked through the kitchen into a sunroom with an ornate, crystal breakfast table at the center. On it were a pair of bifocals, a neon-pink highlighter, and Bible splayed open. The two friends stood at the table. "She's gone to prepare us something; she'll be right back." Sarah couldn't hide her excitement. Minutes later, a little woman entered, carrying a tray of lime drinks and turkey sandwiches.

Ches was instantly rattled by her presence. It was a familiar thing, a sweetness he'd come to recognize, but lately found so unsettling. Her hair was natural black with streaks of gray, flowing from her temples and pulled back. Her dress, modest and tasteful, pointed to a position higher than that of housekeeper. He'd never laid eyes on this woman before this moment, but he recognized her. He began to fidget and sweat profusely. He tried to calm himself with objective thoughts, but eye contact with Sister Fuentes made matters worse. She too was visibly moved by his presence.

"O … sí … sí!" She placed the tray next to the Bible and walked toward the boy. He was taller than she. Sister Fuentes took both of his hands into hers and gazed into his face, nodding with a graceful, knowing smile. "Es nice to meet you. Please … seet heer … eat." She waved her hand to the chair, politely backed away, and disappeared into the kitchen.

Sarah darted her eyes. "Wow! They say first impressions are everything. See! I'm not the only one who thinks you're a weirdy." She smiled sweetly and gave the boy a little nudge. He stared through the crystal tabletop as his body language spoke against his will.

"We can go now if you want," Sarah said. "But not before we eat." She kicked him under the table and slid the lime drink toward his hand. "Try this! Sister Fuentes makes it fresh. It's from El Salvador." The drink was indeed delicious, as well as the sandwich, which proved to calm him a bit.

They finished eating and quietly made their way toward the door. As the door opened, Sister Fuentes called after the two with an urgent tone; her eyes were teary and red. Her left hand clutched a handkerchief, and she extended it slowly and cradled Ches's hands together between her palm and the handkerchief. After a brief silence she spoke, "Señor … God has hees hand upon you. Alwees … sí … sí … God … nambre de Jesus." She released his hand, turned to kiss Sarah's cheek with a whisper, and then closed the door behind them.

Sarah broke the silence as they passed through the guard gate. "She's been with us since I was three. If you've studied Christian history, she is different, believe me. My mother wouldn't have her in our home if she weren't. Christians persecuted my mother's ancestors, contributing to Hitler's dirty deeds. So my father thoroughly researched Sister Fuentes before bringing her aboard. Her type of Christianity has been persecuted too from the first century. My dad says that Sister Fuentes is a pretrinitarian Christian. Pretrinitarian Christianity was founded by Jews, strict monotheists who deny all triangle deities."

Ches was stone silent. He extended his trembling hand to increase the volume of The Cure.

When they arrived at Hanna Park, Ches walked directly to the campfire. Sarah followed, stretching her limbs and staring upward at the gathering clouds. "Can I stay a little while?" she asked. Ches nodded as he pressed a handful of pine needles into the smoldering coals.

Sarah sat closer than usual and watched the boy blow steadily on the fuel. A flame appeared, catching hold of the larger kindling.

With the fire sufficiently burning, he leaned back, turned his face to hers, and relaxed. She blinked and laid her head on his shoulder. "I really like you, Ches." Sarah was serious. Her countenance revealed the hidden loneliness of a world far different from Ches's. "But it's a funny thing," she continued. "When I am with you, I always feel as though somebody is watching."

"You have a cognitive distortion," Ches said wryly, stealing a subtle whiff of her hair as a drop of rain landed on his arm.

Sarah punched his arm, stood, and brushed off her skirt. "You are so mean. I'll come by tomorrow."

After the fire died, he crawled into his tent, tucked himself into his sleeping bag, and closed his eyes.

The waves materialized as forecasted: a solid, four- to six-foot northeast ground swell with onshore winds ten to fifteen knots. He surfed through the weekend. Sarah left a note on his sleeping bag: "You must be seeing things … I think … maybe. Ha ha! See you in the spring. S."

I kneel beside the little chair. How do I know exactly what Brother Brown is saying?

"John writes in his Gospel, 'In Jesus was life; and the life was the light of men. And the light shineth in darkness; and the darkness comprehended it not.' Jesus was apprehended for addressing the confusing issue, the philosophy of myriad possible lights. That is why He said, 'Take heed therefore that the light which is in thee be not darkness. 'If therefore the light that is in thee be darkness, how great is that darkness!' That is what Jesus said! The word of His mouth sheds light on the plurality-of-lights-fallacy. It is darkness. These lights do nothing to save humankind. These lights do not work. Awe, but God has a church that knows what time it is!"

Chapter 16

SISTER PETROSH NO longer tutored the boy on a daily basis. Ches hoped he'd been exonerated, but the tension within the learning center increased by the day. Fellow students whispered as they huddled in small groups while hanging Christmas decorations, stealing glances now and then. The boy did his best to ignore it all. He thought about Sarah.

Throughout the week, Brother and Sister Brown called individual students one at a time to the office. Ches tried to no avail to make small talk at break time with a boy his age. Friday at ten, Sister Petrosh tapped Ches on the shoulder. "Brother and Sister Brown will meet with you now."

The boy stepped into the office and allowed the awkward feeling to run its course as Brother Brown sat in his chair, studying a yellow notepad. After a full minute, the man began to speak with soldierly discipline. "We're going to get right to it! I'm going to ask you some questions. If you respond with the simple truth, we can work with you. If you lie, we can do nothing for you."

The boy's mind raced to a thousand different places, searching for possible answers to who knows what, but eventually calmness prevailed.

The man opened his desk and retrieved a small screw and placed it beside the yellow pad. "Do you know what this is?"

Ches paused. It was obviously a screw, but he was unsure of what the man was asking.

"Answer the question, son! Do you know what this is?" The man slapped the screw to the desktop.

The boy thought the simple answer might be interpreted as arrogance. He began with extreme caution, careful not to appear sarcastic. "It's a … screw … sir."

"Very good. I knew you could do it. Next question. Have you ever offered it to one of our ladies … accompanied with the words *Wanna screw*?"

The boy winced and stared at the floor indignantly. "No."

The man scrawled something on his yellow pad with the red pen.

"Next question. Did you write the graffiti on the bathroom wall?"

The boy searched Brother Brown's face but couldn't see beyond the surface. He'd seen the very expression many times in his own father's face. In this expression, the truth mattered little; the man's mind was already made up.

Brother Brown took a deep breath. "Okay, I will ask one more time. Did you … write … the racist filth about my wife … on the bathroom wall?"

"No," the boy answered softly and clenched his jaw.

The man peeled his upper and lower lips tightly inward until they began to turn shiny from the pressure.

"This is your answer? For the record, I have six names, witnesses, fellow students who say otherwise! You are dismissed from these premises at this time. We will get back to you with our decision."

Ches walked home utterly dumbfounded. His mother had been contacted at her place of work, and she was waiting for him when he walked through the door.

"I have poured everything into you, and this is how you thank me?!" She slung a ceramic coffee cup at the boy, barely missing his head. It shattered the glass clock on the wall behind him. She began to move aggressively toward him. He turned and walked out the door.

It was cold out. The boy ambled into the woods and made his way to his old hiding place, only to discover it had been destroyed. The chair was hanging by a rope high in a nearby tree, with the blue tarp waving like a flag. His surfing magazines and books were all torn and strewn every direction. He shook his head and made his way to the bowling alley. He stepped into the warm building and sat in the diner next to the blaring television.

At six o'clock, he sauntered toward the setting sun and turned along the road that led to the church school. He found the place where he knew of a stack of bricks next to some lumber. He picked up a brick, walked through the dark courtyard, and climbed the steps to the office door. He used the brick to tap the glass lightly just above the doorknob. It shattered. He placed the brick to the side, poked his hand through the jagged opening, and unlocked the door. A small lamp had been left on, which provided adequate light. He entered, approached the bookshelf, and reclaimed his copy of *Crime and Punishment*. On the way out, he gathered the broken glass from the floor, locked the door, and returned the brick to its place.

As he made his way out the dark road, he slung the shattered glass into the ditch and began to cry.

It happened so fast. One week he was expelled from school, the next week he found himself traveling on I-10 west. They were moving. Again. The boy was mystified, curled into a small pocket in the back of the jalopy, which was jammed to the ceiling with stuff. Ches closed his eyes and imagined the brick to be a Molotov cocktail. He smiled as he watched the whole dumb thing burn to the ground.

He'd been robbed clean of autonomy. He could visualize a future in Florida. But now he would be landlocked—landlocked with no future. What is Louisiana? What could be gained by moving to Louisiana? Doesn't a person have a say in the matter of his own future? His hands groped for an anonymous object somewhere amid the keepsakes. He latched hold of part of a plastic bag and squeezed the life out of it. *If I had the power that the delusional preacher accused me of having, I would will him to this mud hole. Wasn't I perfectly compliant and dedicated? That Holy Roller hypocrite just couldn't help himself. He had to wield his pathetic little nugget of power. He sent me packing. My life has been knocked off course. If there was ever a possibility of a career in surfing, there is now none! No chance!*

These thoughts played a continuous loop in the boy's mind for twelve grueling hours until they arrived at his relatives place in Baker, Louisiana, east Baton Rouge parish. The mother and brothers exited the car without a word and made their way into the house. Ches was disinclined to move, curled in a ball amid the family junk, he stared into nothingness. After several minutes, he could hear footsteps from the opposite side of the road.

"What have we heuh? Anybody in heuh?"

"Yes."

"Who dat be?"

Ches reluctantly clambered from his crevice and stood face to face with his cousin, T-Man, whom he hadn't seen since the age of five.

"Yo! Wazzup, cuz? I heard yall wuz comin."

The cousin was two years older than Ches. He sported a teenager's blotchy beard and jet-black hair buzzed along the sides with a six-inch ponytail.

"So, cuz, I heard you dun got kicked outta school. I wanted you to know, Cuz, I know how you be feelin. I knode you wuz sooo low. And knowin you wuz sooo low made me sooo low. And I don't like being low … o … so … fo … sho! I got da medizayne dat is so nice you gonna want some mo."

The boy conjured a faint smile.

"So, yo, you impressed wit my po-e-tray? I heard you wuz one o dem genius brainyacs. Get yo crazy genius sef wit me. I got a lil sump-sump fo yo lil pea brain."

It was almost four o'clock in the morning. The house was dark, and Ches quietly followed his cousin.

"Man, yo crazy relatives went straight to sleep," T-Man said, shaking his head. "See, dey don't know. Les go!"

The boy could barely see as they moved through a variety of wrecked cars, broken-down yard tractors, and indistinguishable piles of rubbish until they came to a building. T-Man opened the door with a screechy spring, and they entered a greenhouse, walked past a row of wilted potted plants stacked around a cat tree, then went out the back door. They trudged through a thicket of waist-high weeds leading to a gated portion of the property. The cousin unlatched the gate, ushered the boy through, and latched the gate behind them.

"Always make sure you close dat gate so da stupid chickens don't escape," T-Man whispered. At that moment a rooster crowed a few feet away, startling both boys.

"Ima keeeyal dat stupid roosta deyaad!"

The cockerel sounded again, and both boys cracked up laughing.

"Shhh! Cuz, be quiet. You gonna wake up da boofaunts. You don't know who da boofaunts is, but you gonna."

Ches was amused. He waited for whatever zany concoction his cousin would invent next.

"Da boofaunts is da three Holy Roller sistas: my mamma, yo mamma, and dey lil sista. Dem's da boofaunts. Wake dem up, and awl mayhem is gonna break loose … not dat I give a flyin flavella, because dey can't do nut'n. How in da world did dem three spazmammies come from our sweet mawmaw? Dats one of life's great mysteries."

The cousin led the boy to a stand of trees. As his eyesight adjusted to the darkness, he could make out a triangular treehouse supported by three large pines. The cousin started up the ladder, and the boy followed. They entered a portal beneath, and once in, the cousin flicked a cigarette lighter over a candle inside a Mason jar.

The candlelight revealed two bunks built into the wall opposite a velvet poster of Jimi Hendrix. There was a hinged plywood box for a table. T-Man slid a boombox from beneath the bunk. "I hope you like Zeppelin, cuz you fidna cruise, Cuz … ovah da heeyells and far away."

T-Man opened the plywood box and withdrew a purple-and-gold cinch bag. Inside it was another ziplock filled with green leaves and buds. Next he brandished a transparent cylinder that was two inches in diameter. The cylinder was opened at the top, and the bottom flared outward, enabling the cylinder to stand independently. Near the bottom of the tube, a small brass tube with a threaded bowl protruded at a forty-five-degree angle.

"I created dis sweet lil mashugy wit mah bare haynds." The cousin opened a bottle of water and poured the contents into the cylinder. He took a pinch of the green herb from the ziplock and packed it into the bowl and fumbled for a lighter in the bottom of the box. He cocked his head in the candlelight, squinted at his Floridian counterpart, and mumbled, "Couyon," as he brought the opening of the cylinder to his mouth. He applied the flame to the bowl and sucked inward with a gurgling sound, held his breath, and then passed the apparatus to the boy as he exhaled. "Don't drawls too hard or yoo'll choke."

The boy lit the bowl and softly drew the contents into his virgin lungs. He held it for several seconds before coughing profusely from the burn.

The boy and his cousin passed the apparatus back and forth until the contents were spent. T-Man increased the volume on the jukebox. "Aw, cuz! Yoo gon luv dis sawng! It's called 'The Battle of Evamo.' Keyaw!"

T-Man retrieved two sleeping bags and two pillows from the upper bunk. Ches was already mesmerized by the driving mandolin and haunting vocal harmonies. Both boys sat on the treehouse floor and surrendered their minds to an ethereal abduction.

An hour later, the cousin turned off the music and lit another candle. The boy stared into the darkness and tried to process the strange contrition gnawing at him. He was acutely aware of the prolonged burning in his chest. He felt sure he'd hurt someone's feelings, someone who loved him deeply, but he couldn't think of who or how. He pushed the paranoia back by reminding himself of his current victim status. After all, it was he who had been disenfranchised. This thought sectionalized the guilt, ushering in a different feeling, a good feeling … really good … as though he'd been imparted a gift. And it was fitting. For this moment he did not care. This moment he had relinquished every notion of the future, and he did not care.

Sunrise revealed the squalid estate of their surroundings. Ches and his cousin made their way along an untenanted road to the local diner, where they would satisfy their voracious appetites. Afterward the cousin showed the boy the shed where he cultivated the cannabis in rows of hydroponic tubes with special lights acquired from the abandoned greenhouse on the neighboring property.

DURING THE FIRST week of January, the mother took the boy to the local junior high school for testing. His reading comp was college level, which prompted several members of the faculty to introduce themselves. The principal and two of the teachers encouraged the mother to enroll Ches in the magnet school twenty minutes from Baton Rouge. In spite of average math skills, his scores landed within the favorable range, and he was accepted into the program.

The morning of his first day of school, T-Man gave the boy an ink pen. "Dis is a magic pen, cuz. If you find yo sef in a crazy sichiashen, find a hid'n place, unscrew the pen, and voila." T-Man unscrewed the pen and revealed its contents: a pen-sized cannabis joint. "Don't forget yo mayches."

Scotlandville Magnet High School offered specialized programs for grades six through twelve. Enrollment was over one-thousand, and the boy was stymied the instant he stepped off the bus. The crowd pressed from all sides as he searched the enormous, echoing halls for stairwell B. He spotted the restrooms and stepped in for a moment to gain his composure. He took one look in the mirror and then walked out of the restroom and headed for the main exit.

The school was in the most crime-ridden section of town, but the boy knew that if he followed the highway north, it would take him directly to Baker. He had walked two blocks when a black man in his twenties stopped the boy.

"Watchoo doin, bowaa?"

"I'm walking home."

"Whuut? I kno you ain't be stayn round heuh. Whays yo creeib?"

"Baker."

"*Shoot*! You lil white honky oui ain't walkn tru heuh. Comone! Ima put yoo on da bus befo somebody dun took yo lil white self. My name's James. I dun did a lotta wrong in my life, but I ain't fidna let yoo git took."

James demanded the boy follow him to the bus stop. Along the way they crossed paths with another young black man. Upon seeing the man, James immediately displayed extreme paranoid behavior. "Trey, Trey, I got it … sho do!" James flashed Trey a nervous grin as they came near one another. "I got it, Boo!"

Trey said nothing, but hauled off and punched James in the eye, knocking him to the ground.

James held his eye and continued to shout, "I got it, Boo! I got it, Boo!"

Trey kept walking. "I know yoo got it, nigga … shoot!"

James lay on the sidewalk with his right eye swollen shut.

Ches helped him to his feet. "I can find it from here, James. Thanks for your help."

"Shut yo mouth, crazy lil white boy. How yoo gong git on da bus?" James insisted on taking Ches all the way to the bus depot, making sure Ches boarded the correct bus destined for Baker. He said a few words to the bus driver and paid the boy's fair.

After a twenty-minute ride, the bus came to a stop. As Ches disembarked, the bus driver saluted with a smile. The boy smiled back.

CHES SPENT THE remainder of the school year cultivating plants with his cousin, never bothering to hide the fact he wasn't attending school, and no one seemed to care.

Come springtime, the family moved into Greenwell Springs Apartments in Baton Rouge proper. As a parting gift, T-Man gave Ches a reddish denim jacket with a giant, white anchor embroidered on the back. The inside pocket bulged with a quarter pound of the winter's yield.

CHES BEGAN TO suffer from an expanding contempt for the world around him. Greenwell Springs Appartments were six hundred miles from the nearest ocean. Even so, the surrounding industrial neighborhood was replete with ways to reclaim his autonomy. There was a convenience store to the east side of the road, a health club on the corner of Greenwell Springs Road and Airline Highway, and horse boarding stables at the back corner. Also, the Oneness Pentecostal Church was less than a mile away. The mother had hinted that the boy would be attending the church school for the ninth grade, or whatever grade. The boy mulled a plan to sneak onto the church property at midnight and lob a Molotov cocktail through the stained-glass window as a preventive measure.

His brother found a job at Dillard's at the Bon Marche Mall two miles away. The boy found a job cleaning stables at the boarding facility.

CHES CULTIVATED A keen sense of his surroundings. He had an animated sense of self and considered himself fortunate that his underadvantaged height was a perfect fit for one who prefers life beneath the radar. But even though he'd trained himself to be objective, he still found it difficult to evaluate his own face. He would stare in the mirror at length but couldn't come to a conclusion regarding his looks. He decided if his looks happened to be above average, he'd probably be better off not knowing it.

As a result of the incident with Brother Brown back in Florida, his relationship to the Oneness Pentecostal Church was seriously aggravated. Interaction with the church was inescapable. He felt himself morphing into the antagonist. He was inclined to don the extrovert's cloak for devious purposes. Since Oneness Christianity was such a tightly woven phenomenon, covertly attacking the Baton Rouge assembly would satisfy his need for retribution. He would become a social Molotov cocktail, special delivery, compliments of Brother Brown.

"We live in the hour of Zechariah fourteen. It is now not clear exactly what is light; it is now not clear exactly what is dark. Up is down, hot is cold, and crazy is sane! This is how we know it is evening. In John chapter 8: 'Then spake Jesus again unto them, saying, I am the light of the world: he that followeth me shall not walk in darkness, but shall have the light of life.' It is evening. And at evening time there shall be light. And in spite of the enormous organized force of confusion and ambiguity, there are still those who are drawn by the light that is infinitely higher than all the other coexisting, coequal lights."

Chapter 17

THE TRENDS THAT were deemed acceptable to the church youth group emanated from one key figure: the pastor's son, Martin Oldham. Ches decided the best way to blend in would be to emulate him. Martin's hair was slick and wavy with a meticulous coif. He wore expensive designer suits and was always careful to present himself as having the highest quality of character.

Ches shook his head at the thought of a seventeen-year-old preacher's son wearing a Rolex Presidential. The boy privately reveled at the notion of a Christian leader so brazenly ignorant to the most notable attributes of the light he claimed to follow. When or where was the light of Jesus Christ ever conveyed through conspicuous consumption?

But Martin Oldham's musical talents were not superficial. He was proficient on several instruments, and his vocal style was classic baritone edging nearer the professional level than one might expect.

Unlike the church in Florida, the majority of the congregation in Baton Rouge was formally educated: alumni of LSU and Tulane, two dentists, a medical doctor, and a large number who worked the white-collar side of oil. The boy perceived a particular arrogance in the parishioner's arm's-length approach to the newcomers from Florida. *Who do these people think they are? Where do they think they are? Louisiana! For crying out loud, this a stinking mud hole north of swamplantis. Wouldn't indiscriminant hospitality be the appropriate calling card?*

In spite of his deep revulsion for flashy trends, Ches had learned to appreciate quality. He shopped at Dillard's with money earned at the stables. His brother gave him the employee discount code, which he used for buying Levi's and understated top-brand footwear. The brother also revealed the code to the cash register at the back corner of the men's suits department. This particular foray would exceed the limits of the boy's conscience under normal circumstances. But there was such a pressure to appear higher on the socioeconomic ladder than the real world would permit, and since the source of such pressure was the church, surely his deeds were justified.

Ches was mostly interested in the psychology surrounding such deeds. He learned that not only was appearance the key to success, but context as well; appearance was relative to setting.

He meticulously prepared for the part. He wore a light-blue Oxford tucked into new jeans with penny loafers. He never darted his eyes to the two-way mirror high on the wall; he always maintained a benign expression, straight ahead, without searching for plainclothes security. He'd walk the parameter once with a sweeping glance from his peripheral vision, then go straight to the register—five-five-five enter, zero enter, scoop the cash, half in each pocket, quietly close the register, and disappeared. He did this twice and no more, as his interests lay with the psychology of the thing, not with the thing itself.

On Sunday he dropped the entire wad of unspent cash into the church offering plate as an abstract token of protest.

Ches applied a similar approach to the local health club on the corner of Airline Highway and Greenwell Springs. The compound was surrounded by a six-foot concrete wall half a block long. There was one main entrance, one back entrance, and three utility gates for authorized personnel only. There were racquetball and tennis courts, a swimming pool, an indoor track with Nautilus machines and free weights in the center, plus a martial-arts training section in the corner with a kickbag and various jump ropes.

Ches would use the exterior maintenance entrance by the back corner. This entrance was accessible from the rear alley in the neighboring block, behind a factory outlet for residential flooring. The gate was almost always open but easy enough to traverse when locked.

He wore quality tennis shoes and appropriate club attire and carried an expensive tennis racquet as he moved through the facilities with extreme politeness. He paid keen attention to the tennis pro giving lessons to various students, including the USTA boys state champ. Ches perfected his forehand and backhand swings through countless hours of hitting the ball against a green, concrete wall. He honed his martial-arts skills on the kickbag with kicks and punches in repetitions of fifty. The staff never questioned the validity of his membership. They treated him like a VIP and called him Jack, even though he hadn't given a name.

He introduced his brother to this innovative mischief, and together they'd swim, do weight training, and play tennis. The brother became infatuated with an older woman who frequented the club's tiki bar. He misread her signals, however, prompting the woman to complain to management. As a result, the two were discreetly dismissed.

On the way out, they passed a sporty red Camaro with the hatchback ajar. "This is her car!" the brother exclaimed. He opened the hatch to find an expensive leather bag in plain sight. Without hesitation, he grabbed the purse and began to run. The boy protested vehemently. They rounded the corner and stopped.

"Don't do this!"

"Why shouldn't I?"

"You will get caught!"

"So."

The boy stood there for a moment, shaking his head. "If you must, then first search the contents, take what you want, and replace the purse."

"But I *want* her to know that *I* did it."

The boy tightened his lips at the prospect of a thirteen-year-old boy trying to reason with an eighteen-year-old.

"Do you want to go to jail?"

The brother paused for a moment.

The boy raised his hands imploring. "Come on! It's my birthday this Friday. Don't do this … please … for me."

The brother opened the purse. There was a wallet with twenty dollars cash, a credit card, her driver's license, and several business cards. He slowly unzipped the side pouch, revealing a Winchester five-shot, .22 mini revolver small enough to fit in a palm.

The brother stared mischeviously at the boy. "I will put everything back but the gun, if you agree to a dare."

There was a long pause as the brother stared. The boy knew immediately there was nothing his brother could think of, short of shooting a human, that he couldn't think of a way to accomplish. The brother grinned as if he held a secret advantage over the boy.

"What's the dare?"

The brother started laughing and shaking his head.

"You have to rob the convenience store next to our apartments … before your birthday."

"Okay. Go put your purse back, now, right now. Go!"

"You have only two days to plan. You're not gonna do it."

The boy frequented the convenience store more than any other spot during his weekly routine. He knew the names and schedules of every employee within the twenty-four-hour work cycle, including Bob, the nightshift guy, though they'd never met. He walked away from his brother. "It's done."

His brother stood there with the purse in his hand and his mouth wide open. He ran to the Camaro, threw the purse into the hatchback, and ducked into the back alley with a jolt of fear.

The boy couldn't think of a more appropriate occasion to wear the anchor jacket his cousin had given him. Appearances are the key to success, appearances in context, appearances relative to setting. He would wear something that the key witness could easily remember and describe in detail. Thursday night he'd set his alarm for two in the morning. The shift change was at 3:59. He would walk into the store at 3:05.

He awoke on schedule, turned on the restroom light, and began to work out his appearance. He remembered a poster he'd seen of the band Sarah had introduced him to. The lead singer was a peculiar artist by the name of Robert Smith—a man with a pasty white face, frazzled hair, and lips smeared with black lipstick.

The boy retrieved a small bottle of acne lotion from the medicine cabinet and smeared it liberally over his face. There was nothing in the medicine cabinet to turn his lips black, so he made them white with the same lotion. He greased his hair with his brother's hair mousse and frazzled it as much as the short length would allow.

Next he donned a pair of his brother's black corduroy pants, rolled the pant legs to fit, and buckled his belt tight. The oversized pants puffed like clown trousers, covering his undersized, ratty Vans. He wore a black T-shirt under the anchor jacket.

It was 2:45 a.m. He stood before the mirror, evaluating his appearance. The thick application of acne lotion was now dry, crackled, and melting from his forehead. He tiptoed into the kitchen, retrieved four sandwich bags, and tiptoed back to the bathroom. He stuffed two plastic bags in his mouth, one on each inside of his jaw, and then eyed his image in the mirror. It was perfect. The sandwich bags altered the shape of his face convincingly. He stood before the mirror and nodded at the appearance of an indescribable lunatic. He checked the clock and retrieved the gun from his brother's sock drawer.

His brother turned on the light. "Holy cow! What kind of a freak are you?"

"Shhh! I gotta go."

"Oh my god! You're really gonna do it."

The boy turned out the light and walked out the door with the gun in his hand.

It was dark, but he knew the area so well, he could have closed his eyes. The small gun fit easily into his front pocket. He entered the backyard of the convenience store by the well-worn path, eased along the side of the building, and slowly peeked around the corner. Bob was sitting on the ice-cream case directly in front of the entrance, reading a newspaper. The boy opened the door, and Bob immediately walked to his post behind the register. The boy walked to the ice-cream counter and pretended to search for something in the case.

"Can I help you?"

The boy nearly reconsidered going through with it, but the clerk's inquiry prompted him to move in.

He walked to the front of the register. "Money, man!"

Bill opened the register. The boy began to relax and attempted to lodge misleading information into the clerk's mind. He altered the pitch of his voice with as much quiver as possible without being misunderstood.

"Don't do nothing stupid … maaann?" He spontaneously tweaked his demands to sound like a question. "Dooon't dooo nothing stupid, maan?"

Without looking up, the clerk scooped all the money from the register: all fives and ones—forty-one dollars—across the counter. The boy snatched the cash and ran.

Within minutes he was at the apartment. He washed his face, rolled the jacket and pants together with the gun, and placed them under the restroom sink behind the Drano. He tucked himself under the covers and closed his eyes.

"Did you do it?" The overhead light came on, and the brother stood nervously over the bunk.

"You'll find out tomorrow," Ches replied as he pulled the covers over his head.

The next day, the brother walked into the store to make small talk with Jerome.

"Did you heuh?" Jerome blurted. "We got robbed layst nayt. Foty-one dollahs!"

The brother quietly made his purchase and left the store without replying.

On the way out the back, the brother ran into the boy. "Don't go near the store! They know they got robbed! Was it you? It was you … oh my … oh god … did you really?"

The boy pulled a sandwich bag from his front pocket with a wad of money inside.

"Oh no! You can't go near that store."

"Shut up! I'm returning the money."

"Have you lost your mind?

"Chill out, you spaz! I found this money at the pay phone outside the store. No big deal. I'm gonna return it. They should give me a reward."

The boy stepped into store with an exaggerated sense of altruism and told the clerk he happened to find the bag stuffed between the pay phone and aluminum housing. The clerk told the boy of the robbery and called the store manager. The manager shook Ches's hand and insisted the clerk give the boy a ten-dollar gift card.

The boy walked straight home and retrieved his other ziplock bag from beneath the bathroom sink. He garnered a pinch of the green from the stash, and then collected the gun, stuffed it in his pocket and made his way outside where he tossed the jacket in the trash dumpster.

The boy ran through the woods as if he were being chased. He leaped fallen trees and palmettos in a full sprint. He saw an opening, the lake behind the stables, and with reckless abandon he slid down the embankment, coming to a stop next to a pine limb at the water's edge.

He snatched the limb and began to pummel the earth. "I hate you, I hate you, I hate you!" Sweat and tears blinded him as he wailed away at the earth until the limb exploded into three pieces. Two pieces drifted over the water; the third piece became a dagger as Ches repeatedly stabbed the earth until his hands bled. He hurled the dagger into the water and forcibly suppressed his tears. Then, he slowly pulled the gun from his pocket, cocked the hammer, and pressed the barrel into his forehead. "Today I am fourteen. What does it mean? Anger and revenge and violence! I wish I hadn't seen that stupid *Scarface* movie. My mind has been violated, and I can't reverse it. If only the pastor in Florida had given me a chance. Now my future is gone. *Stolen!*"

His guts began heaving. He pulled the gun away, rolled to his knees, and vomited. He wiped his mouth with his sleeve but vomited again until there was nothing left. He rolled to a sitting position for several minutes, then stood to his feet and slung the revolver into the center of the lake with a quiet splash.

Ches left the water's edge, desperately wanting to be rid of the toxic feelings for the preacher. *I want to go home. But what is home?* He walked into the convenience store and asked Jerome for rolling papers. "Three point five."

"Whet yoo gon do whit dis?" Jerome said, exposing his gold teeth and tapping the glass counter with manicured fingernails.

"It's for my uncle Spleefy. He rolls his own."

"Uh huh, whatevah."

Ches exited the store and walked in no particular direction until he came to an old laundry mat. He ambled to the back of the building, sat on an air-conditioning unit, and pulled the green contents from his pocket. He smoked half a joint and began walking again.

He thought of Sarah and the unbridgeable differences between them. *Did she sincerely admire me? How? Why? What would a girl like her see in a boy like me?* He would never know.

The day was unbearably hot. Another surge of anger welled up as he kneeled in the shade of an oak tree and imagined a solution: years of frenetic energy exploding all at once upon the arrogance of Brother Brown, his black face turning white with remorse and fear. Ches shook himself. *I have to let it go. Anger is no good in me. I must let it go.*

There was an ant pile at the foot of the tree. He took a twig and began to dismantle the pile, but the ants immediately rallied to repair the damage. A warm breeze began to blow as a mockingbird fluttered past. And then the familiar stirring—but Ches pushed it away again.

"His light is alive and well. Though His light has been malevolently redefined, misconstrued, misunderstood, and misinterpreted, His light still works. His light has never been broken. His light will never die! God has a church … right now!"

The congregation is roaring with praise. Men are running the aisles, and women are shouting. The spirit has risen from the sanctuary floor to the balcony and is billowing through the vent. I am standing; quaking in this dark box as it slowly fills with light.

Chapter 18

It was Saturday morning. Ches completed his duties at the horse stables and walked along the road until he could see the Belmonte Hotel on the other side of Airline Highway. The parking lot was filled to capacity. He ambled haphazardly across the highway to investigate the hubbub. A bellboy hung a giant banner at the head of the driveway: "The National Conference for Interdenominational Christian Dialogue." Ches sauntered past the Doric columns beneath a stone archway with the insignia "The Great Hall."

A diverse array of guests streamed into the edifice from all directions. There were men wearing Jon Wesley–style pulpit robes. Others wore priestly cassocks, or full, gothic chasubles. The women sported boyish haircuts and wore black suits with clergy collars traditional to the masculine gender. There were seminary students from Africa, South America, and Ireland. They filed into a long line that wrapped the main lobby to the center. Conference staff worked the registration tables, assigning nametags and information packets to the registrants. The bulk of participants followed the arrows to a sign above the Great Hall entrance: "Book of Acts Forum, 1:00 p.m."

Ches rushed home and ironed his Oxford shirt. He grabbed a notebook and hooked a couple of pens into his shirt pocket. At twelve thirty he detoured into the patch of woods beside the stables, where he lit a joint and concocted a convincing story for the maître d' to grant him access into the conference.

He rushed past the Belmonte's archway and through the entrance to the Great Hall to discover the registration process had waned considerably. Two of the registration stations were closed. He walked behind one of the tables and smoothly acquired a badge and information packet assigned to Dr. J. Scott Todd.

He pinned the badge to his lapel and stepped through the door to the conference room. An usher handed him a program and motioned him to the left. The place was packed, and the mood was festive. Ches ignored the twinge of paranoia, a consequence of the cannabis, and found a place by the back corner of the room.

The forum featured six Christian panelists representing six different denominations. Three of the panelists, a Greek Orthodox priest, Baptist minister, and the representative of the National Organization of Evangelicals, were big men with matching robust personalities. The eldest of the group, a Catholic priest with gaunt features and a thick shock of white hair, held a commanding presence as he sat serenely in his chair at the center. The Episcopalian priest and the Unitarian, the only females, sat to his right. Each panelist held a PhD in theology. They were all laughing at the perky humor of the Baptist minister. The moderator calmed the crowd as he presented the debate topic.

Moderator: "Are tongues for today? If so, with what purpose, and with what meaning?"

Baptist: "Are what …? (crowd laughter) Tongues? Of course tongues are for today! How could we speak? Who thinks of these questions? I thought we had a bright group. (more laughter) Are your tongues for today? No, they are for next Thursday. (giggles) Yer such a bad boy, ya know. Seriously, seriously, eeaahh, it depends what we're tackling, heh heh."

Moderator: "We are tackling the question of tongues and the whole question of glossolalia."

Baptist: "Certainly what was happening in the book of Acts at Pentecost was a phenomenon unique to Pentecost. What Paul has in mind when he addresses the issue in Corinthians … in the range of AD fifty-three to fifty-seven … is at least … at best, I think, enigmatic. Because most of my friends who, er … uh … speak in tongues describe it as a private prayer language which enables them a sense of intimacy and … ehem … whatever … ehem … with God. In much the same way that … you know … we may have an intimate language we use with our spouse, I suppose … ya know … I could call her coochicoo … or whatever. Um … I'm not gonna really do that in public. Uh … I am not sure what that really does for anyone or even really what it is."

Moderator: "Is speaking in tongues the evidence of coming in contact with the Holy Spirit, or on the other hand, is speaking in tongues explained merely in physical terms akin to the scatting of Ella Fitzgerald?"

Baptist: "Umm, it could be … ehem … described not theologically or biblically … but physically … as the free passage of air over unrestrained vocal chords. At that, it can come out in a number of ways. Where it gets particularly tenuous … ehem … is of course when the explanation or the interpretation of this is then provided. And in the best of circumstances, where I have been on the receiving end of that … is simply … ehem … being rehashed. And usually in the seventeenth-century English of Bible verses and at its best it is being something that is quite superficial and bizarre. And … um, you know, I can think of being in a church … where in Birmingham in England in Yorkshire in England and a number of this happened at the end of some singing. And it went on for quite a while. And the person … ehem … the person spoke … apparently in tongues. And then we all sat in total silence and waited further for the interpretation. And eventually some soul said that … ehem … said, 'God is saying we must give each other … a big hug.' (crowd laughter) No … no lie … no lie … a special revelation, I know. Wow! Ehem … that's a heck of a way to go at it, ya know. (crowd laughter) Ehem … after all, He's already given us in the English language, ya know … said love one another, care for one another, greet one another with brotherly love and affection, greet the brethren with a holy kiss. I don't have to sit around here half the night wait'n on Miss Jenkey's gibberish so that Mister Philbertson's interpretation could tell me I'm spose to give some lady on the front row a big hug. (uproarious laughter) And frankly … and I'll tell you this is not funny. (crowd uproarious) But what happened is … people started giving each other some significantly big hugs. (crowd snickers and giggles) And there were a couple of couples actually left before the next hymn (crowd laughter) … true story, true story. You probably don't want this stuff on tape (uproarious laughter).

Moderator: We'll just run it backward." (snicker)

The audience again roared with laughter as the panelists patted each other on the knee, wagging their heads with mischievous expressions. The two evangelical representatives congratulated one another regarding an inside joke that circulated among the constituency—that speaking in tongues was akin to the satanic rock-and-roll artists who inserted evil messages into their work using a recording technique called back masking.

Evangelical: (wiping his brow, grinning) "You know … the real problem is we don't know how … ehem … we cannot … bridge the gap between the first-century phenomenon and what we're seeing today."

Greek Orthodox: (agitated, jerky motions, beads of sweat on his forehead) "Had glossolalia really been a normal function of worship, beginning in Corinth, and … remained so … which it didn't … but had it remained for every church throughout history, we'd now have a different view!"

Evangelical: (smiling comfortably amid the plethora of kindred Christian doctrines) "But that huge historical gap that exists raises all kinds of questions. *Is this that* that was going on in Corinth? Or is it scatting? Because anybody can scat … uh … scat is unintelligible. Scat is a departure from our normal … uh … vocal functions. And it may sound cool when Ella does it … or when Scooby Doo does it (snort giggle) *scoobidobedobedooooohoohoo.* (crowd laughter)

That's scat! And anybody can do that if they can disarm themselves from their normal inhibitions. But it remains to be demonstrated that, even in the private prayer language, it's anything more than a normal human capacity with groans and unintelligible expressions of yeeaaggh … what? What people want more than anything else … when I talk and was involved with this stuff back in the sixties … is that so many people desperately want to overcome their inability to express themselves to God with how they really feel."

The audience quieted, and the tone became momentarily serious as the Catholic priest, in a faded European accent, eloquently contributed to the discussion.

Catholic priest: "And if I can just bypass the mind, and groan and pray in an unintelligible way, maybe I am able to unleash the profound feelings of adoration … and that is a part of prayer … only this, and nothing more. But that is something, maybe."

Baptist: "No, I just wanted to say that as much as I am being humorous here … I have deep respect … uh … and sincere admiration for friends of mine who are engaged in that stuff. We banter about it, but I have had those people come to my home and they gave … you know … prophetic words in tongues. Ehem. You know in the past … I said to one brother afterward, I said, 'Frank, you know, if you had just gone to Samuel 37:4, you could have said this a lot quicker.' Because what that actually … what he said to me was … you know … in a convoluted way … 'God is saying to you that if you will find your joy and your delight in Him … if you will yield, and so on, he will give you the desires of your heart.' And I said, yeah, well okay, I already got that one because … *it's in the Bible*! And the real issue is … for me … not in terms of the notion of private prayer, but the notion of somehow or another … adding to the revelation of God."

Unitarian: (humble and overly soft-spoken) "Most scholars, as far back as Nicaea … and thankfully, Nicaea does much to address this very issue … most scholars see this in terms of the prophetic word. The phenomenon at Pentecost was the signal that the church age had begun. But the … *continuation of event* of speaking in tongues adds to the canon and undermines the veracity and the sufficiency of the scriptures themselves. And that is what you see in these communities."

Baptist: "Totally agree! I did conferences in the past … and the keynote speaker did a sort of devotional piece, then he would close his Bible and then he'd say, 'And now I am going to do ministry.' And then we moved off into another realm altogether. And what was most striking to me was that the people were far more fascinated by what was happening after the Bible was closed than they were in paying attention while the Bible was open, and that seems to me to be an inherent danger that is represented in that kind of preoccupation."

Greek Orthodox: "If I may just to really briefly, thinking back … uh … languages, tongues. There are plenty of Greek words that could've been used for ecstatic utterances. And … uh … that were associated with the Oracle of Delphi … and ecstatic, religious, mystical expressions. That was Paul's problem with the super apostles. They were looking for a higher knowledge than the knowledge you can get from actually reading … or … you know … having this communication from the circle of the apostles. But really this was the UN at the tower of Babel. God scattered the nations so that they couldn't understand each other. At Pentecost, He was bringing them together, under the gospel, and it was a UN event. People understood the gospel in their own tongue. But we … *must* … understand that it was a *one* … *time* … *occurrence* … at the birth of the church *only*! It was *never* the evidence of a person accepting Jesus as personal Lord and Savior."

Evangelical: "But again, it seems something is different between that and the Corinthian phenomenon. But how do we know? I mean, again, how these practitioners … particularly … the rigid monotheist or so-called Oneness believers who believe it is essential, immediate evidence—how do they bridge the gap between then and today? These Oneness Pentecostals say speaking in tongues is the sign that God has chosen as evidence of receiving the Holy Spirit, because God now controls the most unruly member of the body … the tongue. The bottom line is there is more than one way to be a Christian, period! Oneness Pentecostals suffer from a dogmatic fixation on the concept of … *one*. But you show me a person who insists that Act 2:38 is the one and only door into the church, and I'll show you a heretic! There used to be laws against heresy! We must never forget the mystical thread that connects the whole of classical Christendom is our common embrace of the Trinity—more than one, coequal, coeternal way! Everything outside that creed is heresy."

All the panelists nodded. Applause began to trickle through the audience and gradually expanded to a full-blown standing ovation.

Evangelical: "Wait, wait! No, this is serious! These people are out there telling the world that the entrance into the kingdom is found in Acts and that the Epistles are addressing those who have already complied, literally, with Acts 2:38."

Episcopal: "Well, to be fair, we all agree that the birth of the church does indeed take place in Acts 2.

Baptist: "Yes, but it is outrageous to suggest that the remaining twenty-two books of the New Testament are not for me because I am not baptized in *Jesus*'s name followed with speaking gibberish as evidence of being filled with the Spirit. I mean … furthermore … these people are teaching that in order for a person to be saved … not only is baptism necessary but you actually have to say the name, *Jesus* when you dunk someone under the water. In other words, every theologian on this panel has been baptized … is that safe to say? Yes? But in the ceremony, the baptizer said, not the literal, verbalization of the name, *Jesus* but when each of us were baptized, naturally, the baptizer's exact words were, 'In the name of the Father, Son, and Holy Spirit' … but actually verbalizing the name *Jesus* didn't occur. And *they* say … based on the omission of the name … *they* say the act was invalid, and that I must be rebaptized, verbally, audibly specifying the name *Jesus*."

Episcopal: "Again, to be fair, the scriptural documentation for rebaptism is found in Acts 19, where, in addition to the other documented baptism events, the baptizers really did not say, Father, Son, Holy Ghost. But in the document, they rebaptized, predetermined believers, verbally calling out the name *Jesus*."

Baptist: (nervous laughter) "Whose side are you on, anyway? No, really … I went to seminary and hold a PhD as well as you … but we mainstream Christians mustn't allow ourselves to be seduced by a cultish adherence to the Bible."

The audience applauded again, and the Baptist stood and held his hands above his head, clapping and nodding to his fellow panelists. He hugged the Episcopal priest and shook hands with each of the panelists.

Baptist: "Here, under one roof, we are Catholic, Presbyterian, Baptist, and many others … even trinitarian-Pentecostal. And no matter the denomination, the thing that links us together is our belief in God as a plurality, which is the Holy Trinity. The real issue that we must address today is this issue of legalism and extremism. These Oneness people are telling the world that a person must enter the kingdom through the solitary door opened by the apostle Peter. That is … Acts 2:38. It is heresy! Yes, Jesus gave Peter the keys to the kingdom. But for the life of me, I don't know why Peter utilizes the keys in this manner. He should have obeyed Matthew 28:19, because a plural God is the only God for a pluralistic society!" (uproarious applause)

Ches hurried out the building, relieved of the medieval spirit of the discussion. For the first time he could see the clear divider between the small number of pretrinitarian Christians and the colossal representation of post-Nicaea Christianity. He thought of his grandmother who, in a different time, would have been charged with heresy. "Dis powah is biggah dan yoo lil sword," she would say as the church leaders cut her tongue out.

"Matthew writes in his Gospel, 'Come unto me, all ye that labour and are heavy laden, and I will give you rest. Take my yoke upon you, and learn of me; for I am meek and lowly in heart: and ye shall find rest unto your souls. For my yoke is easy, and my burden is … light.' Brothers and sisters, there is a visual quality to the Oneness Apostolic Church. This church ain't camouflaged! We don't paint our faces and try to blend in. Because the Apostolic Church is bold enough to embrace and proclaim the message of Jesus Christ being the way—the only way!"

Chapter 19

Ches had become so familiar with the school enrollment routine that he could predict the reaction of the test administrators. He chuckled at the fact that his math scores had strengthened solely by the repeated number of placement tests he'd taken.

The principal of the school was a professional woman with a master's in education. Her name was Sister Stover. Her hair was natural silver done in familiar apostolic fashion. She was both confident and congenial. Ches's mother met with Sister Stover and poured out the painful details of their life situation and of how the boy suffered socially. Sister Stover turned to Ches with a wink. "He'll do just fine here."

The school used the identical system as the private school in Florida, but with a professional faculty and a significantly higher enrollment. The mother exited the room, and Sister Stover had a talk with Ches.

"I don't want you to worry about a thing. Our only concern, mine and yours, is that you don't get bored. You communicate honestly and clearly with me. You have nothing to be afraid of. Our task, mine and yours, is that you *stay*. Okay?"

The boy made eye contact with Sister Stover and offered an amenable nod, taking note of how she transmitted the same soothing aura he'd discovered about Gussie Mae and his mawmaw and Sister Fuentes. These women projected a credible safeness in an assertive manner by holding to the purest standard of femininity.

The boy made straight A's his first report card and was instantly popular. The student who sat in the neighboring cubicle was a boy named Brett. Brett constantly peered over the divider, pawing for a glimpse into Ches's daily routine. Brett hoped he might learn the boy's secret. However, Brett mostly found the boy staring into space. "Man, you don't do nothin," Brett would say. "You just sit around all day and do nothin." He often complained to the faculty in this regard.

One Friday afternoon, Sister Stover quietly tapped Ches on the shoulder with an assignment. "God's church is referred to in the feminine sense," she whispered sweetly. "This is why I am careful to let my natural gray hair shine in the color God made it, and I try to keep it all nice and pretty. It is why I take extra care to dress in a manner traditional to a lady, because within those biblical parameters, I have power with God. In the Bible, the church is sometimes called the bride, which might be a parallel to the role of mother."

Ches stared attentively into Sister Stover's face. He studied the way she spoke in comparison to the way of other women in his life: his mother, other schoolteachers.

"I have a special project for you. I want you to write me an essay or poem, eighty to one hundred words, in this context, with your own mother as the subject. I want you to hold your personal perception of the church in the forefront of your mind as you write. Will you do that for me?"

Ches nodded and Sister Stover expressed sincere gratitude. In that moment, the boy would have done anything she asked. He sat for a while cogitating the concepts of mother and church in light of his personal experience. He'd never written in poem form but was excited to give it a try. He closed his eyes, opened them again, and began to write:

> There they run in their plastic days; sometimes I wish that
> I could play that game.
> I pace the shore and contemplate the waves, though I know
> I'll never be the same.
> So knock me down, rip out my tongue, stab me in the eyes,
> and erase my name.

Throw me all the blame, and I'll deny the rising sun.
My balding wings are useless, and my plan is aflame,
How you play so well, how you play that game.
There she stood on her executive plane; I want her to show me the way of fame.
Her face aglow with an artificial taste, seven days my will imitates.

He'd found a brand-new rhythm and could have gone further, but he'd already exceeded the number of words required. After twenty minutes, Sister Stover touched his shoulder. He handed her the sheet, and she began reading at once. Her countenance changed dramatically as she read. Her smile faded, and her expression turned contemplative and serious. When she was finished, she whispered, "This isn't quite what I was looking for. I want you to try again. Only this time make your sayings a touch more … accessible. Can you do that for me?" Her eyes brimmed with confidence as she walked away, and the boy knew precisely what to do.

He grinned wryly and began to write:

I love my mother because she's dear; she's kind in every way.
All the needs I have ever had, she met them day by day.
She brings to my thoughts positive things when negativeness abounds.
She lifts my spirits up so high I can hardly see the ground.
When in the wrong she did correct me, not a moment too soon.
But, O dear Lord, how it hurt, that faithful handle of a broom.
This dear lady is a gift from above, like her there's no other.
And every day I'll express the ways
And why I love my mother.

After a short time Sister Stover approached. "Have we a finished so soon?"

Ches handed her the work, and Sister Stover read it on the spot. When she finished, she stared at Ches, shaking her head. "Of course this is exactly what I was after," she beamed. "Don't you leave! I need to see you after class."

The boy guessed his first piece of writing must've troubled Sister Stover. The words weren't meant to offend. Even so, he prepared himself accordingly, and when class was dismissed, he remained at his desk. Sister Stover informed the monitors they were relieved for the day. She slid a chair near his desk, smiled, and began with carefully chosen words. "There is no need to be nervous. … You are okay by me. But I would ask you a couple of questions." She paused again, unable to hide her fascination as she gazed into his face.

"First, have you ever taken any creative writing courses?"

Ches shook his head.

"No? Really? Because your first piece, while clearly unfinished, simply has it all. It has irony, symbolism, metaphor, sarcasm … especially sarcasm. Definitely not something one would read in a church setting."

The boy sat still as a statue. He'd never been so genuinely complimented.

Sister Stover continued. "I wonder if you would let me introduce you to a friend of mine."

Ches bristled. Was she referring to some kind of therapist? His horror must've shown, and Sister Stover did her best to set his mind at ease. "I promise you, Ches, there is no need to be afraid. My friend is a literature professor at Louisiana State University. He has written several books himself. It's just that I feel you need to speak to someone who can relate to you. Maybe you'll find it a worthwhile experience."

The boy shrugged his shoulders with a blank stare.

"Now, the next question: may I present your second piece, the simpler, more agreeable one, to the congregation on Sunday?"

The boy grew extremely anxious. He didn't know how to tell Sister Stover that the second piece was entirely sarcasm. He didn't wish to destroy her sweet opinion, so he nodded in agreement.

"Ches, you don't have to be present for the reading, as I imagine that would be an uncomfortable experience for you. You have my special permission to dismiss yourself beforehand."

On Sunday morning, the church was packed to capacity, over six hundred in the congregation. After five minutes, the boy quietly exited the building.

He walked slowly toward the woods and found himself struggling with his true feelings regarding the church and Christianity and religion. He entered the tree line and continued walking until he was thoroughly out of sight. Then he sat on a log, lit a joint, and dreamed of surfing.

The following day, the mother woke the boy at dawn in a mad rush. They would travel to Berwick. Something had happened to Mawmaw, and she had been hospitalized.

They entered Mawmaw's hospital room and encountered that familiar ambience. Ches closed his eyes to images of the interior of his grandmother's shotgun house and the peculiar outline of the little woman davening in the dark. He opened his eyes to a different scene; his grandmother lying on a hospital bed surrounded by medical contraptions, intravenous lines, and blinking lights. She was holding the hand of the nurse, praying for the nurse in unintelligible words. The nurse politely pulled her hand free and resumed her duties.

Mawmaw's eyes were barely opened. She motioned the boy to her bedside and struggled to focus on his face through the narcotic haze. She smiled and guided his ear to her lips and whispered, "Sha, you enemy is hidden in dat dawrk place. But dat dawrk place is hiding behind awl dem lights. Dat evil angel of light is really da prince of dawrkness. He done summond his demons to meet in dat dawrk chamber, and he send awl dem demons on a mission. Dat mission gonna spread awl dem lights around da whole world. Awl dem decoy lights, dey gonna confuse dat whole world, yeah. Dat confusion has only one purpose; to hide dat one true light. But dat one true light gonna defeat dat confusion. Dat living light is for awl dem peoples in awl dat world. And you gonna teach dem, Sha, you gonna teach dem awl dat truth." She kissed his ear and closed her eyes.

Ches was slowly beginning to shut down. He knew that running away from home wasn't practical, but he was six hundred miles from the nearest ocean and the one thing he truly enjoyed. He no longer found it within himself to make war or peace with his circumstances or with the church or with preachers. During school hours, he would amble into the back hallway of the church building where there was a telephone on the wall. He would use it daily to call the North Florida surf report. Eventually the pastor summoned Ches into his office to address the significant phone bill that had accrued. Ches had nothing much to say, but he promised to pay what he owed. The pastor raised his eyebrows with a skeptical nod.

Two weeks later Ches knocked on the pastor's office door with one hundred and twenty dollars cash. The boy turned and walked away as the pastor looked on without a word.

The following week offered an anticlimactic meeting with the literary professor at LSU. The esteemed gentleman had forgotten that he agreed to meet with Ches and was on his way out of the office when Ches arrived. The man offered a rueful handshake. "Keep writing, young man. Never quit. Maybe one day I'll read about you in the news."

Near the end of the school year, Sister Stover called a meeting with the boy's mother and suggested that the boy was in urgent need of a change. She handed the mother a report card with straight A's in addition to the necessary transcripts for enrollment into the tenth grade.

The mother had been thinking of returning to Florida for some time as she too had grown dissatisfied with their life in Baton Rouge. During the first week of July, they were traveling again on I-10 east.

THEY MOVED INTO a low-income apartment complex on the west side of town, twenty miles from the ocean. It would be impossible for the boy to surf every day. Even so, he made the trip to Hanna Park within a week.

The boy stared out the bus window, guessing at the slim chance that his surfboard would be in the same place he'd hidden it almost two years earlier. The woman at the park gate waved him through, and he sprinted along the trail until he arrived at the clump of palmettos that once hid his board. He urgently scratched away the leaves ten inches deep, and there it was, wet and mildewed. He carried his surfboard to the ocean's edge and used a seashell to scrape away the old wax and then scrubbed the board vigorously from nose to tail with sand and saltwater. He applied a fresh coat of wax and, without delay, paddled out. He spent his fifteenth birthday camped at Hanna Park.

"In this quality, the oneness believer knows full well the risks involved in proclaiming His light to be greater than all others. We are obligated to stand out as ones profoundly affected by the truth. The Apostolic Church harbors the obligation to spread the message of light because we experienced the light firsthand as individuals. We will not keep it to ourself. We prefer light for our family, light for our friends, light for our community, and light for the world around us."

Chapter 20

Ches's attendance was perfect for the first nine weeks of his sophomore year. His intentions to succeed were sincere. He practiced discretion vigorously as he navigated through the high school culture of cliques and clichés. He made prudent efforts to remain disentangled socially, being careful to avoid distractions such as class portraits, ball games, and pep rallies. Nevertheless, by midyear he found himself struggling against a tide of popularity. Students began to call his name from across the hall. Girls would whisper as he walked past.

No matter how small he made himself, it proved impossible to escape social affectation. In his mind, this pesky phenomenon happened in a concurrence of events and circumstances that had no connection to his personality. His emerging popularity, he deduced, was merely a fluke result of his family's moving habit and the pyramid design of the school system.

Each section within the school district consisted of seven schools: four elementary schools, two junior high schools, and one high school. The section was subdivided. Section 1-A carried two elementary schools and one junior high school, and the other two elementary schools with the junior school made section 1-B. The high school, designated as 1-C, received students from both sections 1-A and 1-B. Typically the average student attended only three schools from kindergarten to twelfth grade, limiting a student's social range to the two schools attended before converging into high school.

By the time Ches reached high school, because of his family's constant moving, he'd attended nearly every school in both sections 1-A and 1-B. Consequently, a majority of the students at the high school knew Ches as the quiet kid from third grade or the smart kid from fifth or the absent kid from seventh.

Ches knew that if he wanted to graduate, he must find a way to endure.

Within a couple weeks of darting through the halls, he observed striking social divides between the various groups: jocks, nerds, preps, etc. Each group shared a pressing need for the external world to be made aware that *they* belonged to *that* particular group. Furthermore, marking certain individuals within a group, the pressing need manifested in a hypermagnified manner. Every moment of every day, the key person's energy was spent screaming out, "Look at me, I'm a football player!" Or "Look at me, I am an artist!" Ches thought of those individuals as *flag wavers*—all style, limited substance.

Two of the most popular flag wavers belonged to two groups at once. They were varsity football players but also surfers, which seemed to Ches an odd mix. These two postulants sought to disassociate themselves from the jock image, in favor of the surfer image, dressing the part of the surfer to a tee: matching surf-brand clothing and matching beach-style shoes. They perfected the surfer lingo too and had perfect surfer hair: expensive, salon bleached, bowl cut, with long bangs. They walked the halls with their heads cocked sideways to emphasize the lengthy bangs and greeted one another loudly across the hall.

"Sup, dude? Did you catch that gnarly swell?"

"Shhiyaaaahahaha … Yeeoo ow ow!"

They valued the surfer image but had no desire to paddle out and surf in the real ocean, in real waves of consequence. They were townies. Townies lived west of the Intracoastal Waterway.

By definition, Ches was a townie too. He'd seen these two at the beach twice, but never surfing, always tanning.

Ches's popularity carried a deeper irony. The group responsible for pushing him into the open did so because of an idealized view of the subversive personality, and they took it upon themselves to promote Ches thusly. This group consisted of the "progressive" or "alternative" crowd. The main thrust of the alternative crowd was "We don't care what anybody thinks," and they expended much energy getting this message across. The group encompassed several subgroups: artists, skaters, surfers, punks, etc. And while other groups might produce a small number of flag wavers, nearly every individual of the progressive/alternative group was a flag waver: spiky hair shaved on the sides; outrageous thrift-store clothing; mohawks, combat boots, and leather jackets stenciled with edgy slogans—but not too edgy as to violate school code.

One student, Jake, made every effort to take Ches under his wing. He was a self-proclaimed neo-Nazi skinhead. Jake wore Levi's jeans tucked into combat boots and offensive T-shirts underneath a tattered army jacket riddled with hand-drawn symbols of anarchy. "You have the heart of a true nonconformist," Jake would say, pointing in Ches's face, exposing the magic-marker swastikas scribbled across his hands and forearms. "But you are naïve!"

Jake would talk incessantly of a fantastic Jewish conspiracy. "Dude, the Jews control the media, sciences, and arts, and you're just another little sheep doing what your Jewish shepherds tell you to do!" Jake constantly petitioned Ches with literature featuring world events orchestrated by the Jews. "Dude, wake up! Reject your Jewish puppet master!"

With a little research, Ches discovered his own beloved Levi's were a Jewish creation. He concluded that Jake's conspiracy theories were dumb. *Why find fault with an individual or group of people who wake up earlier in the morning than their global neighbor? If I ever met a Jew, I would say, "Thanks for the Levi's."*

Ches broke ties with the anti-Semitic flag waver on student portrait day. The yearbook photographer wouldn't allow Jake to wear a T-shirt with a swastika on the front. Since Ches had no interest in the photo session anyway, he unbuttoned his own Oxford, gave it to the neo-Nazi, walked away, and never to spoke to Jake again.

By eleventh grade, Ches was beginning to show signs of fatigue. Jennifer, a reporter for the school newspaper, remembered the boy from a surf contest a couple of years past. She made a telephone call to Sun-up Surf shop, and the owner checked the contest archives. "We thought we'd see more of that kid, but apparently he didn't like the publicity." Jennifer followed another lead and discovered the boy's surfing spot at Hanna Park. Ches spotted her twice on the beach with her camera.

One Friday, after the final bell, Ches hung around and made his way through the empty halls into the darkened newsroom. He turned on the lights for a brisk walk-through, looking for anything with Jennifer's name or initials. There was a workstation with a ten-by-twelve, studio-quality photograph of Jennifer striking an overambitious pose. She wore classic reporter's garb: tweed reporter's hat with a press card tucked into the brim, a white, collared shirt deliberately untucked with the sleeves rolled up, and tweed slacks with suspenders. She brandished a vintage camera and had a dramatized expression of a serious newshound.

"She must be a reporter," Ches said and snickered aloud. He opened Jennifer's desk drawer and discovered a cache of small, black containers of film, each with a date and identifying label. The third container, labeled "Beach Boy," coincided with the date he had seen her on the beach taking pictures. He shoved the film in his pocket and made his way to the photo shop two blocks from the school.

Within forty-five minutes, he was examining the freshly developed photos. There were ten pictures of him, three of which were surfing shots. The rest captured him either in a melancholy gaze from the back of the lunch line or sitting at a desk, staring into a textbook. He pocketed the negatives and prints of himself and returned the remaining negatives and prints to the newsroom drawer.

Jennifer ran the story anyway, without the original photos and without interviewing Ches. She borrowed a snapshot of Ches from another photographer. The headline read, "Is 'A' student a totally awesome surfer?" The last day of school couldn't come quick enough.

That summer Ches landed his first official job, as a grocery store bagger. The store was in the historical section of town along the river.

His first day was slated for three hours of training. However, two employees called in sick, and Ches immediately offered to work a double shift. The manager decided to work over too and familiarize Ches with the routine of gathering carts, filling bag holds, sweeping, and emptying trash.

The manager had a good manner that set Ches at ease as they worked side by side. They bagged the groceries for a man who walked with short little steps and stared straight at the ground. Ches greeted him, but the man didn't respond. At once, Ches recognized him as his fourth-grade teacher. "That's Mr. Coffee," the manager said. "The man lost his mind several years ago when his wife died."

At lunchtime Ches sat alone in the break room, eating a banana. The television volume was high, a bothersome game show blared, and Ches started to turn the thing off when a special news report interrupted the show. It was the president's speech. Ches recognized the man at once from the mask he wore to the Ramones show. He listened intently as the president said,

> We welcome change and openness; for we believe that freedom and security go together, that the advance of human liberty can only strengthen the cause of world peace. There is one sign the Soviets can make that would be unmistakable, that would advance dramatically the cause of freedom and peace. General Secretary Gorbachev, if you seek peace, if you seek prosperity for the Soviet Union and Eastern Europe, if you seek liberalization, come to this gate. Mr. Gorbachev, open this gate. Mr. Gorbachev, tear down this wall!

The audience erupted in applause.

Ches turned the volume all the way down and pondered the power of words. He wondered how people get to a particular place in life. How did *that* president get to *that* place, considering all the variables that can knock a person off course? He thought of Thomas Paine's forty-six pages. Paine couldn't have known that his forty-six pages would knock a monarchy off course, He couldn't have known that over two hundred years later, this present dynamic would unfold because of his few words. And what is happening in this moment? Is it possible to know? What does it mean to tear down a wall? Ches understood the concept of walls and lines of distinction. Will the nations morph into one giant, culturally ambiguous blob?

He wondered again where he might have been, surfing-wise, if the preacher hadn't knocked him off course. At that moment the break room lights went black. He could see the narrow strip of light at the bottom of the door and the human feet on the other side. He waited. The door slowly opened, and a hand reached in and turned the switch on. A coworker entered, smiling. "You keep watching that stupid boob tube, and it'll rot your brain." The young man was at least a year older than Ches. He wore a green grocer's apron over a blue Oxford with the sleeves rolled above the elbow. He was tan with bleached hair. Ches was guarded.

"I'm Joe." Joe extended his hand and gave Ches the surfer's shake. "I checked your schedule, and you're off tomorrow. Boss has us down for the evening shift. We've got two full days. The surf report called for a descent groundswell, two to three with four-foot sets. I'll pick you up at five tomorrow morning."

"Who are you?"

"I'm Joe Fullerton. I grew up with Sarah and Aaron and Chever. Caveman too for the most part, although I am not supposed to associate with Cave, which I often don't! Gotta go, brah. Be ready at five. I already know where you live."

"We are not naïve people who lack the experience to make informed decisions. Our zeal for Jesus will not be swept under the rug. We were hungry enough for light; now we're bold enough to proclaim light. It is evening time, but ye are the light in this dark hour! We see the light because the light appeared to us; we experienced the light personally; we call the light by name.

Chapter 21

A CIRCULAR RAINBOW formed around the street lamp that shone above the boy. It was 4:55 a.m. He sat on the curb and peeled a banana in front of the sign for the Virginian Arms Apartment Complex. His heart raced at the thought of a full day of surfing. Within three minutes a blue, late-model Hyundai turned into the parking lot with the horn honking in unison to The Cult blasting from the stereo. The car came to a screeching halt with its headlights burning into the boy's face. Ches grinned as he slid his surfboard into the hatchback next to Joe's. He buckled his seatbelt, and they were underway.

"My dad bought this rice burner for my graduation present. He makes me pay him payments though, and he's dead serious. He'll repo this sucker if I miss one payment. He's a self-made man. A guy in my neighborhood got a brand-new Mercedes convertible for graduation. He goes out of his way to ride real slow by our place, flittering his fingers, as if I'm impressed with his stupid car. Freaking hilarious! I think he's a gentle-reader. I hate being a townie. My sister and I ran into that same guy at the gas station. He smiled gloriously when Hope complemented his cashmere sweater. Holy free-zone, dude! Be thankful you live in Virginian Arms Apartments and not Yuppie-ville, Ortega."

The waves pumped all day as forecasted. Chever and Caveman were in the lineup, and the four friends surfed until sundown. They stood on the beach in the waning light and gazed at the ocean as another set rolled in. Chever gave Ches a shake of the shoulders.

"Grommet, you're surfing as good as ever after your little disappearing act. Louisiana huh? How was that? Did you learn to speak Cajun?"

"Cajun?" Caveman chided. "He hasn't mastered his telepathetic dialect of Einsteinian! Who's hungry? Let's go to Singletons."

"Ches and I brought food," Joe said.

"Preciate it! Groms always got food. If he only knew how many times I've raided his stash while he was surfing, he might actually verbally express himself. Where are you townies crashing? I know you're not driving all the way back."

Joe slung his leash Caveman's direction, showering him with moisture trapped in the spongy anklet. "If your place didn't smell like duck butter, we'd crash with you. Maybe we'll camp out in Chever's uncle's greenhouse."

"You won't find anything green in there," Cave retorted. "Maybe a little *Tradescantia albiflora*."

Chever snapped his leash at Caveman. "I thought we were hanging with Brannon and Mark?"

Cave snapped back with a wry grin. "Oh yeah, Grom and Brannon can do the Vulcan mind meld while the rest of us hold a conventional conversation."

"Hey, did you hear? Apparently the band has garnered a significant following beyond the surf community. A major record company out of Seattle offered 'em a contract.

Joe exited the highway and turned toward the town's historical district along the river, and then down an alley that emptied into a row of dilapidated industrial buildings. They parked in front of a giant sliding door covered with graffiti.

Caveman led the crew single file between two buildings toward the sounds of live grunge music. They entered a dimly lit hallway that smelled of grease and clove cigarettes and walked five paces until they came to a door with pencil writing and coffee stains over its surface.

Caveman rattled the handle. "DEA, open up!"

The music halted abruptly. Rustling and urgent whispers could be heard just beyond the door. Caveman rattled the door again. "This is the DEA! We have a warrant!"

Thirty seconds passed, a girl with strong perfume slowly opened the door, just enough so that her face could be seen, and then a little wider to give show of her style. Her hair was spiky, jet black with a streak dyed silver, and slick to one side of her head. She wore an eclectic array of studded bracelets and a tattoo of a star under her jaw with thorny rose vines intertwining from her right upper arm down to the wrist. She darted her eyes from Caveman to the backside of the door and back again, but when she realized it was all a joke, she tried to slam the door. Caveman grabbed the handle and placed his foot in the frame to prevent it from latching.

"Um, excuse me!" The girl glared at Cave with her chin cocked "This is a *private* studio!"

Caveman forced his way in and turned on the overhead lights. The place was a grimy mess of old car parts and a forklift with the guts spilling out. There were two grocery carts with piles of clothes in each. There was a bookshelf in one corner plus a refrigerator, a table, and a filthy cloth loveseat. The other corner had been cleared and was covered by an old carpet unrolled as a place to store sound equipment, speakers, a drum set, and various guitars. Another place had been cleared near the back of the garage by the window, where a painter's easel stood next to a small shelf with a variety of painting supplies.

The girl was shocked by Caveman's boorish entrance. "Oh my god! Like, you can't barge right in here like you own the place!"

Caveman ignored the girl and searched under the table and then under the forklift. "We know you're in here, you freakazoids. Come out with your hands up."

"Who are you people?!" The girl harangued as she followed Caveman's nefarious plundering. She replaced every item that he displaced. She was not smiling. "Answer me or I am gonna call the cops!"

Caveman spun lightning fast and stood face to face with the girl until their noses nearly touched. "*What*? It is I who must call the police on you! My dad is the owner of this place!" He turned and walked to the painter's easel and cocked his head sideways. It was an oil painting of a swastika, brown and crumbling, with green, leafy vines all around.

"Like, whoa, is this you?" Caveman asked. "Like, totally visceral!"

The girl scowled at Cave's sarcasm. "You know nothing of artistic expression you disgu—"

Just then a water balloon smashed into the wall above, raining water onto the painting, causing it to bleed. An instant war broke out between the six males, as if by a secret signal. The girl held her hands to her ears, stunned by the ensuing mayhem.

Caveman ran the direction of the hurling water balloons and joined forces with the hiding musicians. Joe and Chever ducked behind the forklift. Joe found a can of tennis balls and tossed one to Chever, who threw a ball with extreme force. It ricocheted off the stack of amplifiers and into the drum set, knocking the ride symbol into the line of standing guitars, which tumbled like dominoes. Brandon, the musician, came out of hiding. "Holy cow, Chever, you're not freaking Babe Ruth!"

"You mean Tom Okker," Chever replied. "Babe Ruth wasn't a pitcher."

"You mean Sandy Koufax," the boy retorted. "Tom Okker played tennis." The room went quiet, and everyone turned to the boy who sat on the couch, reading a musician's magazine. He stood and walked casually to the artist's corner, where the girl stood aghast before her bleeding masterpiece. The boy helped the girl pick up her paintbrushes. Mark righted the instruments, and Joe gave him a hand and said, "Let's go to the COC show, nine o'clock at the Window Pain."

Brannon, Mark, and Ches hopped into Joe's car, leaving the girl to ride with Caveman and Chever. "Oh, so you make me ride with these jerks," she mouthed, while reapplying a thick layer of bright-red lipstick.

Joe pulled into the parking lot and Brannon fired one up while they waited for the others.

"What's taking them so long?" Mark asked.

"They probably took a detour so Cave could propose to Brenda," Brannon said, as he passed the glowing spleef.

The show was in full swing. They passed through the turnstile into an eccentric venue converted from an old gym into an over-the-top, artsy dance club. Hundreds of empty picture frames of varying sizes and styles hung on the walls and dangled from the ceiling. The black-and-white checkered concrete floor had been seasoned with a decade of spilt beer and vomit that stuck to their shoes as they walked. There were two short stacks of bleachers and a few tables and chairs either side of the dance floor, with a liquor bar to the rear. The dance floor was wide open to the stage. Ches and Chever moved immediately to the far edge of the crowd and climbed to the top row of bleachers, ten feet from the floor.

The music was hard and fast fusion. State-of-the-art lights flashed with a hypnotic pulse as the crowd crammed toward the stage into a violent, swirling mosh pit. Ches studied the logistics of the stage and counted the beats of the driving double base. Caveman climbed after Chever and Ches with two tall glasses filled with beer. He offered one to Chever, but he declined. He offered the same to the boy, who also declined.

At the end of the show, the lights came on, and the guys made their way down the bleachers. Caveman had consumed both glasses of beer, and he was snickering loudly. He playfully poked the other two surfers in the ribs and pointed out various individuals in the eclectic crowd.

"Look! Over there! It looks like Chever! Chever told me he secretly wants that dude's hair." Caveman blatantly pointed to a guy sporting a twenty-four-inch, red Mohawk and wearing a cobalt blue, shiny leather jumpsuit. "That's all you, Chever ... and look, there's Grom twenty years from now. Hi, Grom." Caveman waved at a man in his sixties with multiple facial piercings. He wore skimpy, seventies-style tennis shorts and a Spandex, cutoff tank top with the word *Jazz* printed in a multiplicity of fonts. The man waved back and smiled. Ches and Chever shook their heads at one another as their tipsy friend led them to the rest of the group.

Brenda was hanging on the shoulder of a big, shirtless skinhead with red suspenders. His body was covered with tattoos. From his chest to his navel, an elaborate triangle of serpents framed three fire-breathing skulls. A Nazi *SS* was tattoo'd over each shoulderblade, with another serpent inking down his spine. Both shoulders were stamped with a five-inch Nazi Iron Cross. The skinhead wore Levi's with the pants legs rolled up to accentuate his patent-leather combat boots. Caveman zeroed in on the guy.

He whispered into Ches's ear, "Tell the truth, Grom. You secretly want some tats like that guy, don't you? Check out the artistic detail of the spiderweb on his elbow. It symbolizes the web of life that entraps our arms at every bend. I know you be wantin the body art like that guy. Come on! It's a shortcut to higher intelligence. You can be an instantaneous deep inker. Come on! Say it! I know you want some tattoos. I'll lend you a couple grand to get you started."

Ches pushed the drunken Caveman out of his ear as Brenda and the neo-Nazi embraced in a passionate kiss.

Ches pondered the whole outlandish scene. *Why do we humans feel we must forcibly produce individuality? Why do we waste creative energy trying to prove to the world and to ourselves that "I am unique; there is no one like me?" Isn't it possible that an individual may genuinely realize himself to be unique, inherently unique, without props?*

Ches imagined the guy peering curiously into the mirror. He wondered if the Nazi had ever come close to discovering the magnitude of unadulterated uniqueness beneath his hokey façade. *Can't this neo-Nazi perceive the truth that the colossal proportion of his own uniqueness dwarfs all forced efforts to prove himself unique? Isn't every individual fantastically unique without even trying? And so our measly efforts to try to be different must be a tragic waste of time. Has the Nazi ever held a magnifying glass to his eye and counted the little flecks around his iris? Has he ever really, deeply observed his own hand, awakened to the fact that there has never been another hand like his hand? Isn't it a misappropriation when we make dogged efforts to be different when we already are—enormously so? It's like spearheading a campaign to declare water wet. Such ignorance merely funnels the individual into ritual face painting and body alteration.*

The boy imagined the skinhead at his home, smarting off to his flesh-and-blood mother who folded his clothes as she thoughtlessly gazed into the latest TV sitcom. He visualized the skinhead disrespecting the twice divorced schoolteacher as she solved student problems on the chalkboard. He imagined the skinhead cursing the police officer who arrested the drunk—the police officer himself oblivious to the misguided quality of human behavior. And yet, in spite of raging efforts to separate himself from the pack, this young skinhead who wore Levi's was blind to the double irony. *Wouldn't such rigid adherence to nonconformity and individuality call for trousers made of sharkskin? Or better yet, no clothes at all.*

Ches began to laugh aloud at the absurdity of the conversation in his head. He laughed at his choice to have this conversation in such a setting, and how ridiculous he must look to everyone else. The underage kid who spends countless hours *trying* to look normal is the only one who doesn't. He mocked his own self-absorbed notions: *my effort is no less artificial than the effort of this eclectic crowd.*

Caveman realized Ches was smiling and scooted closer until his nose touched the boy's ear. The snickering between them increased. Cave perceived Ches's rare outward expression as a green light to raise the volume of his own drunken jeering.

"Guys, we gotta go," Caveman said loudly. "I'm late for my appointment at Bob's Skin-Canvas Tattoo Parlor. I've converted to the proto-Aryan society of race fakers. But unless I invest sixteen hundred dollars worth of permanent anti-Semitic symbols into my skin, no one will take me seriously."

Caveman giggled more as he looked at Ches, searching Ches's face for another approving smile. Ches was smiling, but not at Caveman. His eyes were focused beyond his friend, and his smile was one of greeting, one of diplomacy, as the two-hundred-pound, round neo-Nazi walked menacingly toward them, staring right at Ches. In a flash, the brute pushed Caveman aside and delivered an open-handed slap to the boy's face.

Rhythm. Slow motion. A blistering array of movements. Ches delivered a head-spinning series of lower roundhouse kicks to the outside of the giant's left knee, stepped back with casual efficiency to avoid the brute's pugilist flail, and then made a forward thrust into the attacker's straightened knee again. Like a curtain that returns little resistance, the man crumbled forward to receive a torrent of uniform blows. Methodic strikes peppered the fleshy side of the attacker's neck and head. The man collapsed on the rock-hard dance floor, defenseless, as the swift stomp to the back of his head smashed his face into the concrete.

All at once a decade of pent-up frustration burst from Ches's lips. "*You are wearing … Leeevi's*!"

The music stopped. A hush washed over the crowd. Ches screamed at the barely conscious lump of humanity, "*You are wearing Leeevi's!*", again and again. The crowd gasped as thick, red fluid oozed from the man's left ear into bloody tracks across a pale, sweaty face. One side of the brute's suspenders broke loose as he moaned unintelligible gurgling sounds, bare-chested in the pooling blood. Chever and Joe ushered the hypercognizant Ches to the door as the boy struggled to keep his body positioned toward the broken man. The boy quaked at the absurdity. "*You are wearing Leeevi's!*" he screamed, "*Leee … vi's!*

Ches leaned against Joe's car, too embarrassed to speak. Chever and Joe stood a short distance away, locked in a discussion until Joe got in the car and turned the ignition. Chever squeezed Ches's arm affectionately and opened the door for his laconic friend. The wheels screeched onto the main road as an ambulance blasted past with lights flashing and sirens blaring.

After a ten-minute journey, Joe navigated confidently through the upscale neighborhood. Ches sat in the passenger's seat with his hands clasped, squirming beneath the lucid memory that unfurled: fists pounding meat, and the warm, fleshy feel of the skinhead's neck and face. The violence flashed again and again, pressing the ugly truth to the forefront. He could feel the man's left knee reverse bend in compliance to the striking force of his right heel. He could hear the cracking ligaments and tendons and the repulsive groans of a creature shocked with piercing pain and desperately clinging to threads of consciousness.

He opened Joe's glove compartment and stuck his hand into the light. Blood poured from his middle knuckle, swollen and split, forming the shape of an eye. His whole body was shaking. "I hurt another human being."

"Dude, don't worry about it. The dirt bag got what was coming to him."

Ches broke down weeping profusely. "Joe, you don't understand. I shouldn't have been in that place. I don't belong there, and now I have hurt another human being."

"Listen, brah, I have seen that guy before. I watched him walk into a party and randomly KO totally unsuspecting strangers for absolutely no reason. And to tell you the truth, I don't think he even knew you and Cave were there. He simply chose you at random. That's how he is."

Joe pulled into the posh driveway of his parents' residence. Ches was shaking his head. "Joe, I don't want to inconvenience you. I've got gas money. Please take me home."

"No way, brah, you're hit'n it with us tomorrow. You'll regret it if you don't. It's gonna be epic, a foot overhead. Wait right here while I make sure the coast is clear."

Ches sat alone and tried to block out the ever-present gruesome deed. He could hear the sirens as a dark reality flooded his consciousness. He realized now that his thoughts weren't the same as his friend's. The Freudian whispers grew louder as he opened the car door and ambled quietly along the driveway to the road out.

"Grom, what're you doing?" Joe hissed. Ches turned back, shaking his head, embarrassed by Joe thwarting his escape.

"Dude, you're flipping your wig for no reason. Turns out my parents took a spontaneous trip to the Bahamas. They do that sometimes. We have a cottage there. Come in. We'll chow down on leftover pizza from my sister's soiree. She'll bandage your hand. Here she is now. Hope, come get this guy. Maybe he'll listen to you."

Ches had never slept in such an opulent setting. He remembered the half hour he'd spent at Sarah's place two years ago. Joe's house was equally inordinate. The guest room alone was as big as any house the boy had ever lived in. Adjacent to the bed was a sitting area, a couch and loveseat, and a hi-fi entertainment center. Hope cleaned and bandaged his hand, then inserted a CD of Mendelssohn in the player. "Sarah told me you'd appreciate this," she whispered sweetly.

Ches eased onto the herringbone duvet covering the king-size bed. He felt awkward holding his bandaged hand to his chest. His head buzzed, not from the THC, but from utter shock. As he sank into the rich goose-down pillow, a sinister genetic predisposition came into full view. Ceremonious voices chanted from the periphery, recounting the evil of which he was capable and the sin he'd committed this night. Images of his father brutally beating members of the family danced vividly before him. His mother too—the time his brothers pinned Ches to the floor while the mother rained blow after blow upon the bewildered boy. *I am inherently bound to such bouts of violence, and there is no escape.* He stirred and pressed his face into the pillow, wishing not to know these things.

In a moment of reprieve he felt the other voice quietly enter from that inexplicable place as it had so many times before. He strained to open his physical ears, wanting the stereo music to neutralize his piquing awareness of that familiar angelic sweep, so different than he, now filling the room where he lay. He wanted the presence not to be so real, for the contrast was the cause of his knowing, his certainty. The very presence of holy light commanded obeisance to all other lights. But the boy would rather all of it be merely his imagination, or the culmination of coming down from the weed together with crashing adrenalin, or maybe an irrational dose of remorse.

He listened to the layers of strings from Mendelssohn's "Spring Song." Even so, the other spirit persisted sweetly, washing over him for comfort and gentle admonition. Ches stood abruptly, walked toward the blinking stereo, and turned it off. He pulled a pillow from the bed, dropped to his knees upon the hard, cherry wood floor, buried his face in the pillow, and wept.

"In these hours of darkness, all the difficult questions swirl in all of our minds. And while I have learned to love the question, I cannot even pretend to have an answer to some of the questions we share in this moment. Even so, we Oneness Pentecostals are drawn by a higher light that is far more powerful than every unanswered question. Our light is far livelier than every global effort to fasten us to the philosophy of myriad coexisting, coequal lights. You can't hold me down when I got the Light! I am baptized in the name of light because it matters. And I don't worry about any trinitarian that argues against saying the name of Jesus at baptism. Besides, I am not filled with the spirit that argues against verbalizing the name of Jesus. The spirit I am filled with came to me precisely because I said the Name of Jesus."

Chapter 22

By summer's end, Joe had talked Ches into surfing a couple of contests. He made the final in both, with a fourth and second-place finish. But Ches was fairly certain he would never adapt to the competitive arena. Besides, the move to Louisiana had cost two crucial years. He enjoyed following the ratings of professional competitors though and was awestruck by surfers who actually performed better in the heat of competition.

The start of his final year of high school was only a week away. Ches had $1,400 in the bank. He traded his job at the grocery story for a higher-paying one with the local newspaper. He began his senior year with little heart for the insufferable trappings of high school, where he found himself the stranger. Dances, clubs, sports, gossip—he was ready to say good-bye to all of it forever.

Joe, having graduated the previous year, made an agreement with his father to work for a year and pay off the Hyundai before enrolling at the local university. On his days off, Joe would rendezvous with Ches outside the school grounds, and they would head for the beach. When Ches's absentee tallies exceeded the allowable limit, he would sneak into the dean's office, pull his file, and replace it with a clean sheet.

Come mid-November, the dean of boys summoned Ches to his office for a discussion. The befuddled dean stared at Ches for five minutes, trying to dissect the species sitting before him. Ches's hair was short and groomed. He wore a starched button-down sharply tucked into a new pair of Levi's. He was very articulate, and his manners were impeccable.

"I am convinced of your innocence," the dean remarked with a sarcastic grin. He moved closer to Ches, and his countenance changed radically as he stared down at the boy. "Now you listen to me, young man! The president of the United States is coming to town to give a speech. Select students throughout the county will have the privilege to attend. You are on that list. So help me, God, if you are so much as one second tardy between now and the first of the month, I will strike you from that list so fast, it'll make your head spin!"

"Yes, sir," Ches replied, demurely. He bowed his head with wanton eyes that strained to meet the dean's face. Ches exited the office with his hand to his mouth, thinking of how awful it would to miss an opportunity to see a politician, and instead have to spend a day surfing a six-foot groundswell. He also wondered how the dean missed the fact that, for the present quarter, he was slated for straight Fs.

The president spoke to students at the Veterans Memorial Coliseum, an 11,000-seat, multipurpose, circular dome. He opened his long-winded speech with "I'm going to keep my remarks brief. I'm not going to take a chance on being voted in your yearbooks the president most likely to talk until June" (crowd laughter)

"You know, it's good to get out of Washington, where we spend a lot of time worrying about things only important there. Here you have perspective and realize what the important issues are … who's got a Christmas dance date and who hasn't."

Ches couldn't help his fascination. From the midlevel seating, he scanned the audience of students, government officials, and parents.

"But now, before I get started, I have a special message from Nancy. Whenever I speak to students, she asks me to remind you: For your families, for your friends, and just for yourselves, just say no to drugs and alcohol."

Ches pondered for a moment the theory that marijuana is a gateway drug, ultimately leading to drugs of a more destructive nature. He remembered his fellow students in the restroom sneaking puffs of a cigarette. *Cigarettes are dumb*, he thought, *and alcohol isn't convenient to surfing.*

"Today is not just a high school convocation; it's a family day as well. So, let me ask the parents who are here today, could you stand for a moment just so we could see you? (applause) I'll applaud that too. Mothers and fathers, your dedication to your children and the schools has made this community what it is today. Your support is the foundation on which the success of Duval County's schools has been built and on which your own children's success will be built throughout life. Today all of us say to you, for all you've done and for all you are doing and for all you will do, from the bottom of our hearts, thank you."

Ches considered the state of his parents' marriage as he watched the multitude of parents rise in support of the students throughout the arena. His parents' divorce would soon be finalized, and the mother would relocate to another state, perhaps to be with another man. Ches had to make a decision soon.

"Teachers, principals, parents, and students, you have made your mark on American education. You've sprinted to the head of the class in improving test scores, cutting dropout rates, winning teaching awards, winning more National Merit scholarships, and winning a better future for every student and for this entire community. I've heard that you have a slogan around here: *Winners are finishers*. It means stay in school, stick it out through tough times as well as good, finish, and you'll be a winner too. America wasn't built by people who said, I can't. Every pioneer who crossed our frontier said, I can. Every man or woman who ever started a new business, discovered a new invention, explored a new idea said, I can. You will graduate from high school because you said, I can."

Ches slipped from his seat and made his way to the highest levels of the auditorium toward the upper exit. The crowd grew thin the higher he climbed, and the president's speech progressed from a direct address to the students to issues of freedom and small government: more decisions outside of Washington, fewer inside, fewer federal rules, and more opportunity.

"And while we're talking about the American people making choices, not Washington, don't you think that each morning when you start your school day you should have the same voluntary choice every member of Congress has every day: to bow your head to God in prayer?" (applause)

Ches stopped in his tracks. With the highest row of seats completely empty, he slowly turned and sat down.

"The federal government does a lot to shape the future. And there are many times when it would be helpful if government just left things alone. Our goal should be to make government the servant of the people and not the other way around."

Ches listened intently as the president began to speak of present and future threats, not only to human freedom but even to human existence. The man outlined in simplified terms the global dichotomy between the Soviet Union and the United States of America: Soviet expansion and American expansion; oppressive governance and the urgency of nuclear arms reduction.

"For the first time in history, we will wipe an entire category of American and Soviet nuclear weapons from the face of the Earth, but in the excitement of the summit, the treaty signing, and all the rest, we must not forget that peace means more than arms reduction."

Ches was transfixed by the power of the nuclear bomb. He had not considered such a reality before that moment: an ICBM that could deliver, not a kiloton warhead, but a multimegaton warhead.

"But for all of you, this threat that's alive in the world today of missiles that can … well, I've said that a nuclear war can never be won and must never be fought. By never being won, I mean that, by the time two great nations exchange thousands of nuclear missiles … firing at each other … where would those people who weren't blown up … who still remained left … where would they live? The very soil would be poisoned radioactivity."

The president's words echoed behind the swinging doors to the coliseum. Ches walked past the long row of yellow school buses to the main road beyond and followed it for three miles to the local community college. He eased along the campus corridor until he found a sign that read, "Student Services."

"May I help you, sir?" A little women with silver-blue hair and bifocals appeared behind the counter. She spoke with a genteel accent and greeted Ches with a warm smile.

"Yes, ma'am, I would like information regarding GED testing."

"Yes. But did you know we also offer a high school equivalency diploma? You may qualify for a high school equivalency diploma."

During the short interview and character assessment, Ches disclosed the turbulent circumstances of his academic life, having attended fifteen different schools from kindergarten to tenth grade. At the end of the meeting, the women offered to administer the HSED test on the spot.

"We can do it now or make an appointment, and you can come back. It's your choice. The test takes about four hours. The office closes at five, and it's twelve thirty now. If you've already eaten lunch, we can get you in and out before closing."

Ches agreed to take the test right away. He settled into the test and finished by three thirty.

"I can grade the math and writing portion now. But if you don't mind waiting, the remainder will be graded electronically within thirty minutes."

Ches nodded. The administrator directed him to the student lounge, where he leafed through the various college brochures and course catalogs. The average cost per course was ninety dollars plus books. He borrowed a pen from the end table and checked courses of interest: World Religions, Sociology, Writing, and Oceanography 101. He folded the schedule, tucked it into his pocket, and grabbed an *American Literature Magazine* featuring an article of Mark Twain.

As he read the article, he was reminded again of the way his favorite writer irreverently deromanticized the herd mentality.

> All the territorial possessions of all the political establishments in the earth—including America, of course—consist of pilferings from other people's wash. No tribe, however insignificant, and no nation, howsoever mighty, occupies a foot of land that was not stolen. When the English, the French, and the Spaniards reached America, the Indian tribes had been raiding each other's territorial clothes-lines for ages, and every acre of ground in the continent had been stolen and restolen five hundred times.

Ches laughed aloud, recalling his first-grade teacher's infatuation with indigenous cultures, "paragons of peace and harmony."

Before long, the administrator came into the lounge, smiling. "Young man, I have been administering this test for seven years. Your test scores are exceptional! But before I congratulate you, I must encourage you to consider taking the SAT. You really need to take the SAT. It could mean a substantial academic scholarship. Otherwise, congratulations, you're a graduate of FCCJ High School."

It was spring term, one month since Ches dropped out of high school and received his diploma—both in the same day. His parents' divorce had been finalized, and within thirty days he entered the life he had dreamed of for so long.

He paid four hundred dollars cash for a lime-green 1975 Toyota Corolla, enrolled at the community college, and signed a three-month lease on a single-bedroom apartment at the beach, one block south of the pier. The oceanfront townhomes across the street were all that separated Ches from his passion.

His boss arranged for a transfer to the newspaper distribution branch a few blocks from the young man's residence. To Ches's surprise, he not only received a transfer, he also received a promotion to assistant branch manager. His hours would be two to ten in the morning, Monday through Friday—convenient for both studying and surfing.

It was surreal. No more arguing, no more fighting, and no more anxiety over being uprooted at a moment's notice. Ches was seventeen, on his own, and free to pursue a normal life undeterred by mitigating circumstances.

"Jesus is my King! I am not baptized into a plurality. I am baptized in His name. There are other spirits, waving the banner of Christianity, who hate that we are baptized in His name. But that is all right. He is still our King! This world and its governments are under the influence of the plural god. But Human philosophy cannot save you. Your first job is to pray for your leaders. Because if the earthly leaders don't have people of the light praying for them, what hope is there?"

Chapter 23

THE PROFESSOR WORE tinted bifocals and spoke with a permanent, sarcastic sneer. "I have been teaching world religions now for two decades. In my class you are encouraged to voice your opinion." The man's blue polyester shirt was soiled at the underarm, and his wiry, shoulder-length hair was disheveled and pulled to one side of his head. "Both objective and persuasive participation requires the ability to think critically. The student needs to be able to clearly present information in a format that is logical to the class."

He paced in front of his desk with an unceasing circular nod that left the class constantly second-guessing. "That said, my students should be prepared to think about the subject and *draw their own* conclusions after thinking critically about the information. And in the case of persuasion, it is highly advisable to study the opposing argument before you open your mouth. If you pass this class, you may well discover that your little religion, if you are religious, is merely one of a myriad of beautiful religions in this great big colorful world. By the end of this semester I believe you will discover … that god is indeed … a plurality."

The psychology professor was in her mid-fifties. She was a pretty woman wielding an earthy style with a subtle hardness in her eyes. Natural blond hair with streaks of gray accentuated her dewy, uncovered complexion. "I have been married for twenty-two years. I did not take on my husband's last name, because such traditions are reminiscent of a culture where the woman is the property of her husband. Nobody owns me! I am my own person."

The woman's frame was youthful, and she spoke with fits and starts like a schoolgirl. "Critical thinking is the ability to apply reasoning and logic to new and unfamiliar ideas and situations. Thinking critically involves seeing things in an *open-minded* way. My students must examine an idea or concept from as many angles as possible. This will allow you to look beyond your personal view of the world and demonstrate the ability to affirm the opinions of others. The open-minded approach and the aptness to think critically are essential to problem solving. Being open-minded allows a person not only to seek out all possible answers to a problem, but also to accept that there are many right answers to every question. Open-minded thinking requires that a person does not assume that one way of approaching a situation is best, or necessarily right."

Ches immediately recognized the common theme in the professors opening remarks. He understood it as introductory language necessary to first-year college students.

The sociology professor could have been related to the psychology professor except she made obvious efforts to conceal her softness. "Most of us in Western society have been inundated with the Judeo-Christian worldview with little consideration to the social sciences. Unless you have an open mind, you will probably be greatly offended at some point in this course. But before you drop the course, I want to remind you that we live in a pluralistic society, and there are millions of ways to be a human being. And when a particular way doesn't align with your narrow Western experience, don't give up … get real!"

Ches immersed himself in the college process. He'd never taken formal education this serious, but now things were different. Now the onus was squarely on his shoulders, and he welcomed the long-awaited opportunity to fit in with the mainstream. In college, there was such an emphasis on the notion that there are millions of ways to be a human being.

At first Ches was intrigued by the fact that success in the classroom hinged on a student's broad-minded reception of information. And while he understood these concepts as essential to subjective fields of study, he couldn't understand why the math teacher brought these concepts into various discussions. He found himself growing skeptical of the sociology professor's noncritical attraction to indigenous cultures, as though indigenous peoples were higher than human, as though being the first one to inhabit a particular land automatically exempts one from the same fleshly shortcomings suffered by the rest of the world. Are the aboriginal occupiers mystically impervious to inclinations toward cruelty, war, greed, ethnic cleansing, and other universal human flaws? Aren't we all the product of the native?

By midterm, Ches had grasped the college system handily. His first papers returned good scores. His professors wrote notes with suggestions and little red circles marking his errors in punctuation. Nevertheless, he slowly began to perceive that college success had less to do with merely testing for levels of knowledge. Rather, with the exception of math, college success seemed more about the student demonstrating that he or she could communicate the concept back to the individual professor, using a customary language in a manner the professor deemed acceptable. In Ches's mind, the system was inherently corrupt because it was less about the book and more about the professor. Rubbing the professor the wrong way might well decrease one's chances of making the grade. To achieve success, a student need only pinpoint the professor's personality and language, and then feed the subject matter back with an appropriately crafted language that gelled with that professor's disposition.

Ches reined in his inclination to write a strong piece. Instead, he gave each paper a tailored and condescending twist that landed quietly beneath the sensitivity of the professor. As a result of this subtle subservience, he achieved the Dean's List, begrudgingly.

Ches began to resent the system more every day. In his mind, the constrictive energy of college culture forced students to ignore the obsolescent nature of knowledge itself. He could no longer look into the faces of his fellow academicians. He was repulsed by the self-absorption, the dark circles under the eyes, and the conceit overlane with a thin veil of false humility.

He imagined the same delusion shared by scientists long ago who smugly insisted the world was flat. He began to see college success as something ugly, like an invisible cumbersome crown laid heavily atop natural insight. He became increasingly offended at the idea of packaged, marketed knowledge, and he began to abhor the image of himself wearing a graduate's gown, standing in a long, passive line of identical graduates wearing dumb hats and tassels. He imagined walking across the stage to receive a diploma that represented an approved box of knowledge, as the royal academic paragons extend congratulatory nods.

He knew that any person could possess testable knowledge identical to that of a person holding a degree. But so many are denied the opportunity to support themselves, to eat and have shelter, because they can't purchase the approved box of knowledge.

Ches was convinced he was no more intelligent than the average student. He attributed his academic success to an ability to exploit the system's whopping weak spot: its uncritical view of itself. He found it all too revolting and moved willfully away from the opportunities inherent in a degree, though he gave some consideration to the possibility that his views were somewhat extreme, skewed by powerful mechanisms that tweaked his early years of development. *How deeply is a person's perception shaped by a single life event?* he pondered. *Is it possible that the image of my mother's head being bashed by my father affects my rationale? What about the many negative experiences throughout my adolescence? My mother beat me bloody with an extension cord. Am I now cursed in the way I see the world? Have I finally been delivered to the hour of self-sustenance and freedom, but have been sabotaged by a deformed worldview: a toxic loathing of systems—even those that function?*

The answer to these questions mattered little in the here and now. Even from a reasonable perspective, the peace Ches longed for, the genuine peace he'd experienced in another dimension, could not be realized within the confines of formal education.

Ches was not a conspiracy theorist. Conspiracy theories drained his energy. He reckoned that something similar to genuine peace is discovered while surfing. Surfing offers all the struggles and challenges of life without bias, without insider privilege. During the autumn, the ocean delivers six-foot ground swells, and northeast winds whip the coast at twenty to twenty-five knots. Every surfer, regardless of skill and strength, takes a pounding. All surfers are welcome to paddle through the impact zone. And every surfer who makes it through is rewarded with the sweetness on the other side. That sweetness is not guarded by or subject to judges who decide, once the surfer successfully makes the lineup, that he must meet *their* approval. No such approval is needed to partake of the ocean's bounty of swell.

Ches began to despise occasions when well-meaning professionals pointed out his potential to succeed in the system. "Mr. Ches, a Dean's List academic standing is achieved by a small percentage of students nationwide. You're gonna go far."

This grudge transferred to his place of employment. His boss got wind of his grades through his daughter, with whom Ches had two classes. The boss would put his arm around him and give inspirational advice on how not to miss opportunities. "Now, if I had it to do over," the man would say, followed by a tired story of exceptional athletic prowess forfeited for love.

Still, Ches could do no wrong in the workplace. He tested the limits of this by sending a clear message that being present in the lineup took priority over being present in the workplace. His boss would respond with "Now, young man, everybody knows you are going to go far with this company. I know you like to go out and ride the gnarly waves. But really, there is no future in surfing." Ches would nod graciously while thinking of the incoming tide.

"Dude, it's time you move out of this dump," Joe declared.

The seedy flat was infested with cockroaches and smelled of wood rotting in the extreme humidity and salty environment. Joe pretty much lived with Ches, and he finally convinced Ches to colease an oceanside townhouse across the street. Caveman agreed to part ways with his camper, since he worked as a cook at a nearby restaurant. With a third roommate, Ches's rent decreased.

The place was nicer than anything he had ever imagined. It had central air-conditioning, new appliances, and three bedrooms with three full bathrooms. A winding staircase opened into an airy, upper-level living area. Each room had a balcony and ocean view. He immediately positioned his mattress by the window so he could check the morning surf without rolling out of bed.

I slide from the tiny chair to the floor and draw my knees tight to my chest. I am involuntarily rocking back and forth, davening to the preached words that pour through the vent. I have no choice but to reckon with that thing that has kept me from hiding away in the islands of the South Pacific, or the Indian Ocean. An invisible hand has held me fast, guiding me to this, pressing my face to the louvers. Brother Brown, the man I should hate, is preaching in musical notes with deep sincerity and raw emotion, "Sommme … bodaay … tell … me what time it is?! It's time for you to lift your head, my son!"

Chapter 24

A TROPICAL STORM was brewing in the Atlantic basin, but the swell wasn't expected to arrive for another week. The residual pulse from a previous swell produced two hours' worth of fun waves at sunrise. Ches could smell the coffee and bacon as he clambered up the boardwalk still wet from the morning surf session.

The Pier Restaurant was a greasy dive built on pylons at the head of the fishing pier. Its salt-faded walls were adorned with dried starfish, sand dollars, and conch shells. A large painting of Elvis framed in fishing net hung on the back wall next to a bright-orange mural of a sunset. The floor was made of pier planks with cracks in between—through which, at high tide, diners could see the waves crashing below. Rhonda, a waitress with leathery skin and a raspy voice, winked at Ches and pointed to his table by the window. She served his usual broccoli omelet and morning paper.

The front page featured a twelve-year-old Palestinian boy in the middle of a road, hurling a stone at a Merkava Mk-2 Israeli tank. The picture captured the essence of grave inequality and invoked feelings of anger. Ches had seen similar images in the past year on the front page of a number of mainstream news magazines.

The Palestinian boy wore a slick rugby shirt and Levi's jeans. His was a palpable feat of courage: a small boy willing to sacrifice his life for a cause. Ches imagined that his own mother might have permitted such a sacrifice. He stared at the photo of the child facing a giant tank. *Maybe we are a lot alike. Maybe in a comparable affair, my family would've found a precedent for unity. And instead of compulsive fighting among ourselves, we would've aimed our weapons at a common target*. Ches found it difficult to picture a circumstance where, if he was a father, he would encourage his own twelve-year-old son to take the path of the sword. Still, the picture of the audacious twelve-year-old boy attacking a tank was spellbinding.

When the ocean was flat, the surfers involved themselves in unorthodox forms of entertainment. Most of them rarely watched television. But during flat spells, it had become commonplace to get high and watch the daytime soaps or the PTL Club televangelists, purely for the comedy. Eight to ten surfers would gather around a television set with the volume muted. Then each surfer would do an ad-lib voiceover that fit the expression of the actor or televangelist. Ches applauded those sublime protests, especially when Caveman played the part of a televangelist wearing one of Joe's pinstripe suits. Joe laughed so hard he puked all over the floor.

Ches found it interesting that he had happened to land among such a likeminded group. They were linked not only by an irrational dedication to the ocean, but also by a common revulsion for mainstream culture. They rejected a world where millions of people wasted away, addicted to television. The surfing crowd considered it extremely inappropriate that society fashioned itself according to the dictates of artifice, complete with the painted faces and personalities of the actors it worshiped. "Fake muscle! Fake hair! Fake lips! Fake body parts! Fake faces! I know a girl who videotapes all her TV shows," Cave said. "She'll spend an entire day catching up on the soaps she missed. And she laughs exactly like Valerie on *Beverly Hills 90210*."

The townhouse had become the hangout for many members of the surf community. During surfing contests, traveling competitors opted to stay at the townhouse instead of a cheap hotel. Two more surfers, Ron and Mark, moved next door, and new friendships were forged as they often contributed their extra space to the cause.

The gatherings were hardly a sixties-style version of conscientious objectors or indolent hippies whose main indentifying feature was *protest*. True, the surfing crowd appreciated music and cannabis and shared strong aversions to mainstream society. But unlike any other subculture, the surfers demonstrated a disproportionate passion for riding waves— an activity more labor intensive than possibly any other. Rarely would they find occasion for an organized complaint or political rally, especially during a swell.

Sometimes the flurry of new faces in the townhouse was too much for Ches, so he sought solace amid the sand dunes. He'd sneak along the newly worn trail to the place where he kept a weatherproof ziplock bag that contained his writing material, buried near an L-shaped patch of sea oats.

By coincidence, Caveman discovered Ches's sanctuary, and he repeatedly barged in when Ches was writing. "Have you laid any eggs?" Caveman would say mockingly. "Let me read it! Is it poetry? Is it a love letter?" One day he unearthed the notebook and was immersed in the words when Ches walked in. "Holy flan, Grommet, this is seriously heavy stuff!" Cave declared with a nervous twitch.

Ches tried to snatch the pad from Cave's grasp, but he dodged and began to read aloud. "When the water falls, I'll see my sinful ways begin to fight my shame. And the grinding night is covered with blacken, melting winds. For the beginning is near, and with power to flee I'll shed my sight so sore from the breaking day." Caveman shook his head, wide-eyed. He finally handed the work back to Ches. "Straight-up Edgar Allen Poe, my boy." Ches snatched the pad, disturbed by Caveman's fluid sense of boundaries.

On Friday afternoon Ches sat in the library, reading a science magazine. Doctor Leon Lederman was slated to win a Nobel Prize and had written a brief paper chronicling his quest for the smallest subatomic particle—a foundation-particle so small it might connect everything.

Ches had been on his own secret quest. He strongly believed there must be a logical explanation for the disembodied presence—a presence he never spoke of, a voice that calmly narrated his every coming and going. From the very day he moved to the beach as a young man on his own, something changed, and the voice assumed a more active role. He never mentioned the companionate whisper, for fear he might be diagnosed with schizophrenia and condemned to a life of antipsychotic meds. But now things were different. His life was no longer controlled by the desultory guardians of his adolescents.

Ches's nighttime ritual of hiding in the sand dunes, gazing into the vastness of space, seemed to elevate the whisper. He wanted to shake the bothersome concepts he'd been taught during his semester at college, those discomfiting awkward cubes of state-approved doctrines forcibly crammed into the smooth, round shape of his mind. These too had become a nattering voice. He recognized the woeful directives everywhere: *There is more than one truth*! *There are many paths*! *This is a pluralistic society*!

Escaping these other voices proved more difficult than dodging raindrops in a torrential downpour. *There are a million ways to be a human! God is a plural! God is a plural! God is a plural!* The world around Ches was sinking into a sea of antidefinitives.

He'd read Mikhail Gorbachev's *Perestroika*, and studied the idea of glasnost, or "openness" policy reform. He'd studied the philosophy that insists there are many coexisting, coequal pathways that lead to the same spiritual mountaintop. He wondered if mainstream societal structures as a whole might be under major reconstruction. *Is it a global, spiritual bait-and-switch? Because the notion that billions of individuals can travel any random path yet arrive at a single identical destination has nothing to do with the real universe.*

Ches stared at the clock on the library wall. It had a traditional face with sixty little dots marking the seconds. He imagined the center of the clock as the starting point from which one might travel outward on a decided path toward any particular dot around the circle. He wondered how many additional trillions of microscopic dots would fit between the seconds, representing infinite possible pathways into outer space.

He concluded that the domineering many-pathways mantra was deceiving. He knew that the idea that all candidates start from a specified point, travel outward in any random direction, and still arrive at the same predecided destination was nothing more than preposterous. In reality, the mathematics applied to a moon landing cannot be used for a Mars landing. In this universe of infinite possible trajectories, it is necessary to have verified, precise coordinates for a specific destination.

It was six in the evening. As Ches exited the library, he saw Caveman across the street, riding a bicycle toward him. Cave nodded to Ches.

"Put this on your tongue," Caveman said, as A1A traffic whizzed past.

"Whatever for?"

"Seriously, stick out your tongue."

Cave waved a sandwich bag with small bits of what looked like paper confetti. "Lysergide." Cave handed Ches a solitary quarter-inch square, and the young man placed it on his tongue. Cave placed two on his own tongue and grinned at Ches. "Want another?"

"Sure."

"Dude, we are going on a trip tonight. Hope you didn't have plans for the next twelve hours or so."

The two talked of the latest swell and the rising stars of surf competition as they wondered toward the Oceanside Boardwalk. Within forty minutes, a foreign sensation began to creep into their consciousness. Within the hour, a full-bloomed strangeness replaced all chatter. Their ability to speak had been overpowered by a heightened state.

They ambled along the endless row of souvenir shops, arcades, and taverns, staring at common things they'd never noticed before.

They had loitered along the boardwalk countless times, but this night everything was balefully crooked and seedy. The endearing aromas of popcorn, hotdogs, and cotton candy had been corrupted with the stench of human waste as merchants lit flashing signs to attract passersby unapologetically. A palm reader sat beneath a giant neon triangle, holding the hands of a sharply dressed, middle-aged couple.

The aged wooden planks beneath Ches's feet turned rotten, and the filth attached itself to his sandals, with every step, and slowly crept up his legs to his thigh. A man wearing a three-piece suit clutched a liquor bottle as he wallowed in his own vomit. He pointed to the surfers and began to sing "Amazing Grace" as they passed. The two friends darted glances at one another, astonished at the man's uncanny crooning ability, but they didn't smile. Cave attempted to make a comment, but his words were formless.

They weaved through the morbid sea with bewildered expressions. Ches detected a spark of fear in Caveman's face and tried to convey a sense of well-being, but he secretly wondered if they could endure the grinding sense of expansion much longer?

At the end of the boardwalk, the mood lightened. The deafening sounds of pinball machines, skee-ball sirens, and carnival amusement faded, but there were still no words between the two. The boardwalk emptied into a sandy trail lined with giant boulders. A psychedelic blend of sand fleas and cockroaches parted like the sea as the path evolved before them. They turned on a dark road along a row of shops and businesses, and walked until they could hear the music pounding the white brick walls of their destination: Einstein-A-Go-Go, an all-ages alternative music club at the farthest end of the boardwalk.

Einstein's put north Florida on the alternative club circuit, drawing bands such as Nirvana and Aleka's Attic. Cave handed Ches a ticket with a cartoon sketch of a boy with spiky hair and the inscription "Red Hot Chili Peppers."

A girl with purple lipstick and silver hair half-shaved stood in the doorway, checking tickets. It was a packed house with a dual theme of homely and grunge. A sparse array of colored lights hung from the black ceiling, and the walls were white with amateur artwork painted on bedsheets draped all the way around. Each patron received a green or purple glowstick; little luminescent worms floated around the room appealing to amplified senses of sight.

As Ches knit through the revving crowd, the lights dimmed, followed by a flash of a strobe, and for a moment Ches thought he'd caught a glimpse of Sarah. He turned and started to leave the building, but someone grabbed his arm and spun his torso into a forced hug. It was Chever. Chever held fast to Ches's arm and led him to a back corner, where he was instantly swamped by friends and unknown others who shook his shoulders and ran hands through his hair affectionately.

Joe's sister took Ches by the hand and delivered him to a small couch in the corner. The strobe flashed again, and Sarah's image blasted into his amplified space—then darkness, and a soft hand slid into his. He felt embarrassed and dirty. He didn't want Sarah to see him like this. He was verbally paralyzed, though she didn't notice, seeing his wordlessness as nothing unusual. Suddenly, out of the blackness a hush washed over the crowd, and then the accidental crash of a cymbal as the band members readied themselves. Sarah started to speak but was interrupted by a musical explosion as the kaleidoscope of color unveiled the most incredible sounds Ches had ever heard.

He stole glances of Sarah in the blinking colored light. Her elegant presence was a perfect contrast to the grungy atmosphere, but when the lights blinked off again, the young man's heart sank. Sarah had changed. Her hair had been dyed. The striking line of brownish makeup along her jaw extended to the top of her nose, thoroughly concealing her delicate wisps of freckles. Her eyes were painted with a montage of purple fading to the outside edge of her eyebrows. She turned her smile toward Ches and exposed perfect teeth with flecks of lipstick glowing in the fluorescence. She darted her eyes nervously under his studious gaze.

Ches turned to the music. The four musicians were too young to be so good, or maybe it was the lysergide. He wondered at how vast the underworld of obscure talent was. *There are unknown artists with abilities far beyond the narrow scope of commercial endorsment.*

The crowd throbbed to the beat as one vulcanized mass of fleshy discharge, oozing and flowing rapidly together in oscillating rhythms. Ches felt his own body vibrate to the extreme decibels but suppressed the impulse to move. Instead, he scanned the crowd, studying the faces of the affected from the safety of his perch next to Sarah.

United though the crowd was, there was a striking disparity—the same disparity found in all crowds. Those who strove for a more alternative look were preoccupied with subtle glances, hoping to catch the attention of others, while the unassuming portion, mostly surfers, behaved without fear of any kind.

The musicians stood apart from the swarm. They played as ones literally possessed by their craft, immersed in the effect of their music on the lurching congregation. The vocalist, drummer, and bass player shared a jovial contempt for the spectators. Between songs, they mocked and jeered at different ones. This was a huge hit with the surfers, who roared with laughter as the band called out a guy with a tattoo of a spider on his forehead. Chever and the rest returned hoots with gusto.

The guitar player was markedly different from the other three members of the band. He was not the front-man, but he was clearly the brains of the operation. His gestures were subtle as he stood at a distant angle to his fellow musicians. His guitar work was exquisite and energetic, yet his countenance was sad and aware. He had the face of a good boy who probably should have been doing other things with his life. Ches began to grow unsettled at the wayward quality of this guitar player.

He slid from the end of the couch, cautiously weaved through the swarm of glowing worms, and walked through the door into the ocean breeze beyond.

The townhouse was thirteen blocks south of Einstein's. Ches inhaled the ocean air and walked east until he found the public entrance to the beach. He took off his sandals and padded along the edge of the Atlantic, taking inventory of his synthetic mental predicament. At one point, back at Einstein's, he'd felt as though he would snap from the effects of the chemical inflation within. And now every possible sound seemed to vie for his attention: night birds, chirping crickets, blowing breezes. Every stirring spirit of dark called his mind to a different direction. He tried to determine the time and distance of his journey in an effort to outpace an encroaching panic. *How long have I been walking? How far away could it be? Is that the pier up ahead?* He began to laugh at himself, and the panic receded. *What is time and space anyway?*

Ches brushed the sand off the pages of his notebook, slipped it into the ziplock, and buried it again.

Caveman passed the spleef, and Ches inhaled the stuff without a word. He could feel the hot smoke billowing downward, deeper, burning its way into each chamber of his lungs. It was three in the morning, and the lysergide had begun to release its grip on their ability to articulate. For the first time in eight grinding hours, Caveman broke the silence.

"Holy cow, I was tripping my brains out."

Ches nodded.

"Those guys rip! Chever told me all about 'em; he knows the guitar player."

Ches nodded again.

"Something occurred to me during the show, Grom. I was listening to the lyrics. Ches … you can do that. I mean … you can put words together … creatively. And your stuff is … deep!"

Ches turned his body to avoid eye contact with Cave.

"You see, Ches, the thing is, you and I are cut from the same socioeconomic cloth. We are, like, way down here among the bottom dwellers. I mean, the deck has been stacked against us from the beginning. Ches, I have no idea how I am going to finish college. I pretty well screwed up my scholarship, and I refuse to apply for any more student loans. I owe thousands already. I mean, Chever and those guys have no idea what it's like to have no way out, and that's cool. I don't resent them, because none of us gets to choose his birth situation. But man, you and I have gotta come up with a plan. I mean … I want to surf forever, but how can we support it."

Ches began to relax, realizing the seriousness of his friend.

"I know your stuff is a private matter, but would you mind if I finished reading one particular piece?"

Ches shrugged, and Caveman gingerly dug the writing pad from its hiding place and squinted into the pages. Ches retrieved the green glowstick from his pocket, gave it a crack, and passed it to Cave. Cave began to read aloud.

From Us to I Am

Hate me so bitterly, I love you anyway, kick me in the face
a thousand times

I walk naked in the street in the middle of the day

So come out, come out, wherever you are, don't be shy

Now I don't know how to not hate you, and I don't know
how to not cry

And I don't know how to not love you, so I can't see your
face all over the place

But I have kissed your cheek a thousand times

Slipping away, over and over again, more to come, chipping away

Until I find the middle I'll be in this confusion to stay

But I'll spread some lies through a couple of friends because when I sin I die

I only want to know you, I only want to see your face

Look down on me and I'll show you how to never turn away

Life, love, money, just for more, I'll give my soul

Give me a steamroller for this rocky road

Together I know we can fly so high, so I'll throw away my wishing marble

And wish away the sky

"Dude, what … is that? Grommet, I have never been more serious. I know you. I know something stirs deep inside, something that far exceeds the passions of we mere mortals.

Ches turned to Cave and took a deep breath. "The piece is nothing more than a basic socioreligious comment. It's my view, in a word picture, of the global society's response … to a God they refuse to acknowledge … on His terms."

"Ches … do you know God?" There was a palpable desperation in Caveman's words, a sense of longing, and hope.

Ches stood, brushed the sand off his jeans, and bolted into a blinding sprint down the beach.

It was the voice again. Ches ran until he knew he was completely out of sight and then fell to his knees in the darkness. The voice brushed aside the effects of the trifling, filthy offal and began to flood its holy mandate into the young man's consciousness. Ches covered his head, self-aware and embarrassed. The name was on the tip of his tongue, but he resisted the impulse to speak it. "Why are You touching me? I am dirty. Please don't touch me." He closed his eyes to the little boy sitting on a chair and the funny man with the thick shock of hair shaking the boy's hand, bidding him to laugh. The boy tried to wrench away, but the man opened his mouth and a painful light poured from his tongue.

As the sun cracked the horizon, Caveman found Ches face-down by a tidal pool, speaking unintelligible words.

That day, after a five-hour surf session, Ches retired to his room. But his sleep was hardly restful; it was riddled with strange dreams of Caveman's face, the face of the Chili Peppers' guitar player, the face of Sarah, and multitudes more. No matter where he turned, the faces appeared, staring at him.

Brother Brown is closing his sermon. The congregation is responding with waves of worship. Brother Brown is worshiping too. He is weeping. "I am just a man called of God. I feel the Holy Ghost stirring. There is somebody in this room right now. You've tried to hide but you just can't hide. You've tried to run, but no matter where you run you can't get away from His voice. Because God is calling you! You have been fighting it, like Pilate, the voice of God has been right there all along, and you have turned the other way. Come on friend. God still has a work for you, but you gotta come out of hiding."

Chapter 25

THE SLEEP DEPRIVATION wasn't intentional. Ches wanted to sleep, but it was the most active storm season in a decade. His pattern consisted of surfing during daylight hours and bed at eight, with intentions to rest until midnight and to be ready to clock in at the newspaper at two in the morning.

Einstein's became a nightly ritual for Joe and Cave and the rest of the crew. With bands like Rein Sanction and Firehose playing six nights a week, the townhouse became an after-hours gathering for surfers and musicians.

Ches often entered the workplace in an altered state. But his coworkers never seemed to notice, and he was careful not to expose his dilated pupils.

The extreme demands of his new life ultimately required Ches to review his priorities. He quietly traded his job at the newspaper for more flexible means of sustenance, such as laying sod or construction-site cleanup. A ritual use of substances was necessary to neutralize the recurrent dream of the waiting faces. And another dream began to occur; a dream within a dream. Or maybe it wasn't a dream at all. It had happened several times, mostly in the morning. He'd feel himself stirring at the sound of the alarm clock, but he couldn't wake up. He'd strain with all his might. His breathing would grow rapid, his heart rate would increase, but he couldn't wake up.

Ches did everything he could to stay occupied, believing the flurry would drown the voice. Flat-spell activities evolved from lampooning television sitcoms to real life shopping-mall excursions.

The surfers would mob a cheesy, pop-culture clothing store and choose the most outrageous outfit, try it on, and then step out of the fitting room into the open to compete in a mock fashion contest. Cave would always push the limits with something like a skintight, powder-blue, sequined jumpsuit with gold chains and a snazzy matching hat. Usually these charades were halted by a fuming clerk with gaudy makeup, jewelry, and giant hair threatening to call security.

One Friday, Caveman convinced Ches to attend the World Religions Conference hosted by the Beaches Pavilion. The two friends outfitted themselves at the neighborhood thrift store. After sifting through the vintage suits and ties, Ches hit the jackpot with a navy-blue Brooks Brothers two-piece and a matching Cambridge striped tie for ten dollars, plus a pair of tattered wingtips tagged for fifty cents. The slacks were several inches too long but they covered the old shoes.

Cave was going for a more pernicious look: a seventies, double-knit, brown plaid suit, white belt, and white patent-leather shoes. He resembled a faith healer who swatted seekers with a healing handkerchief. Ches diplomatically talked his friend out of the plaid hat.

With one hour to spare, they ran into the neighboring grocery store to the cosmetic aisle for hair gel, a comb, and a mirror. It'd been so long since Ches used a comb that his hair had grown into a poof of sun-bleached ringlets. Cave approved. "Dude, I never noticed before, but you're a straight-up Rastafarian."

Ches applied a generous glop of gel to slick his wavy locks straight back with a perfect part to the side. Cave's hair was already short, since he regularly cut it himself. As the twosome inspected one another, their next-door neighbor, Mark, who worked in the produce department, happened to turn down the aisle. He shook his head without a word and pointed to the exit.

The snickering surfers replaced the items and ran for the sliding doors. As they weaved through the parked cars, a familiar voice called to Ches. He turned and beheld the face of his former teacher, Sister Petrosh, as she opened her car door. She hadn't aged a minute, and she greeted the surfers with timeless elegance.

"Wow! You look … nice," she said, eying the twosome's clashing outfits. "What's the occasion?"

Caveman extended his hand, discarding all euphemisms and sarcastic surfer slang, calling on his articulate manners. "I'm Thomas."

"Nice to meet you, Thomas." Sister Petrosh greeted him with a wise smirk, appreciating the farcical quality of his outfit. "Your friend here, Mr. Ches, was once my student. He holds a very special place in my heart."

Cave subtly ogled the woman. "Indeed he does, which makes him all the more special." Sister Petrosh's contnenance glowed with keen and sincere interest.

Cave cocked his head suavely and spoke with a debonair cadence. "Ches and I are making our way to the Beaches Pavilion to attend a conference of interfaith dialogue. Will you join us?"

Sister Petrosh politely ignored the invitation and focused on Ches. "We never quit praying for you, my husband and me, and Brother Brown as well. He asks about you often." She paused and reached for the young man's hand with a motherly affection. "There is no denying that you were hurt. Human beings make errors. But human fallibility is dwarfed by the urgency of it all."

"What of my classmates?"

Sister Petrosh paused again, glanced at Cave for a moment, and back to Ches. "After you were expelled, a girl came forward with the truth regarding the information given to Brother Brown. Apparently the student responsible for the awful graffiti happened also to be the one who gave Brother Brown the false list. The kid lied! Ironically he is serving a prison sentence for a terrible crime.

And of the eleven of your peers, only one remains faithful, and he will be moving to Panama to do humanitarian work."

Ches stared at the ground, and Sister Petrosh let go of his hand. "You have a calling on your life, Ches." She lightly touched his shoulder and then opened her car door. "That calling will never go away." She looked into his eyes one more time and drove away.

"Dude, that lady was hot!"

"You're sick, Cave. She's old enough to be your mom, and she doesn't wear makeup or pants."

"Exactly!" Cave retorted with a dreamy expression. "That whole … ultra-holy-girly image triggers something primal. Man, I would devote my life to such a woman … all circumspect … and commanding … unadulterated feminine power."

Ches shook his head as they veered into a vacant lot and ducked behind a patch of palmettos to burn a spleef. Cave held his smoke as he surveyed his friend's dapper outfit. "Hey! You look real! I mean, you look like you're supposed to wear a suit, except your pants are as baggy as a four-man tent." Ches returned the compliment, and side by side they made their way into the conference.

The two surfers meandered incognito into the auditorium to the infectious beat of live African percussions. The place overflowed with Christian men and women in modern attire. Buddhists adorned in orange-yellow saffron sat in their designated section. The first four rows were filled with an eclectic array of colorful robes and headwear that neither surfer recognized from their world religions class.

"Uh, uh, uh, Grom, that would be my seat, next to the Hindu hottie." Cave's vociferous comment caused bullets of perspiration to explode from Ches's forehead. They sat beside a woman in a purple and orange silk sari.

The multicultural music extravaganza came to an end with applause and cheers, and as the crowd quieted, the emcee introduced the keynote speaker, a former UN dignitary with an undetectable accent. He began,

> Political walls are crumbling and the pluralistic societies of the world are integrating en mass. Connectedness between the great religions of history must be the burning priority as we respond to the recent conflicts. We need look no further than today's headlines and the recent fighting and religious divisions in the Middle East to understand why this mission is so vital. And in the West, too many narrow-thinking agencies have hijacked religion to propagate hate. Yet we know these divisive, rogue policies, of castigating "the other" are improper strategies for a healthy country, continent, or world. Religious leaders have immense influence. They can be a powerful force for global cooperation and learning. They can set an example of interfaith dialogue."

The speaker's voice reverberated over the rapt crowd. Ches was mesmerized. Caveman nudged his friend, and when Ches turned, Caveman immediately pretended to be mesmerized as well. Cave turned to Ches again with a melodramatic furrow and sarcastic shaka.

> Our mission is to abolish philosophical doctrines that yield themselves to straightforward analysis. We must ferret out those few dogmatic elements threatening the harmony of global society. We will lay the responsibility squarely upon the shoulders of those who hold rigid loyalties to singular truth and exclusive doctrines of specificity. We will encourage the religious legalist to take up a more flexible, generic cross for the benefit of the majority.

Cave was now nodding and shouting amens so loud that the Sikhs in the next two rows smiled at him with affirmative nods.

> Faith is a reality too great to ignore, and we do not seek to supplant or eradicate those who are engaged in the essential organizing structures of religious faith. Nor do we want to interfere with the appropriate religious doctrines which unify the world community.

Ches was growing uneasy as Cave shook the hand of the smiling Hindu woman next to him.

> We live in a pluralistic society in which the embrace of myriad, coexisting, coequal systems of belief will rule the day. Isn't this the essence of Christianity? Isn't the Christian god a plurality? The great country of the United States is but a melting pot, and it is our view that the world at large will be better served as faith is gradually refined to meet the needs of the whole. We will do this through education at all levels, from grade school to university, and through every media outlet available: radio, television, music, news, and theater. Our projections for the next decade are extremely positive as we build and expand the movement.

Ches was near the point of walking out. Cave had begun a game of clapping his hands off-cue and giggling with delight when his clapping spurred isolated awkward applauses.

> This interfaith movement has the full support of the United Nations because the recent attacks have proven to all that religious leaders and religious ideas have enough power and passion, by themselves, to destroy the world. But together, through education, we will achieve peace. Please join us.

A standing ovation erupted from the audience. Ches and Caveman hurried out the back.

The two surfers stood tall in their fancy suits atop the sand dune, checking the surf. "What a nasty little tagiversation that was," Cave remarked.

Ches pointed to a sizeable set south of the pier. "What does tagiversate mean?"

Cave squinted wisely. "Exactly! If you've ever studied ancient Rome, I mean, that guy literally plagiarized the ancient Roman text for law and religion. In Rome, the citizen is free to worship whatever god he chooses. But the citizen is not free to declare one particular god "the only" valid God. Basically, our little global government bureaucrat was laying out the identical policy, which facilitated the execution Jesus Christ."

Ches was taken by surprise by the comment. He'd always been entertained by Cave's haphazard intellectual scope but wouldn't dare participate in this type of discussion. Any other time Ches would've dodged the issue, but the diatribe quality of the interreligious conference left him uncomposed. He removed his tie and jacket and sat on the dune. "What do you know about Jesus?"

"Yeah, when I read Jesus, I find it difficult *not* to respect Him. I mean, what can anybody say against the one who would give his life for those who hate Him? I mean, isn't that the true and only recipe for peace? His power is greater that the sword. Remember when Jesus was arrested? Peter tried to split the arresting officer's head open. Jesus was like, dude, you're embarrassing me; put that silly thing away. Then He plugged the poor man's ear into his head. Above all else, using the sword to enforce faith is the dumbest thing I have ever heard of. If I kill the infidel as a gesture of devotion to a god I believe to be so wonderful, I have permanently eliminated the infidel's chances of ever knowing my wonderful God. No, Jesus is fine. It's the Crusades and the enforced laws against heresy and the Spanish Inquisition that I ain't signing up for."

"So, you find no fault in Jesus?"

"Ooh, scary, scary! That is Pilate's position, which is the globalist position, which is not my position. My position is, I refuse to have a knee-jerk reaction against the validity of Jesus based on the atrocities of the church. One of my college professors, a man who claimed to be an atheist Jew, whatever that is, emphasized the free pass we give Pilate, while laying the execution of Christ squarely on the shoulders of the Jews. He said Jews could penalize Jesus only by exploiting the spirit of Rome, as the spirit of Rome diplomatically spins Jesus into a Roman plurality."

Ches couldn't talk. He couldn't move. Inadequate footing hindered any meaningful response. He stared at the ground, shaking his head at Caveman, who lay in the sand, chewing a sea oat like some wild enigma wrapped in a plaid leisure suit, turning an esoteric dilemma into a comprehensible plaything.

Cave sensed the conflict within his trembling friend. "Look, my dad died of alcohol poisoning when I was four; my mom died in prison when I was eight; and her mother, my only living relative, is an extreme alcoholic. I have been searching my entire life. How in the world did I get here? And why?"

In that moment, Ches was obliged to reckon his friendship with Cave to an occasion orchestrated by a higher force. Ches was to the point of having to control his emotions.

Cave continued. "One time I extended my hand to help Chever's eighty-five-year-old Bubbe, but she looked at me as if to say, 'How dare you assume I would touch your filthy hand.' But I wasn't offended. Everybody knows I am nondiscriminatory when it comes to places I put my hands. Besides, Bubbe happened to be the one who discovered I was squatting in their greenhouse. So, old Bubbe doesn't like me. So what? Sometimes I don't like me."

"Have you ever been to church?" Ches felt weird as the words came out.

"Here's the question! What must I do to be saved? That's the elephant question, because the cult of easy believism gives me nightmares. I have been to lots of churches, and they all present the same happy-clappy-sign-this-card remedy to the dilemma of my soul. Dude, according to mainstream Christianity, I am saved! Look at me … you know! I'm a four-fifty-four, full-throttle hedonist, and I'm likely to die this way. But they insist I am a believer. To the precise point where the mind makes the mental ascent … shazam! Nothing more is required.

"Look, I am no theologian, but it seems to me that the door to the church opened, with earsplitting, splendiferous glory, in the book of Acts. And the guy who stood on that day, and preached the first sermon, was the very man Jesus gave the keys to. And when Peter opened the door, explaining *the one and only* had been crucified, the spectators were pricked in their hearts. It is impossible to be pricked in the heart unless one believes. I am pricked in my heart every day of my life. And when the guilty pricked-hearts asked Peter the big question, *What shall we do to be saved?* Peter didn't tell them to do nothing but believe, nor did he tell them to accept Jesus as personal Lord and Savior."

Ches was sweating profusely and fidgeting. "What is your point?"

"Isn't it obvious? The door to the church is Acts 2:38: repent, be baptized, call on the name of Jesus, and receive the gift called the Holy Ghost. But every deacon, every pastor, every priest and theologian I have posed this question to literally suggests that Peter misinterpreted the Great Commission—which is to say that Jesus made an error giving Peter the keys. I mean, anybody who surfs knows there is a living God, but we aren't exactly saved. Ours is a lifestyle of circumventing the world's dancing elephants, avoiding all things meaningful and superficial alike in exchange for a surf trip. And still my heart is perpetually pricked."

Ches wanted to comment. He wanted to share with his friend what he knew of the pre-trinitarian church and how the original church in the book of Acts was simultaneously persecuted and strictly monotheistic. He wanted to tell Cave that several centuries after the church was established, a doctrine palatable to Rome's pluralistic view of God was invented, with sweeping legislative reforms and the use of the sword to enforce the religion. He wanted to show Cave the striking difference between those who were persecuted for their unflinching commitment to the name of Jesus, and those who discarded the definitive term, favoring the ambiguous triadic formula of three separate, coexisting, coequal persons. Ches wanted more than anything to show Cave how near to the truth he was. But Ches remained silent, because he knew he wasn't in the boat, and he couldn't push someone else into the boat when he too was drowning.

Chapter 26

A CATEGORY-FOUR HURRICANE wobbled erratically past the Leeward Islands and tracked a course toward the Eastern Seaboard before it slowed to a stall five hundred nautical miles east of Nassau, Bahamas. Except for the occasional afternoon thunderstorms, the crystal-blue Florida skies gave no indication of the monstrous spiral feeding on warm, moist air above the Atlantic basin. They called it Hurricane Alley for a reason. And this is precisely the meteorological phenomenon Florida surfers live for. The long-range outlook was off the charts, forecasting six- to eight-foot groundswells with ten-foot sets over seven days.

Mark, the neighbor, used the last of his leave time while his roommate, Ron, took advantage of his employer's five-day bereavement benefit; he had an aunt who passed away five years previous. Joe took a week's vacation, and the rest of the guys either quit their jobs or finagled their schedules to accommodate the historic swell.

Few Florida surfers had experienced a swell of this magnitude. Chever, Ches, and Cave paddled out south of the pier. The lefthanders barreled through like freight trains, clipping the top of the pier, which was a solid fifteen feet from the surface at high tide.

Ches was on fire. He surfed with the confidence of a seasoned professional, dropping in fearlessly under the lip to a committed bottom turn in a low, tight center of gravity, exploding off the top and back into another bottom turn with lightning speed. His transitions were crisp and seamless. Fellow surfers shouted their approval as Ches's powerful backside carves displaced chunks of water in a twenty-foot liquid fan.

At noon he took enough time to consume a banana and a peanut butter sandwich, washed down with several gulps of orange juice, and then paddled back out straight away. By the end of the week, Ches was one of the few surfers who hadn't broken a board, though he'd come close. When the surf is big, even the best get pulverized and held beneath the surface—sometimes to the extreme that he can hear voices calling from the other side.

On Friday night, a significant crowd gathered at the townhouse. The crew had been thoroughly ravaged by five days of solid groundswell; noses were raw and limbs ached. The entire right side of Caveman's face was severely scabbed from getting slammed onto a shallow sandbar. There was a palpable excitement in the air, and the surfers fully intended to celebrate the season's bounty of waves.

Mudhoney was scheduled to play at Einstein's, while Fugazi was the ticket at a basement dive called the Milk Bar, in the heart of downtown twenty miles away. For several days, Caveman had whispered of a special prank he'd concocted; he met with Ches on the balcony and presented his plan.

Ches's writing was no longer a secret. Sarah, Hope, and Joe, with Cave and Chever, had been discussing Cave's idea. Sarah knew of an open-mic poetry contest at an artsy joint downtown, two blocks from the Milk Bar. As a dare, Cave agreed to enter the contest. The girls would dress Cave as a poet, and he would recite Ches's material before the captive audience.

Ches felt his blood pressure rise. His forehead and ears grew hot, and his fists balled involuntarily as he focused on Cave's chin. Cave's total disregard for boundaries was intolerable.

The crew filtered onto the balcony as Cave waited for Ches's reply. No one noticed that he was on the verge of losing it. Sarah tiptoed behind him and ran her fingers through his hair, which miraculously neutralized the meltdown. She and Hope cracked up laughing as they exchanged ideas for Cave's costume. Within minutes, everyone had approved of the escapade and unanimously decided for a night of imposter's poetry. Sarah pressed her hands to Ches's cheeks, and said, "I am so mad at you for letting Caveman read your stuff before I got to."

Ches exited the balcony, and the party erupted with hoots and cheers. As he made his way to the dunes, the ocean breeze cooled his temper considerably. He took a moment to stare out to sea and then to retrieve his writing pad from its hiding place.

Everyone in the townhouse was cracking up laughing. Caveman sat in a folding chair in the brightly lit dining area, surrounded by adoring fans. Ches adored Cave too. He studied the scene as his friend subjected himself to the creative input of the spectators. Caveman wore a purple French beret, a paisley scarf, and fifties-style, horn-rimmed glasses with Ches's Brooks Brothers slacks and a white tank top.

Sara and Hope pushed through the party carrying a set of makeup pencils and a variety of colored ink pens. Together the girls methodically outlined a fake tattoo scheme. The crowd huddled over the scene, craning their necks, and offered suggestions:

"Dude, thorns will make him look like a deep thinker."

"Yeah! He's got to appear *open-minded*. Do a yin-yang!"

"No, triangles! Gotta do Egyptian triangles."

The girls agreed that a conflicted theme would be most appropriate, considering the charlatan spirit of it all. They painted an anchor on his right arm, wrapped with barbed wire. They drew a purple MOM across his chest, framed by an intricate spider web. His left arm was covered with over-the-top Oriental symbols and sarcastic surf lingo, such as "like," "whoa," "totally awesome," "dude," "whatever," and "shyeah."

The place was called the Metropolis. It was a small coffee shop with pricey desserts and an exclusivist ambiance. The owner was a tall woman in her late forties who projected unsubtle Buddhist-esque feminism. She wore Native American–themed jewelry and a silk sari. Her face gleamed with exuberant makeup encompassing the middle third of the color wheel: dark orange to browns to plush reds. She sported a bright-red, boyish hairstyle, thickly gelled into a spiky, militant flat top. Her multiple silk scarves whirled and twirled as she showered her regular patrons with syrupy affection and complementary cubes of gingerbread biscotti

The tiny venue was jam-packed, and the cherished regulars huddled to one side, close-knit and overconscious of the sharp increase of newcomers; word had spread fast through the surfing community of Caveman's poetic debut.

Ches's eyes darted back and forth. He could tell that most of his friends were already under the influence of lysergide. Cave shook Ches's hand and spoke with a Jamaican accent as he offered Ches the quarter-inch square. Ches shook his head and placed it on his tongue.

The air was electric with giggles and whispers. Chever motioned for Ches to sit with him beside the band members from Rein Sanction and three other musicians from the UK. Sarah and Joe and the neighbors sat closest to the stage. Ches found an obscure place by the corner, near the exit.

The first reading would be performed by a girl of about thirty. She wore an all-white dress, and she called herself Fate Galloway. The crowd quieted as Fate stepped to the mic and stared at a spot in the distant corner of the ceiling for half a minute. When the whispers ceased, she began.

"Trees, O trees … how doth thy bark so sing to me

Thy leaves sustain and still thy enemies wage war against thee

I shall stay in the shadow of thy ark and bend of thy bark like a dog and be …"

The girl stood motionless for a moment and then moved into a prolonged curtsy. The surfers erupted with shouts and applause and unsavory hoots. The Metropolis regulars clapped with less enthusiasm, craning their necks, envious of the abundant ardor poured upon Fate Galloway. The poetess made a valiant effort to maintain a blank expression, but her eyes and the corners of her mouth betrayed her insatiable lust for the praise lavished upon her.

The owner of the Metropolis stiffly seized the microphone. "In the words of Anne Waldman … *Wow*! Ha, ha, ha, haaa! Simply glorious! Thank you, Fate. You're beautiful, Fate … courageous and beautiful."

The woman waited condescendingly for the cheers to subside before introducing herself. "For the few here who do not already know me, I am … *Jade*." She brought her hands together and calmed her face with a graceful scan of the audience, and then turned to Cave. "Next … a male poet we've not heard of. He is a newbie to our night of magnificent dilettante expression. His name is … well … um … okay … we welcome you … Caveman."

The crowd went bananas. Caveman the poet hopped onto the little stage. He looked outright bizarre under the spotlight, standing there a solid minute, staring at his feet. It took an enormous effort for him to gain his composure once he realized the hilarious brightness of his white, patent-leather shoes.

Cave looked extraordinarily fit under the stage lighting. The entire upper half of his physique rippled with lean muscle, revealing the unthinkable hours a surfer spends in the ocean, paddling and harnessing the most powerful forces known to man. The troubadour outfit might have been better matched to a beer gut and a cigarette behind the ear. Ches wondered how in the world Cave could stand in front of this crowd without collapsing in fear. The crowd silenced, and Cave began.

"We must shift our weight, and consider the lateness of the day.
Feel the cold wind blowing in the darkness.
Flowing rivers of pleasure-filled decay …"

Cave's fake tattoos had begun to melt under the heat and perspiration in a psychedelic metamorphosis that contributed to his intended effect.

He had entered into the character. He paused expressively in the perfect place, raised his hand outward as a prophetic gesture, as though touching the crowd, and then turned his hand at the wrist, face-level with shoulders lifted.

"I've taken the plunge, I don't want to be myself, I want to be you and everybody else

I am now a runner in this race; a beautiful smile will hide my face"

Cave had taken ownership of the words, and with an exquisitely timed quiver to his voice, he shifted his weight to a more sanguine pose, head cocked valiantly.

"O, how you play so well. O, how you play that game

You will never recognize me. A crown of knowledge on my head will hide my face.

Your funny shanty reminds me, the diamonds in my hand must remain.

O, how you play so well. O, how you play that game."

He employed a seething vocal inflection now to key phrases. The technique persuaded even his co-conspirators to ignore his ridiculous costume as he pointed at the silent crowd accusingly with a stiffened, trembling forefinger. The crowd froze, mesmerized. Cave realized that the surfers had forgotten the original intent of the shenanigans, so he changed his accent to an awful attempt at British and spoke louder to wake them from their stupor.

> "I caused an earthquake yesterday, but you know … it didn't faze me. Tornadoes and hurricanes are all part of the game … famine and hunger sustain me.
>
> So nail me down, tie my head in a knot, spear me in the side, and drive thorns through my face. Once again I'll rise

and hide behind the unsung sun. The world will never know
I am the creator of the game."

Cave finished with an over ambitious bow. "O, how you play so well. O, how you play my game."

The crowd exploded with laughter. They laughed at themselves for being momentarily seduced by the prank. They laughed at the outrageous image of Caveman, who played the part impeccably. Someone began to stomp and chant, "Encore!" The rest of the crowd joined in.

Jade, clueless about the goings-on, wrenched the mic from Cave in an urgent effort to gain command of the zany group.

"Yes ... ehem ... thank you. That was really special ... er ... em ... Caveman."

The few indignant regulars sat near the monitor, refusing to join the exuberant response. Cave stepped to the little stage again and began to haggle with Jade, his body language pleading, "One more, just one more," until she surrendered and huffed off stage. The crowd roared.

Cave waited again. The tattoo on his chest now spelled the word *NOM*, and the spiderwebs were a blurry, black blob. He adjusted his beret and glasses and waited for silence so his voice could break forth jarringly. He lifted both hands, and with an evil whisper deep into the microphone, he began.

"When the sun dies I'll remain ... and the birds will fly right by."

He pulled the mic free and tweaked his accent to something like French seasoned with hellfire preachy fits as his attention was drawn to the back of the room. The guys from Rein Sanction had jumped the back counter and were filling a backpack with muffins and various sweets from the display case. Cave fell to his knees and pleaded into the mic like a televangelist, loud and expressive.

"And the beast will change its name-ah, and the prophet will fall for a lie

I've waited for this day-ah, throughout my eternal life-ah."

A couple of other surfers leapt the counter in suppressed giggles. Ian the musician forced a tug-of-war with Mark the surfer over an apple pie. Another musician tiptoed behind and crammed a chocolate-dipped banana into his best friend's ear. Jade was growing suspicious. She bobbed and weaved and shot glances to the back of the venue. Caveman worked the crowd with rising intensity, morphing his unstoppable guffaws into dramatic sobs with real tears.

"No, the Rock is not my name-he-haim, when it crumbles I will shine

And the four corners of the earth shall worship my beautiful face

And I shall lead the world as one."

Jade suddenly stood with her hands on her ears. "Aaagh! Robbers! Thieves! We're being robbed!"

Chapter 27

It'd been seven months since the big blowup with Cave, seven months since Ches's decision to leave the townhouse. He hadn't severed ties with his friends; quite the contrary, the parties with Joe and Cave increased. Ches found a job washing dishes at a Chinese restaurant near his new residence. As a random gift, Joe gave him his personal mountain bike for transportation.

Ches had lost his temper with Cave for the first time in an explosive manner. "You had no right to do that! I cannot understand how it is that you have no sense of boundaries!" Dozens witnessed the event. Ches immediately regretted it, but it was too late.

"I thought you'd be happy!" Cave screamed, as guests trickled into the townhouse, drawn to the spectacle. Cave had taken it upon himself, without Ches's consent, to present the young man's writing to an up-and-coming music group.

"They recently signed with a major record label. It's an opportunity to be something! But for some reason you've suckled yourself to some silly subversive façade, and you've failed to notice that your friends might actually care! I just seized an opportunity. You should be grateful. Maybe I've been wrong about you all along."

The place was now packed with onlookers as the two friends stood face to face in the center of the living room, looking as if they would come to blows.

"I … it … it isn't … that I am ungr … grateful. It's j … j … just that I cannot."

Someone turned the stereo to Echo and the Bunnymen as the two argued vehemently. Bodies began to dance in Ches's peripheral vision. His own body quivered. He wanted to implode or run away, but he was cornered, literally, with his back against the living-room wall and Caveman standing inches from his face as everyone stared. Caveman had seized the upper hand in a senseless psychological coup d'état.

Everyone knew that Ches was barely scraping by. Most of the group had already completed their second year of college, including Cave, but Ches stood obstinately against conventional measures of progress. Moreover, Joe sometimes carried Ches's portion of the utilities and rent. Ches had sold his car to make things right with Joe. But in this moment, he felt betrayed by Caveman's selfish ambition, as though he himself should be the ticket to the good life. And Cave was determined to expose Ches's unorthodox reasoning.

Caveman was growing aggressive. His head was cocked back, exposing the bulged veins in his neck as he poked Ches in the forehead. Ches tried to back away. Cave's shameless glare revealed an irrational resentment for Ches that had been building for some time. Cave looked to the crowd to garner approval before shouting into the young man's face, "If you have a gift, why can't you share it? Why? I want to know? Why do you have to hide, huh? Tell us! Did you plagiarize? Are you a fake? Answer the question!"

The walls closed in. Ches had no response to this awful intrusion. He knew the answer, sure, but the thing that made this exchange so hurtful was that Caveman understood to a small degree as well. Cave was also aware that none of the spectators were capable of comprehending the answer, which would cause Ches's response to be perceived as that of a crazy person.

Caveman refused to release Ches of the call to transparency. And with no escape, Ches faced the crowd and gave the best reply possible: "I … cannot … share my work, because … it's not … the truth!" The townhouse was stone quiet except for the exasperated breathing of the two friends. Ches turned and walked out of the townhouse, utterly broken.

The Sunshine State was in a thawing trend. The drawbridges had closed for three days during the freeze, and the waves were all-time. The frigid air colliding with the warm coastal water caused steam to rise. Surfers doubled their wetsuits. Soon it would be springtime again.

Kathryn Abbey Hanna Park had been faithful to Ches. Such a large, mature hammock is a rare find along Florida's heavily developed Atlantic coast. Ches pitched his tent amid a woodsy no-man's land—twenty acres of untenanted city easement along the densely wooded 447 acres of Hanna Park. An eight-foot fence divided the park grounds from Ches's patch of woods. His campsite was beneath a perfect dome of dwarf oaks in a tight valley of sand dunes thirty feet tall. This geographical arrangement provided 360 degrees of privacy and protection. Smoke from a campfire would do little to draw attention to the area zoned for three hundred campsites.

The nearby army surplus store served as a thrifty supply center where Ches purchased a camouflage tarpaulin plus 150 feet of quarter-inch nylon line. He pitched an A-frame secondary cover over his dome tent to keep dry in stormy weather. Forty-five dollars bought a military-issue wool blanket, a sleeping bag, a hatchet, and a folding shovel. The showers at Hanna Park were fifty yards from his retreat—along the wooded trail over the dune, and just beyond the fence line. Ches cleared a path through the weeds and vines to the boundary corner and dug a hole for passage beneath the fence, which he kept covered with branches and leaves.

The young man spent more and more of his time alone by the beach. Determined to extricate that other voice that had become terribly persistent, he filled his mind with alternative philosophies and an excessive use of marijuana. Such efforts proved futile though, as the voice eased to the forefront like an emerging inner compass, daily pulling against the young man's preferred direction. And the voice was no longer neutral or banal but compelling and impossible to predict. If anything it was uniform in effect, separate from all things earthly. No matter the time of day or Ches's mental or emotional state, the voice was always the same, producing the same tears and trembling.

In an effort to identify correlating factors that might be attributed to the voice, he began to document the occurrences. Surf sessions at dawn were his happiest moments. But often at sunrise, as Ches kneeled in the sand to attach his leash, it would happen. There, on his knees, beneath the sound of crashing waves, the whisper would come, inciting tears and trembling.

He recalled the afternoon Cave helped himself to the money in his top drawer. Ches was so incensed that he locked himself in his room at the mercy of an involuntary savage picture. His body convulsed from the realness of the vision of bludgeoning Caveman mercilessly. And the whisper would come, rendering Ches a cognizant yet hapless puddle on the floor, begging forgiveness for entertaining thoughts of hurting Cave.

He recalled the night the voice occurred as he viewed surfing videos with a group of traveling competitors. Ches quietly excused himself and bolted up the stairs. By the time he reached the door of his bedroom, it was too late; that name had begun to roll off his tongue. He shut his lips and put his hand over his mouth as tears poured down his cheeks. He fell across his bed, sobbing in obdurate resistance. "What do You want with me? I don't know what You want!"

The voice would heed no philosophy, no particular emotional state, or time of day. The voice would heed no drug, or combination of drugs. There were nights, under the influence of five or six different drugs at once, Ches wondered how close he might be to an overdose. *How much can my heart withstand before shutting down?* And then that voice would enter, part the haze like a curtain, and distinguish itself from the illicit chemical cocktail at work in his system. The voice would come, not because of any particular emotional or chemically altered state, but in spite of it. The voice would come and gently settled itself between Ches and the dangerous alternative philosophies, psychological patterns, and destructive behaviors. The voice would come, whether day or night.

The young man sometimes wished he could be an atheist. He tried, to no avail. He tried to believe that all other voices were equal and valid. He tried to believe that serious and honest interfaith dialogue was the need of the hour. He tried to believe that peace could be found by coming to terms with God as a plurality and with the millions of other ways to be human.

The only thing he could come to terms with was that somehow, somewhere long ago, of his own volition, he'd opened himself to a seed, a light like no other light, and it was now beginning to move him indescribably. Notwithstanding delusion or cognitive distortion, he was genuinely, identifiably different from the world in ways beyond physical or social. How else could it be explained? Both he and Caveman shared a similarly challenged life. Yet Sarah and many others were no longer on speaking terms with Cave. And in the spirit of charity, shouldn't Cave receive the greater attention? He had raised himself in a camper. He had nobody to care for him. So charity wasn't really a satisfactory explanation for the affection Ches received above Cave.

Ches was now a vagrant, a squatter whose life direction pointed only east, to tread upon the stormy seas. Ches was a surfer—exactly that and nothing more. If there were warning signs of his faculties slipping away, Ches's friends—students of social science, and medicine, and the law—were none the wiser. These social elite, this top 1 percent, genuinely adored Ches to a disarming degree.

Sarah had tracked him to his tent and would often fold his clothes and bedding. She brought little designer wooden crates to organize his books. Chever and Joe would visit too, if only to chat by the fire until daybreak. They would invite Ches to the annual gala ball or various high-world gatherings, but he always declined.

Sarah insisted that he come and meet her family, but he always declined. She would solicit his advice for school and for social or family dilemmas. Ches's friends discerned something in a deeper place, acutely hidden behind the young man's effort to blend in. These unlikely souls sought warmth by the unassuming glow beneath the obvious mess.

Caveman sensed it too. He mentioned it numerous times through the years. "What is that, Grom?" Cave would say affectionately. "Everybody knows you're from a different planet."

One night the group congregated around the beach fire steeped in another abstruse discussion. This time they pondered the biological connection to visceral things, such as the physical aspects of an awkward moment; the weird inexplicable feeling in the shoulders when you're at a wedding and you realize there is dog poop on your pant leg, and you further detect that other people smell it; or the feeling in the neck and throat when you're on a date and you realize you have no money.

Cave stopped the conversation, flailing his hands and shouting until he had everyone's full attention. "Now everyone in this group knows that Ches and I have always had it hard, relative to most of you." Beads of sweat immediately pushed from Ches's forehead at the comment. Cave's voice sounded like his throat was swollen, septic, and quivering as the group stared silently into the fire. "And it's pretty obvious … Ches and I are way down here, while all of you were born with a silver spoon, have never really experienced what it's like to go without." Cave tried to look into the faces of each person, but none dared lift their head. Suddenly Cave cracked up laughing. "That! There it is! I created it! What is that?"

The group erupted with burdensome moans and dry laughter.

"Cave, sometimes you're too much," Chever said. "But seriously … seriously! I've got one. Cave and I have discussed this for a long time." Chever faced Ches as he spoke, "Cave—"

"Yeah! Yeah!" Cave interrupted. "No, I know what you're gonna say, Chever."

"Okay," Chever continued starring at Ches. "So … we are interested in the group opinion. Everybody … look at Ches. Isn't there … something—"

"Let me say it first." Cave insisted that he'd spent the most time thinking on this particular matter.

Chever stood his ground. "Wait, Cave. Let me set it up." Chever shared a look with Cave and set out to shed light on the tacit perception of the group.

"So, Cave, remember that party you guys had a couple years ago at the townhouse? Most of us dropped a couple hits of lysergide, including Ches, and it was a super-intense night. I mean, twenty-five people sat in the living room, and no one spoke a single word for three hours, tripping so hard."

"That's the night I quit smoking weed," Joe chimed in. "We silently passed the bong, and Ches began whispering like some demon: *pay attention when you inhale, and the smoke is drawn into each chamber of your lungs; you can feel your alveoli burn.* My trip went south from there because I had a sort of out-of-body experience. I could see myself as a little boy, scorching my own precious lungs merely for the pleasure of the high. I haven't smoked since."

"Exactly!" Chever stood facing Ches. "So, this particular night, everybody is in outer space. Ches had migrated to his melancholy nest in the dunes, and Caveman decided to lock himself in his room, hoping to curb the intensity. But for some reason, Cave turned on the television. Big mistake! He starts freaking, rattling on about the dark sarcasm of syndicated programming. He tried to change the channel, but the screen turned to fuzz, and then things got really bad.

I was sitting on the couch grooving to the Hoodoo Gurus, and Cave kept peeking from the bedroom door. 'Go find Ches … please,' he would hiss. 'Now! It's an emergency! Please, I need

Ches.' I mean, we tried everything to calm him, but he wasn't having it. Finally, I walked to the beach to inform Ches of the *urgent* situation that apparently only *he* could attend to. Ches didn't even go inside. He just stood in the street, facing Cave's bedroom window like some aboriginal shaman, the Venetian blinds open, and the next thing Caveman is slinking outside all subservient as Ches leads him to the dunes without a word. The thing I find interesting is that most of us have had similar frightening experiences. And who was the first person we thought of? Ches!"

Ches stared at the ground as though his secret had been uncovered, and yet he had no idea precisely what the secret was.

"And when you look at it from Cave's awkward demonstration of socioeconomic disparity," Chever continued, "it proves our point. I mean, those of us on the high side of the socioeco divide have every advantage, every possible means available to deal with the weird stuff of life. We privileged darlings have therapists, lawyers, financial advisers, and the generational support of wealthy, educated families. I could have any kind of car I want. I drive a jalopy. It's my overambitious attempt to connect with the underprivileged. My compassion is conspicuous at best, but Cave is correct: I really don't have a clue. All Cave and I are saying is, we have noticed that when things get weird, the first person we all think of is Ches. So our question is … what is that?"

After a brief silence, Cave shared his theory. "I have determined Ches must be … Ches … is … the devil."

Ches peddled into the woods with a backpack full of tangerines, oranges, and bananas. A ten-mile bike ride to the farmer's market and a ten-dollar bill had purchased a week's worth of fruit. Just as he entered the trail, he heard the familiar honk of Sarah's BMW. He unloaded his pack and hurried to meet her. "Let's go, you phonon! We're scheduled to view the exhibit of the masters—original paintings of Monet, Rembrandt, and Picasso."

Ches and Sarah moved thoughtfully, shoulder to shoulder, before the gallery walls with few words between them. Both could hardly contain the awe they felt staring at a masterpiece, the farthest reaches of human creative expression, hanging casually by a nail.

As Sarah dropped Ches off, she tried again to convince him to come to her place and meet her mother. He politely declined. Sarah was more than beautiful, but Ches tried to maintain a sensible view of the dynamic between them. She received his decline sweetly and watched as he disappeared into the woods.

Chapter 28

Ches hadn't seen his reflection in a mirror for some time. Sun bleached ringlets hung to his shoulders, and he hadn't shaved in months. Not to neglect personal hygiene, he showered every day, sometimes twice, and brushed his teeth obsessively.

He warmed his hands by the fire, and the clouds above parted like a curtain to a velvet-black, sparkling sky. A gust of wind blew his hair back as he climbed to the top of the dune and gazed seaward. He thought about the common misconception that there is no substance in art and that a work of art becomes significant only by chance, as though any random individual may arbitrarily splatter some paint on a canvas and then commit suicide for guaranteed widespread notoriety. "Anyone who has ever had the privilege to lay eyes on a real van Gogh or listen to *Beethoven's Ninth* should think otherwise," he whispered to himself. "How did a painter like Jackson Pollack stir such extreme emotion that one is compelled to assuage the artist? And that response is precisely what the artist intended."

The sadness of the one who communicates from the deep places moved Ches; how disconnected, how marginalized to be confined in a chamber of breathtaking creativity, to live life on the fringe. And yet it is only the one who inhabits the whirlwind of disparate brilliance who is able to capture the essence.

Is this a picture of God? Ches wondered. Does God feverishly aspire to connect? Is God the ultimate dreamer driven by an unsavory degree of passion, with an impossible yearning to express what is on the inside? Or is art only human? Are symbolism, irony, form, and figure mere human tools applied with human craft in an effort to connect to those beneath the chamber? Could God actually be the original artist who creates as a means of making known the depths of love and hate, and of loneliness?

And what of this beast called loneliness? How does it entice humankind to error? It looms in dark, palpable shadows, whispering words of hopelessness, persistently laying traps and dangling illusions of light that would lure any unsuspecting soul into another spiraling path. To be sure, loneliness has the power to persuade one to make some choice that always leads to a deeper lonely and disconnected state.

"Man may well be least himself when he talks in his own person. Give him a mask, and he will tell youth truth."

"But Oscar Wilde missed something vital," Ches said aloud. "God is always there."

Ches focused horizontally over the dark expanse of sea. The light of a lone fishing boat faded into the celestial reflections and the unthinkable distances beyond. And there, just above the fishing boat, was Earth's planetary neighbor, Venus, approximately thirty million miles away. A voyage from here to there at seventy miles per hour would take half a lifetime with no human contact, no gas stations, no art museums, no gatherings of friends and confidants. If there is life out there somewhere, the space between is impassable by reason of the loneliness. But no scientist would consider loneliness a physical thing—a tangible, obstructive force that depletes the passage maker of energy, desire, hope, reason, and motive. It's the origin of romance. The universe, as a creative expression, must evoke loneliness. And so, alone the artist must be.

Ches returned to his tent and searched for a Bible to no avail. He recalled a passage in the book of John depicting an iconic moment during the feast of tabernacles. It was the moment when Jesus stood before a Jewish crowd, and just as the priest prophetically poured the water over the altar, Jesus cried aloud, "He that believeth on *me* as *the scripture* hath said, out of his belly shall flow rivers of living water."

The scripture? The scripture! Considering the Jewish audience, was Jesus referring to the Shema? "Believe on Me as that … One!" Ches said aloud. "If I believe on Jesus as *that* One, then the next verse of the Shema will occur. Love for *that* One will flow from my heart, soul, and might. To hear the voice say, 'I Am One, I Am the One, I Am the Savior, I Am the Artist, I Am the way, the truth, the life … I Am … the Light,' hearing is connected to believing. And when I respond to that voice, *I Am One, I Am One*, as it echoes through the ages … everything changes."

Ches began to tremble. He clutched his heart and fell face forward in the sand. "Jesus Christ, I know who you are! O my God! You are one and the same person as the Alpha. You are the Alpha and the Omega without being more than one person. You are the same yesterday, today, and forever. You have humbly squeezed yourself into the tiny cell of human conception: begotten flesh seen by mortal eyes. Your Spirit pours from your side. You have displayed your art and introduced yourself with a bow and revealed a name that is above every other name."

The boy sat on the dune, davening back and forth, soaking the earth with his tears. The Friend was there next to Ches, surrounding him with a presence far more majestic than the gentle breeze and ocean waves lapping the shore. For the first time since he was small, Ches began to willfully say the name. "Jesus, Jesus, Jesus. How I have pushed You away. And still You touch me. I am not holy. Forgive me. Please forgive me."

The wind subsided, and Ches scanned the horizon. "I don't know what You want me to do, but I know who You are. I remember when, as a boy, I was immersed in Your identity. You were always there. Still, I am afraid I don't fit in with those who gather together in Your name. But I know that I need the gathering. I need those people. But how can a guy like me ever assimilate into the opposite extremes of my own peculiarity?"

A small flock of birds flew overhead, barely discernible in the night sky. "The world will never flourish under the dogma of pluralism. Sure, we are all different, but we are all nourished or poisoned alike. We all smile in the same language and frown the same, and because of you, we all have the opportunity to speak the same language. O the depths of sorrow that comes to a pluralized mind—the turmoil, confusion, and violence. To embrace the One with one saving name is to invite clarity, peace, liberty, and healing.

Ches retrieved his notebook from his bag. "You reached for me even when I disdained You. You are not two, You are not three, and You are not many. You are One, and Your name is One."

Ches opened his notebook and began to write:

> All alone once again, everybody's gone, and finally I can peel away this old façade. It's wearing thin and ever heavy. I look into the mirror and my face has changed from years of lies. My eyes are hard and cold from turning away from light that never dies. For so long now I have reasoned away the simplicity of truth and its happiest details. Now I'm so empty.
>
> But every time I'm alone, the light comes and speaks to me—the voice that time just cannot change, warm and power whispering.
>
> Please forgive my insolent ways. I want to give my life to You, but I don't even know Your name. Who are You, God. What must I do? I've thought so hard to comprehend such majesty, and why would You speak to a man like me? I'm so tired. No more delay. I surrender.
>
> I'm so glad you've turned to me. I've died and live just for this day. It makes me happy when you're free and when you know just who I Am. What I say you must do to be the man you long to be. Totally immerse yourself in My revealed

identity; I Am that I Am, the crucified One, Father, Son, Holy Ghost, I Am that I Am! I Am Jesus.

Ches pulled the marijuana from his pocket and threw it in the fire. He crawled into his tent, closed his eyes, and declared, "Tomorrow I will tell Caveman the truth."

The following evening he clocked out at 6:45. After quick shower, he began the ten-mile bike ride to the townhouse.

"I will tell Caveman everything," he said aloud as he pedaled along A1A. "Jesus Christ strongly rebuked the literal use of the sword relative to the gospel. And yet centuries after the birth of the church, a duplicitous theological view emerged. This view unfolded parallel to the use of the sword as a means of preserving confessions and creeds, but Jesus is not one of three in the Godhead. It's the other way around. All the fullness of the Godhead is in Jesus."

A car with surfboards on top sped past from the opposite direction. The driver honked the horn, and the inhabitants yelled the boy's name, but he peddled on, talking to himself with increased madness.

"*Jesus died for all that they which live should not henceforth live unto themselves, but unto him which died for them, and rose again*. I will share everything with Caveman … how the first-century church, as opposed to the classical church, clearly followed the example of Jesus, spreading His message, not through the use of the sword, but through an unflinching commitment to *self-sacrifice. Self sacrifice!*"

Ches sped through a bus stop where a dozen people stared as he rolled furiously past, preaching to the wind. "I will show Caveman the point on the timeline when Christianity split, and when they began to cruelly enforce faith in spite of overwhelming evidence that such practices depart from the teaching of Jesus. I will show Caveman where they abandon the uncomplicated model of dying for the sinner, in place of the cryptic mode of dealing with heretics. *Heretics!*"

A taxi driver slammed on his brakes and yelled expletives as Ches cycled forward without lifting his head. He began to shout with all his might, "I will expose the sinister element that turns the simple truth of Jesus Christ into labyrinthine strings of controversy! *Controversy!* I will tell Caveman he was right about everything! *Everything*! All people everywhere must repent and be baptized in the name of Jesus Christ for the remission of sins, and ye shall receive the gift of the Holy Ghost!"

The place was dark and quiet. Joe's car was in the drive next to Chever's. Sarah's car was parked on the curb.

"Joe!"

Silence

He knocked on the window. "Cave!"

Silence.

He ambled to the beach and walked south to the old fire pit. He could smell the smoke from half a block away, and he could see a dozen people standing around the flickering light. He noticed the eerie absence of spirit where there had always been revelry.

He whispered from the edge of the crowd, "Where's Caveman?"

Nobody answered.

Joe and Chever stood opposite the flames, facing Ches. Their bodies formed strange shapes in the flickering light as each person around the fire turned toward Ches without a word.

Joe was markedly sober. "I think you should have a seat, brother."

Chever held Ches by the arm as they pressed through the group. Sarah sat motionless on a log with her face in a handkerchief.

Joe clenched his jaw. "There is no easy way to say this, Ches."

Ches tried to make eye contact, but Joe only stared at the ground, shaking his head. "Cave robbed a bank."

Ches immediately bowed over as his diaphragm went into spasms. It had to be a mistake. Maybe Cave was playing a prank. But somehow Ches knew it was real. He slowly pulled himself together and tried to think of a way to help Cave out of the situation.

Sarah reached for Ches's hand. Chever draped his arm over the shoulders of his laconic friend. "Grom, there's more."

The boy shook his head violently.

Chever held him tighter and continued. "Cave tried to escape."

Ches let go of Sarah, brought his hands to his ears, and slid from Chever's embrace.

"They shot him in the back, Ches. He's gone. Caveman is gone!"

The blood drained from Ches's face as all the hands around the fire reached for him. He wrenched away and disappeared into the darkness.

At three that morning Chever found Ches in a fetal position at the edge of the tide. He was soaking wet and shaking uncontrollably.

"Come on, Ches. Let me take you home."

Ches looked up. His eyes were swollen; his face was contorted and barely recognizable; and his hair was caked with sand and seaweed. "What is home, Chever? I wish somebody would please tell me, because home has been calling. Always calling. But I have no idea what home is. It seems to me that all of this life, my life, is only an obstruction keeping me from home. What is home, Chever? You gonna take me home, Chever? Are you the chosen? You gonna take me home, Chever?"

As the tide receded, Chever began to share what had been on his mind for far too long. "Ches, I don't know how I see it, but I do. You have a calling on your life. You don't belong here. There is more to you than the foolish dregs we grovel in."

"No, Chever! It's too late!" Ches held his hand rigidly outward, weeping profusely, but he couldn't stop Chever's words.

"Whatever that thing is, Ches, you can't hide. Everyone sees you. Whatever you have to do to embrace that calling, whatever you have to endure or sacrifice, be it surfing or separating yourself from all of us, do it and do not be afraid. Ches, I will never forget you."

The sun cracked the horizon as Ches rode his bike toward his camp. He kneeled in his tent, rolling fresh clothes into his pack, and then made his way to the showers. The warm deluge splattered on the floor and formed into streams that spilled down the drain, but the boy couldn't muster the will to step underneath. He lay on the grimy floor and watched endless particles of steam billow downward until the warmth turned cold.

Without changing into fresh clothes, he ambled outside and tried to keep his thoughts neutral. At noon he slipped on his backpack, rode his bike toward Atlantic Boulevard, and turned west.

He pedaled lithely toward the far side of town against the ebb and flow of Sunday traffic. Within two hours he crossed the Main Street bridge. After another hour, he entered the area of town where he'd grown up. He ignored the former places of residence and passed two former elementary schools without lifting his head. He stopped at a convenience store that had a pay phone by the exit door. The phonebook dangled, and he opened it in search of the address of his destination. The sun was low on the horizon. He drank from the bottle of water in his backpack and continued slowly westward.

At 5:45 p.m. Ches made his way into the back lot of the church grounds. A car was moving his direction, so he pushed his bike into the woods and hid behind a tree. The car passed, and he started again just inside the tree line, stopping within fifty yards of the church to study the activity in and out. The entire back section of the building was still under construction. Doors and windows hadn't been installed and the clear plastic sheeting that covered the openings puffed in and out as if the building were breathing.

He hid his bicycle under a pile of pine branches and eased his way undetected to the back of the building. He stepped through the plastic sheeting. There was a lumber staircase splattered with drywall mud, and at the top of the stairs, a door. He climbed the chalky stairs and slowly opened the door to a dim hallway. A solitary light bulb dangled above another door at the end of the hall. He tiptoed along the hall twelve paces to the light. The sign on the door read, "Utility."

I step inside and closed the door behind. It is dark and dusty, and I can barely hear beneath the roar of the giant air-conditioning unit. I rest my head on the wall next to the return-air vent and peer through the slats, but I can only see the carpeted floor of the balcony. My fingers aimlessly run the length of the electrical conduit. I can see a child-size, wooden chair in the corner, and the moment I reach for it, the air-conditioning unit cycles off. The silence gives way to a plethora of voices rising through the louvers and reverberating high throughout the small hidden space. There is soft, low weeping and speaking in tongues. The people below are praying. I hear the voice of the old black preacher calling out my name. I am trembling. I wipe the tears from my unshaven face with a dirty, determined hand, and whisper, 'Jesus,' through stammering lips.